PLE CROWN PUBLICATIONS PRESENTS

DISCARD

K'WAN'S GANGSTA

TRIPLE CROWN PUBLICATIONS PRESENTS

Published by Triple Crown Publications
P.O. Box 7212
Columbus, Ohio 43205

K'wan Foye Fan Mail
P.O. Box 7212
Columbus, Ohio 43205

Library of Congress Control Number: 2002114275
ISBN# 0-9702472-1-4
Cover Design: Vickie M. Stringer
Editor: Joylynn Jossel
Graphics: Apollo (Steve Berry) Pixel
Consulting: Shannon Holmes

Second Edition printed March 2003

Printed in the United States of America

"Thanks"

First and foremost, I would like to thank God for it was He who planted the seeds through which I gained the inspiration to write this lil piece. On many occasions I wanted to give up and take the easy way out, but each time I doubted myself, you lit that fire under my ass and motivated me to push on.

To my mother, I tried to be the best son I could be while you guided me down the road to manhood. I also thank you for passing on to me the gift of expression. The ability to put words to paper to create a story is a beautiful thing. You were always supportive of my dream and encouraged me to hang in there.

To Nana, How you put up with me and my odd ways is beyond me. Yet you never turned your back on me, and I love you for it.

Tee Tee, you already know so I ain't gotta tell you. You stepped up to the plate and held it down when your sister fell on hard times. Your strength and good heartedness should be the mold to craft all human beings after.

To my aunt Les and my three uncles, Eric (Uncle Elroy), Frankie (Crumb Louie) and Darrell Foye. Told y'all all that drinking would pay off.

To my pop's, I ain't salty with you no more. All I can do is learn from your mistakes and make sure I don't repeat them with my seeds.

To my unborn, your daddy made something out of nothing. I will do any and all things in my power to make sure you do not make the same mistakes or suffer through the same adversities as I have.

To my baby mamma, Denise, if it wasn't for you I'd have probably finished this book a lot sooner.

To my family, Pop, TM, High Water, Queen, Coo-Coo Kilz, Killa Free, Swayze, Smiles Davis, TSC and everybody else I might've forgot to mention: Love is love y'all. It took a while, but I'm up in here.

Vickie, you get a special thanks. You saw something in me

TRIPLE CROWN PUBLICATIONS PRESENTS

that nobody else did, talent. You gave me a shot, and this is what it has become. Let's make a million.

A Special shout out to Shannon Holmes, Jerome Howard, Thomas Martin, Steve Berry, Apollo Pixel Graphics, Tracy Taylor, Tamera Fournier, A&B Book Distributors, Nikki Turner, Rob Eiletes, Ms. Jones and Tei Street.

Last but not least I would like to acknowledge the haters. Y'all know who you are…the people who had no faith in my dream. Without you I couldn't be here. I thank you for all of your doubts and negative words. Look at me now.

'For my folk'

Dolores 'Auntie' Yarrell: I miss you and if heaven got a liquor store, put me a fifth on hold.

Donald 'D-Black' Best: I stayed outta trouble long enough to amount to something. You said I could,and who am I to make a liar outta you?

Jamel 'El Jamel' Johnson: Ya jello pudding pop eating mafucka, I'm still hanging in there.

Michael 'Mizo' Mack: This is what I've always talked about and now I've done it. I only wish you were here to see the finished project. There's a new product in town and I got that weight. Feel me?

This here goes out to my loved ones lost in the struggle we call street life. For every one of y'all they take, two more of us pop up. For my niggaz that's still here, keep ya heads and let's make something outta nothing.

" For you, mommy. I told you I'd do it."
Brenda M. Foye
10/55 - 9/02

TRIPLE CROWN PUBLICATIONS PRESENTS

Gangsta

An Urban Tragedy

A word to the reader

The tale I'm about to run down to you is deep, so please pay close attention. It is a tale that reflects a lot of what we go through today as being young men of color. We struggle every day trying to make ends meet, in a world that doesn't have a whole lot of love for us. We do what we can when we can in hopes of a better tomorrow that never seems to come. We do what we have to in order to get the things we need for ourselves as well as our loved ones. Whether you hustle, pimp, whore or pull heist, I feel you. It's all in the name of survival. I feel you because I am you. The endangered species...the young black man. Whether this book sells one copy or one million, it is what it is. Only God can dictate fate. But if I can help somebody by putting my thoughts to paper, then I've accomplished something. To those who came up under me, peep game. To my elders, I've learned from your mistakes, so your lessons weren't wasted nor your warnings unheeded. To those who feel misunderstood or unwanted, walk with me and know that you're not alone. To those who feel that life has only given one option, there's light at the end of every tunnel. I don't knock nobodies hustle cause survival is rule number one. But you gotta understand that we do have options. All we have to do is look. I know to a lot of people this probably sounds like some ol' bullshit, but I'm speaking from the heart. A heart just like yours. The heart of a man who has fallen time and again only to rise and continue on, so you know its possible. Walk with me, my niggaz, as I tell you about my peoples...

...THEY CALLED HIM LOU-LOC, AND THIS IS HIS STORY

"THE BEGINNING"

"*L*ou - loc," a female voice boomed from the other side of the door. "Lou - loc! Don't even try to play like you don't hear me. St. Louis Alexander, are you awake?"

Slowly Lou - loc pulled his head from under the pillow. His long wild hair was all in his face as he tried to wipe the sleep from his eyes. The first word that popped into his mind was "drama." Whenever Martina called him by his full name, it meant drama.

Drama was the last thing he wanted at that moment. His head was still throbbing from the party the night before. He knew that he would be no match for Martina in an argument, especially in his drunken condition.

All the homeboys and girls from the hood got together and threw a welcome home party for Pop Top. Top was an older homeboy who ran with the PAC (Park Avenue Crips). He had just come home from a three-year bit. Lou - loc didn't know Top that well. He had only met him a few times when Top came through California a few years back. That still didn't deter him from going to the party.

A lot of people thought Top got his name from those damn fifty - cent sodas he was always drinking, but that wasn't the case. Top got his name for his ill temper. The boy was certified nuts.

The day Top caught his bid he was only in court on a steering - directing drug traffic charge. The public defender wanted Top to plead guilty and take one year on probation. Top wasn't trying to hear that.

The "lip" Lawyer didn't listen to Top and plead guilty anyhow. That was a bad mistake, at least for the public defender it was. Top lost it. He started beating on the lawyer right there in front of the judge and the entire courtroom.

Out of nowhere Top just went off. It took three bailiffs, the D.A. and Top's sister to get the boy off of him. The judge wanted to throw the book at Top, but he had papers documenting that he was crazy. Top did a little over a year on Rikers Island. There he stabbed a Blood over a chocolate chip cookie. The rest of his time was spent in a nut house on Staten Island.

Lou-loc rolled his sleepy eyes over to his clock. Ten thirty-three a.m. is what the digital numbers read. Once again, Martina had broken his sleep. He knew the only way for him to possibly get any further rest was to simply listen to her and not argue.

"Damn, fool, you deaf," she shouted as she burst into the room. "I been calling you cause you got a phone call." Martina tossed him the phone and went back the way she came. "And tell your stupid ass friends to have some respect when they call my house," she said as she slammed the door.

"Bitch," Lou-loc mumbled under his breath. He loved Martina, but she was a pain in the ass. He couldn't figure out why he even got with her in the first place.

Martina was a typical hood rat: No job, no education and a foul mouth. Though she had faults, she was fine as hell. Even at six - months pregnant the girl was gorgeous.

Martina was a Dominican girl born and raised on 149th between Broadway and Amsterdam. She was a shorty, but not real short. She stood about five feet five inches in flat shoes. Her skin was a reddish brown, which blended well with her straight brown hair. She wasn't built like the regular Spanish chic either. She was built straight from the island. Her legs were firm and muscular from her days of running track back in high school. She had nice round breasts and a slim waist. To cap the package off, she had an ass that men would die to be next to. A few almost did thanks to Lou-loc.

Martina was definitely the bomb. By looking at her you could hardly tell she was pregnant, let alone had two more kids. Martina was a pain in the ass indeed, but she was his pain.

Lou-loc cradled the phone and spoke sleepily into the receiver. "What's cracking?" Lou-loc spoke.

"Brims, blunts and bottles," replied the voice on the other end. Lou-loc recognized the voice immediately.

"My nigga, Gutter. What it be like, cuz?" Lou-loc said.

"Everything is blue, homeboy." Gutter replied.

3

Gutter and Lou-loc grew up together as children in Los Angeles. They were crime partners as well as best friends. When Lou -loc made his move to New York, Gutter was right there with him. Lou-loc came out east because he wanted to become a writer and give the street life up. Gutter came because he wanted to be a kingpin.

Upon their arrival they found out that there were Crips in New York. The only thing was, the Crips on the east coast didn't know a thing about being Crips. Gutter and Lou-loc thought it their civic duty to set them straight so they started their own chapter of Crips. They called it Harlem.

"What you on today?" asked Gutter.

Lou-loc paused to light his Newport. "Can't call it fool. How bout you?" he said.

"Glad you asked," Gutter replied, "I gotta go see the boy Roc out in Brooklyn. Roll wit a nigga, cuz?"

"I don't know, Gutter? I got a mean hangover, and I had just planned on kicking it on the local side of things."

Gutter burst out laughing. "What the hell is so funny?" Lou -loc asked confused.

"Ain't nothing," Gutter said trying to catch his breath. "I'll understand if Martina won't let you out. I'm your boy. You ain't got to lie to me."

"Man, fuck you crab," Lou-loc shot back. "I'm grown, fool. I do what I want when I want. Just because Sharell be kicking yo punk ass don't get it twisted." The two friends enjoyed a laugh.

"Nah," Gutter said a little more serious, "I need you to watch my back. You know how these New York niggaz is, especially in Brooklyn. Shit, they worst than them fools in Compton. I'd end up having to blast one of them fools for trying to jack me."

"Okay," Lou-loc moaned finally having enough of Gutters snow job. "I'll roll with you, 'G'. Pick me up in two hours, not one hour, not one and a half. Scoop me in two hours, Gutter. You hear me?" Gutter repeated the instructions and hung up the phone.

He and Gutter had been down since they were both just lil shorties. Gutter was already a full fledge banger while Lou-loc was still trying to get in. Shortly thereafter, Lou-loc's father died and he started getting into all kinds of shit. He figured if he caused enough hell the homeboys from the local Crip set would notice him.

After hearing about the wild ass lil nigga from up the street, the G's decided to approach him.

It was Gutter and his uncle, Big Gun, who stepped to the young Loc. Lou-loc was in an alley with some local hard heads shooting craps. When he saw Gun he got all excited. He knew who the OG was, but he had to play it cool.

"What up, homey?" Gutter asked mugging Lou-loc. "Where you from?"

"Ah...," Lou-loc began nervously, "I don't claim no hood, cuz. I just hold down where ever I'm hanging."

"I hear that," Gun added in. "Say, we been checking you, homey. We see you out here kicking up dust and shit. Even heard you cut up some nigga from Cabbage Patch Piru?"

"Can't stand them, marks," Lou-loc said spitting on the ground.

"Slobs blasted on my old man a while back. I bust on them niggaz every time I get a chance. Kinda personal you know?" Lou-loc said.

"Sure you right," Gutter said giving him some pound. "Say man, how old is you?"

"Thirteen, homey."

"You just about the right age to join up. Ain't nobody crack on you yet?"

"Yea, a few niggaz. Too many hoes done got at me though. I ain't really feeling they style. Them niggaz like chasing them bitches. That ain't really my thang, cuz."

"Oh, yea? So what's yo thang, homey?" Gutter asked.

"I'm trying to get money and blast slobs," Lou-loc replied.

"I hear that. You talk tough, but can you hold yours?" Gutter asked.

"Man, I get down. The hood know about Crazy Lou."

"That's what you call ya self?"

"Yep."

"A'ight, Crazy Lou. What if I gave you a chance to belong to something big?" Gutter asked.

"Man, what you rapping bout?" Lou-loc questioned.

5

"Homey, they call me Lil Gutter. I'm claiming Harlem Gangster," he said flashing his set. "This hear is my uncle, Big Gun, from Hoover 107."

"I know who the big homey is, but your set, never heard of it," Lou-loc said nonchalantly.

"Most square ass niggaz haven't," Gutter capped. "We small now, but we on the rise...banging and slanging, cuz."

"Man, what the hell make me wanna joint yo set?" Lou-loc asked.

"Cause, lil nigga, we more than a gang. We ain't like these other mafuckas. We a family," Gutter affirmed.

"I got family, thanks," Lou-loc said.

"Nigga," Gun said, "who you think you fooling? I see it all in your eyes, loc. You been through some shit in ya life, as have most of us. You out here kicking up dust causing all this shit and for what? You ain't gonna do nothing but get yo ass locked up or bodied," Gutter said.

"Listen, youngster. Ain't no shame in being lonely. Yo daddy gone and I know ya mama don't understand how it is in these streets. Instead of being destructive about it focus that energy and make something of ya self. My nephew and his little shit kickers are doing big thangs. Hear him out," Gun added.

Lou-loc pondered what Gun was saying. Since his father's murder, Lou-loc had always felt like there was a piece of him missing. His sister was younger than he was so it was like he was alone in the world. He longed for a sense of kinship amongst his peers. This could be what he was looking for.

"A'ight, homey," Lou-loc agreed, "let's talk about it."

"Listen," Gutter picked up, "we putting it down in Cali. We got allies from Hoover 107, 83, East Coast Block Crips and Victoria Park. Harlem gonna have it sewed."

"A'ight then. What I gotta do?" Lou-loc asked.

"Listen," Gutter said leaning in to whisper, "meet me out by the Ikea mall around 10:00 p.m. Can you do that, stud?"

"Yea," Lou-loc said sounding surer than he actually was. "I can do that."

"Come prepared to scrap, cuz. We fixing to see if you as cold as you claim?" Gutter stated.

"Ain't nothing but a thang, cuz. Ya boy gets down," Lou-loc said.

Lou-loc stood there trying to look hard as Gutter and Gun strutted away. Inside, his tiny little heart was beating out of his chest. Getting down with Harlem would definitely put him in the big leagues. No more of this petty shit, strictly paper. With a small army behind him, he could avenge his father.

For the rest of that day all Lou-loc could do was sweat and ponder. He wasn't no coward, in fact he had whipped some of the older kids in the neighborhood. This was different though. See, there's different ways of proving ya self to get, "Quoted", more commonly known as getting in a gang a.k.a. "jumped in".

Lou-loc knew he had to put his thang down. He knew damn well what Harlem Crip was. Them niggaz was rowdy as hell. He figured he'd have to square off with at least 5 other niggaz. That's if he was lucky.

At around 10:15 p.m. Lou-loc came strolling into they alley. He was late because he had to take 2 busses from his girl's house in Culver City. At first he didn't see anybody. Inside he breathed a sigh of relief. Maybe Gutter had changed his mind? Just as Lou-loc was about to turn back around he heard footsteps.

The first cat to step out was this lanky dark skinned kid. He wore a pair of creased blue Lee's and a black sweatshirt. His blue bandanna was tied off to the side on his baldhead.

The next figure to appear was a squat lil fat nigga. Lou-loc would later come to know him as Pudgy. They would become close friends as well as brothers at arms.

Gutter came next, slithering out of the darkness. His charcoal skin and black jump suit made him appear to ooze from the shadows. He had a blue bandanna wrapped around his head as well as the lower half of his face. A pair of black sunglasses covered his eyes. He looked every bit of the thug mafucka he was.

Lou-loc stepped up stone-faced. He was decked out in a pair of black Levi's and a gray sweatshirt. He wore a black Raiders hat over his tiny box-braids.

"Sup, loc?" Gutter said stepping towards Lou-loc. He was flanked by two other blue clad soldiers. "Thought you wasn't coming?"

7

"Nah," Lou-loc said. "I decided to come see what you niggaz was rapping bout."

"So you think you can hold yours in a circle of your peers?" Gutter asked looking Lou-loc dead in the eye.

"I guess we'll find out," Lou-loc said matching his stare.

Without warning, Pudgy stole off on Lou-loc. The surprise that was added to the impact itself almost knocked Lou-loc off his feet. He managed to stay on his feet and land a hard shot to the fat man's gut. Lou-loc didn't wait to see if the blow had fallen. Lou-loc swug high and hit Gutter in the mouth. It was on now.

Gutter shot a jab to Lou-loc's cheek staggering him. Before Lou-loc could counter, the dark skinned kid popped him in the lip. Lou-loc lost his balance and collapsed on his hands and one knee. He knew he was done if he didn't get up.

One of the other bangers tried to kick Lou-loc in his head, but he was waiting on it. He grabbed the kid's leg and sucker punched him in the nuts. The kid halted his attack, giving Lou-loc the precious moments he needed to get on his feet.

For every punch Lou-loc threw, he took three. His lip was busted and he could feel one eye trying to close. He had to fight through it though. If he failed the test, his street credibility would be shot. Life in the hood is hell for a nigga who can't hold his own. A mafucka always gonna try you. No matter what, he had to prove that he was man enough to hold his.

The homeboys whipped on Lou-loc for what seemed to be an eternity. The homeboys tried to knock his head the fuck off, but Lou-loc stayed on his feet. Lou-loc fought with an animal like fury that willed him to survive the ordeal. The youngster gave as good as he got. He hit one soldier in the mouth so hard that the skin on his knuckle split open. He felt like he was going to fall on his face when Gutter finally called for the homeboys to stop. It was over. Lou-loc had withstood the onslaught and proved his gangsta.

"You see this?" Gutter asked out of breath. "You stood amongst a circle of your peers and held yours. You knew that all you had to do was lay down and it would all stop, yet you wouldn't. Youz a stand up nigga and can't no mafucka tell you different, cuz."

"Word up," co-signed the dark skinned gangsta. "Lou, you get down for yours, loc."

"Lou-loc," Gutter repeated, "I likes that shit, cuz. From now on, we gonna call you, Lou-loc, cause you is one crazy nigga. Welcome to the family, cuz."

The homeboys all hugged Lou-loc and give him some dap. They all either had something busted or lumped up. Lou-loc was a true warrior.

Gutter pulled out a bottle of 100 proof vodka and some weed. The homies got fried that night to welcome their new brother to the fold.

Lou-loc felt proud of himself. He had done something that most niggaz in the hood only strive to do, become a part of something great. In killer Cali, your set is your badge of honor. Technically, Lou-loc still wasn't anybody important. He would have to put in work for his new set to get his status up. Sometime after that fateful night Lou-loc would discover his gift in the game. Murder!

Lou-loc slid out of the bed and onto his feet. As he stretched, various bones cracked and corrected themselves.

"Rough night," he thought to himself as he put on his slippers and shuffled to the mirror. Lou-loc looked at his handsome brown face in the mirror. He had lived quite a hard life to be only twenty-five. As hard and as fast as he lived, he still maintained his boyish features.

His face was completely bare, no mustache or beard. It didn't reveal one trace of his actual age. Sometimes when he went into the liquor store, if the counter person didn't know him, they'd ask for two pieces of ID. I guess they thought his license might have been a fake.

He was dark, but not as dark as Gutter. He had smooth chocolate skin, and when he smiled his teeth pearly white teeth peered from behind his feminine lips. Martina always teased him about that. She would say, "Damn, Lou-loc. Your lips are prettier than mine."

What stood out most about Lou-loc were his eyes. They were a very soft brown, like caramel candy. The only blemish on him was a scar behind his left ear. He got that from a rival gang member in Y.A. Other than that, he was very easy on the eyes.

Lou-loc shuffled over to the closet to find something to wear. When people were lucky enough to get a glimpse inside of the huge walk in closet that he had built for Martina, they couldn't help but to be impressed. Each side of the closet held three rows of hanging bars, like the ones you might see in a dry cleaners. Each row was filled to the brim with designer clothes from all over the world. There was Rocawear, Sean John, Pradda, Dolce, Gucci, and quite a few designers that people had yet to hear about.

On Martina's side, she had minks and leather jackets in just about every cut and color. She had dresses that wouldn't be available to the public for a few years yet to come. When it came to shoes, forget about it. She had every designer shoe you could think of. Lou-loc liked to spoil his boo. His homies used to joke and call him a trick, but it ain't trickin if you got the chic, right?

Lou-loc's side of the closet was a little different. He wasn't no slouch or nothing like that, he had some fly shit. Leather jackets in every color, at least one pair of shoes made from made from different animals and some fly ass hats, like Dobbs fifty's and things like that. But Lou-loc wasn't really into dressing up. He was a street nigga so he mostly dressed accordingly. But even in that department he was holding.

He always got the newest sneakers at least a year or so before they hit the street. For every sports team, including soccer, he had a "home" as well as an "away" jersey. When it came to stunting, niggaz couldn't fuck with Lou-loc, but he was humble about his shit.

On those rare occasions though, you might see him step in the place with his most prized possessions: A full-length electric blue mink coat with a matching mink baseball cap. Let anybody else tell it, the cap was the real showpiece. On the front of the cap was a diamond engraved 'C.' Lou-loc could ball with the best of them when he so chose to.

After a few minutes of debating he decided on an outfit. He selected some black Carpenter jeans, a blue Dodgers jersey and the matching hat. Since this trip was going to be business, there was no need to floss his jewels. He selected a blue-faced Timex for his wrist and a gold crucifix for his neck. To make the outfit complete, he reached up under his pillow and pulled out his nickel-plated 9mm. Chrome matched with anything.

As Lou-loc made his way to the bathroom, Martina's son, Carlo, stopped him in the hallway. The boy was the spitting image of his mother, except his features were more masculine. Even though Carlo wasn't Lou-loc's son, he still looked out for the boy.

"What up, OG Lou-loc?" Carlo said putting on his best mean mug. "What that Crip like fool? We rolling today?" Lou-loc smiled and slapped the boy five.

"Nah, Lil player. I got some things to do. Ain't you got no where to be this morning?"

Carlo raised his right hand above his head. With his index finger and thumb, he made the shape of a 'C.' "Nah, everything is blue."

Lou-loc laughed at the boy's response, but Martina coming down the hall shouting cut his laughter short.

"Carlo!" she shouted. "What did I tell you? If you want to be a thug, you do it when you're eighteen and out of my house. Understand?" With that, she popped him in the back of his head and sent him to his room. She turned her attention to Lou-loc, who was standing there quiet. "How many times I got to tell you, Lou-loc, don't bring that shit around my kids."

"Martina..." Lou-loc said.

"Martina my ass," she cut him off. "Look, if you and Gutter want to run around making asses of yourselves, you're grown and entitled to do so. My kids are a different story. I'm not having it. I don't want it around them or the little one in here," she said rubbing her stomach.

"Listen, Martina," he started. "You know what I am and what I'm about. It was that hood shit that got ya nose open for me from the jump, remember? You got some nerve trying to get brand new on me."

He pulled up his T - shirt exposing the tattoo on his stomach.

"Look at it," he demanded. "OG Crip, you see it? That's who I am, Martina. I'm a mother fucking gangsta. I didn't ask for the shit, that's just how the fuck it is. Where the fuck I come from we ain't got a whole lot of choices, ya heard? It's either you bang or get banged on. We not like these muthafuckas out here who tryin' to get a name."

"Back home, we live, die, and murder for colors. They start recruiting at thirteen, you know that? They snatch the babies and turn them into soldiers, machines and killing tools. That's the only way a lot of them niggaz know how to live. It's about survival," Lou-loc continued. "Martina, I would never get yours or anybody else's kids caught up in this craziness. All this shit is genocide, but I can't deny what or who I am. I'm going to be a Crip until they put me in the ground. I can't change that, but I don't have to poison others with it. Let that burden be mine to carry."

"What ever," she responded. "That all sounds good, but I can't see it. You and those fucking assholes, Kenyatta and Gutter, or what ever you want to call him, always into something. Every time I turn around it's *Lou-loc did this or Gutter shot that one.* What the fuck, yo?"

Lou-loc paused to gather himself before answering.

"Martina, you must be crazy if you think I'm going to be hustling all my days? Yo man got a plan. I'm going to be a writer. I'm going to be bigger than Goines, Slim, and any of them other muthafuckas out there. You watch."

Martina let out a chuckle and said, "Nigga, please. Them people are larger than life in that game. Who the fuck is you? They got publishers and agents. What you got? You need to keep on getting that paper instead of daydreaming. Shit, a bitch got kids and a bitch need thangs. Them funky books you call yourself writing ain't going to put no food on the table." With that last comment she made her way back to the kitchen.

Lou-loc wanted to follow her and continue the argument, but all the liquor he had consumed the night before was raising hell in his gut. He went back into the bedroom to get what he needed. He took a small wooden box from his nightstand, and headed for the bathroom.

When Lou-loc got into the little blue room he stripped naked and sat on the toilet. The liquor was doing a number on his stomach and he needed to get it out of his system. The sooner he did it, the better he would feel.

Lou-loc pulled out some rolling papers and a bag of weed from the wooden box. With the speed and skills of a veteran marijuana smoker, Lou-loc rolled a joint.

"This'll chase the headache away," he said to himself.

Once the joint was rolled, he lit an incense and then the spliff. The weed smelled like sweet perfume to his nose. He inhaled deeply, sat back and let his mind coast.

He silently went over the things he needed to do in his head. He had planned on just keeping himself local today, but Gutter needed him and it was hard to tell Gutter no. He could be very persuasive. Besides, he didn't like the idea of Gutter riding out to Brooklyn by himself. The blacks out there were bad enough, but these people Gutter was going to meet weren't black. They were Middle Eastern. From what Lou-loc had heard of them, they were very unpredictable and distrustful of Americans.

It was a good thing that he was riding with Gutter, that way he would be free to think instead of concentrating on the road. But with the way Gutter drove, he would probably have to watch the road anyhow. Oh well.

It's not that Lou-loc didn't have his own ride. In fact, he had two cars in New York. He and Gutter owned identical two-door Camrys. The only difference was Gutter's was dark blue with gold rims while Lou-loc's was silver with chrome rims.

Lou-loc's pride and joy was his 1979 Cadillac Sedan De Ville. He had that flown out to New York from LA. The body was a forest green while the tires were pearl white with gold hundred spoke rims. He even had his boy Wiz fit it with bullet proof plating in the doors and roof. Even the windows had been proofed. And a Caddy ain't a Caddy without switches-Hydraulics.

When Lou-loc was halfway through his joint, he noticed one of those important looking manila envelopes sticking out of the bathroom garbage. Upon closer inspection he noticed that it was addressed to him. He pulled the envelope from the garbage, and read the label out loud.

"Borough of Manhattan Community College. That bitch!" he snapped. This was no doubt Martina's handy work.

Some time back, Lou-loc decided he would finish his schooling. He had taken some classes at LBCC, but never received his degree. It had always been his dream to become a writer, so he planned to pursue a degree in Journalism and recognize his dream.

"Negative tramp," he said to himself.

Here he was trying to do something with himself and she was trying to sabotage it. Instead of being happy with "Joe Schmo", she had to have a baller. She wanted to marry a drug dealer.

Well her little trick didn't work. He still had time to deliver the forms before the deadline. He would just deliver it in person as opposed to mailing it.

CHAPTER 1

After his shower, Lou-loc went into the bedroom and began dressing. He figured if he dressed and left quickly, he could avoid a confrontation with Martina. As if reading his mind, she appeared in the doorway.

"Daddy," she said in her sweetest voice. As soon as he heard her tone he knew what she was after...paper. "You know daddy, my sister's wedding is next week?" Martina said with no answer in return. "Well, are you still going with me?"

Lou-loc continued tying his sneakers.

"I can't call it," he said still not looking at her.

"What kind of answer is that? What you mean, you can't call it?" Martina said.

"I mean what I said. I don't know," Lou-loc responded.

"Lou-loc," she wined, "how you going to do me like that? How will that look to my family?"

"You *supposed* to be my man, but you would let me go to my sister's wedding solo?"

Lou-loc's anger was rising, but he tried to keep it in check.

"Martina," he said through clenched teeth. "Them people don't even like me. Every time we go by there your sister and her stank ass friends be talking about me. They think that if they speak Spanish I won't understand what they are saying about me. That goes to show how stupid they are. I grew up in LA Spanish is a second language for us. Dumb ass heifers."

"What you mean my sister be tripping?" she shot back snaking her neck. "Don't even go there, especially with the way your sister came out here acting. That little yellow bitch acting like her shit don't stink."

Lou-loc had finally had enough.

"Look, Martina, you know just as well as I do how that girl is, acting all high off the hog and shit. She be acting like she ain't even from the projects. Plus she always bragging on that punk ass nigga she hooked up with. Talking about he a high powered lawyer and all the money he got. I'm surprised he got any at all," Lou-loc said.

"Between your gold digging ass sister and all the powder he snort, they'll be broke soon. Shall I go on?" Martina said with no answer from Lou-loc. "If your sister supposed to be so in love, maybe you can answer me this. If she love her man *soooooo* much, why little Snoopy seen her hugged up with one of them fag ass brims on 112th street? Huh, tell me that?"

Lou-loc felt himself about to go overboard, but he figured why stop now? So he didn't.

"Yo sister just salty because I didn't take the pussy when she offered it to me," Lou-loc said walking over to the mirror and starting to comb his wild hair. He told himself that he couldn't give in to Martina this time. He had to stick to his guns. But when he looked at her reflection in the mirror, his heart sank.

Her full sexy lips were drawn and pouted as she stood looking at her feet with her hands on her belly. When she looked at him, her big brown eyes were rimmed with tears. Martina was a pure hell raiser, but at times she appeared so innocent and fragile.

He stopped combing his hair and walked to where she was standing. When their eyes met, a lone tear ran down her cheek. She had him hooked.

She sat on the edge of the bed and spread her legs. With one hand she was wiping the tears from her eyes. With the other hand she motioned for him to sit between her legs. And he did.

She began to gently finger comb his hair while he rested his cheek on her thigh. As Lou-loc smelled the fresh scent coming from her private place, he remembered all the good times they had when he first came out to New York. She was a pain in the ass, but he loved her.

"Why you always got to go there, Lou-loc? I know you don't like my family, but you don't always have to throw it up in my face like that. A bitch got feelings too, you know?

"I didn't even come back here to argue with you. I knew you'd feel funny about going around my peoples, so I just figured I'd start softening you up for it early. I'm sorry for wanting to be around you."

15

Lou-loc started to feel bad. He honestly thought she had come to hit him up for some bread. Guess he was wrong.

"My bad," he whispered. "Your moms and everybody else is pretty cool (when they weren't trying to get him in church), but me and Mirasol just don't click."

For a long moment they just sat in silence, each lost in their own thoughts. Lou-loc got up from the floor and walked over to the mirror. Martina had parted his hair and put a French braid on both sides. It wasn't much, but it would do until he had a chance to get it done by the Africans on 125th.

Outside of their five-story walk up, somebody was beating the hell out of their car horn. Lou-loc's ride had come and it was time for him to hit the streets, but not before Martina put her bid in.

"Daddy," she said as he gathered his keys, and wallet. "I was going to wear those Pradda shoes you bought for me to the wedding, but being that my feet are swollen I can't get into them. You think you could hook a sister up?"

"Don't this just beat all?" Lou-loc thought. All this time she was just setting a nigga up for the pay off. That's a female for you.

Lou-loc put on his best phony smile as he pealed off five fifty-dollar bills from his stack and dropped them into her waiting hand. He didn't want to part with the money, but if it could get her to shut up, it was well worth it.

As he was leaving, she stopped him short with a question.

"That's it? You must want your lady to roll up in there half ass?"

Lou-loc gave her a "you can't be serious stare." He loved her and she was his future baby's mama, but it was her ways he didn't like. No matter how much you gave her, it wasn't enough.

"Listen, Martina, you said you wanted some new shoes, not a trip to the Dominican Republic. If that ain't enough, you're just assed out. Later."

*

On the Lower East Side it was business as usual. The fiends were out looking to score and the young soldiers of the Latin Connection were more then willing to serve them the poison. It wasn't personal, just business.

The Latin Connection was a fraction of the Bloods. The difference between them and the rest of the Bloods was the fact that their members were all Latin; Puerto Rican, Dominican, Salvadorian, Mexican. You name it they had it.

As the soldiers continued to serve the heads and dope fiends, a long red El Dorado pulled up to the curb on Avenue D. The driver got out and made his way to the passenger side. He was a beast of a man. When he stood to his full height he was well over six feet four inches. His shoulders were almost the entire length of the Cadillac. Maybe that's why the passenger sat in the back seat.

The man who stepped from the back seat looked pretty average. He had clear light skin and a full beard lined his jaw. As he stood to his full height, which was only about five foot nine inches, his white linen suit hung loose on his body. He brushed off his red Fedora and placed it on his head.

As he made his way towards the little Spanish restaurant on the corner, people moved to get out of his way. Although he didn't appear to be very powerful, especially next to the driver, you could tell he was important. He was Michael Angelino, leader of the Latin connection. Also known as El Diablo in the streets.

"Como Esta?" he said shaking the hand of Marco, who was standing in front of the restaurant. Marco was one of Angelino's workers, and Cisco's lieutenants.

"Angelino," Marco said with a smile. "Everything is Buenos. Muy Buenos. Cisco's inside waiting for you."

Angelino brushed past Marco and went into the little diner. When Angelino entered, every one started to cheer and clap. He was somewhat of a local hero. They called him "the man who cleaned up the streets". What that really meant was he forced all the non-Hispanics out of the area. Some hero.

Angelino smiled at everyone and bowed.

"Please, please," he said motioning for silence. "I am just a man. Save your praise for someone who deserves it."

With another bow, he made his way towards a table in the back where his Captain was waiting for him.

"The people love you, Michael," said Cisco standing to greet his leader and mentor. "You make the streets safe for poor business men such as myself. You deserve your praise."

With all the flattery done, the three men seated themselves.

Angelino was the leader of the connection. But it was Cisco that the soldiers answered to. He was the Captain and El Diablo was the general.

The two men embraced.

"Cisco," said El Diablo smiling. "My most trusted soldier and dearest comrade. How have you been, amigo?"

"I cannot complain," Cisco said reseating himself. "What can I say, Michael? Tu es muy heneroso, mi amigo. You make it possible for my family to eat."

El Diablo removed a cigar from his jacket pocket, which the giant readily lit for him. "So, my friend," El Diablo said exhaling the smoke. "How is business? Everything is good, no?"

"Si, si," Cisco replied. "We are indeed prospering. Our sales have increased by over thirty-two percent just over the last six months. Don't worry, Michael, you left your business in good hands."

El Diablo smiled at his Captain. "Very good, Cisco. And our plan to expand. This is also progressing, no?"

Cisco shifted in his chair and said, "Well, yes and no. Mostly yes."

El Diablo gave his captain a strange look. Cisco in turn moved his chair a little further away from the giant.

"Cisco, forgive me for being a poor dumb country boy, but I do not understand. This yes and no, is it some sort of new slang? I didn't know there was such a response. Explain please?"

"If you'll permit me?" Cisco said reaching into his inside pocket. From the pocket he produced a map, which he laid on the table. It was a map of the city with color lines dividing certain areas.

"These are our main borders," he said sliding his fingers from Thirty Second Street to the tip of Brooklyn. "With the exception of China Town and Little Italy, we are the controlling factors."

Cisco paused to see if El Diablo was still with him. El Diablo motioned for him to continue. Cisco took a deep breath and did so.

"We also now have territory in the Bronx," he said tracing his finger from Third Avenue to Fordham Road. "Our soldiers are turning profits there, but it's still a little slow."

El Diablo looked at the map closely.

"And what is this area marked fire zone?" he asked pointing at Harlem. "What do we have there?"

Cisco made a face like he smelled something foul.

"Harlem, that's no good, Michael. Those blacks up there," he shook his head. "They are killing each other in the streets."

El Diablo scratched his chin.

"Cisco, I thought Harlem was Blood Hood?' If this is the case, then why have we not spoke with our Negro Primo's about an arrangement?"

Cisco shrugged his shoulders.

"Michael, I spoke with Scooby personally. He assured me that if we did indeed migrate to the area, we would receive a cut of the action."

El Diablo shrugged his shoulders.

"If you have their support, what's the problem? Why do we not have soldiers in Harlem?" El Diablo said.

Cisco knew this question would come. He had gone over it again and again in his head. Now that the time had come, his mind drew a blank. There was something about the way that El Diablo looked at him.

"W...Well, Michael," Cisco stuttered. "Things have changed. It seems that the Bloods in Harlem are losing their hold in some areas. Harlem is falling under new management."

El Diablo's eyes bulged with disbelief. "Who?" he demanded. "Who is so bold as to tell Bloods we can't eat?"

Cisco paused before continuing.

"Crips, Diablo. It is the Crips who are gaining a foot hold in Harlem."

El Diablo sprang to his feet. Cisco braced himself for the blow he knew was to come, but instead he was shocked by El Diablo's reaction. El Diablo burst into a fit of laughter.

"Crips," he said trying to calm down. "You mean to say that you allowed a handful of disorganized gang bangers to stop us from invading one of the most profitable drug areas on the east coast?"

El Diablo back handed Cisco to the floor. Before Cisco could gather his wits, the giant scooped him up by his collar.

"Michael," Cisco pleaded. "These are not the same people you remember. These two black kids from LA came here and everything has changed."

El Diablo motioned for the giant to stop squeezing Cisco's neck. "Release him," El Diablo said evenly. The giant reluctantly dropped Cisco into a chair.

"Don't play me, Cisco. The Crips are too busy killing each other to unify. What are you talking about?"

"All true," Cisco said gasping for air. "From what I gather, they came out here about two years ago. Maybe more."

"At first they were just working the corners like every one else. They weren't getting major paper, so we paid them no mind. Over the last year or so things have changed. They started speaking to all of the Crips and their allies in Harlem. They were saying that since the Crip sets in Harlem were so small and thinned out, that it would be more beneficial for all of the smaller individual sets to unify under one set. They are calling it Little Harlem, named after the original set in LA."

El Diablo sat back in his chair.

"Cisco, why has this problem not been dealt with? If these men would unite the C-nation, why do they still live? Who are these two dead men you speak of?"

Cisco straightened his suit jacket before continuing.

"Believe me, Michael, there have been attempts. A while back some Bloods from up around the Gun Hill section of the Bronx decided to get rid of these two. Much like you, they had a desire to take Harlem. Well, they sent down three of their best killers. I mean these guys were pros. Bad asses, Michael. Any how, these guys roll up on one of them, Gutter, I think that's what they call him. They're all surrounding him in front of the bodega on 125th and St. Nicolas. They figured he was alone so they could get at him. They're out there waving their guns and popping mucho crap. The whole time this Gutter character is just laughing. He started off giggling and then it turned into laughing, like somebody waving a gun at him was funny. So while these muthafuckas are trying to figure out what the hell is so funny, this other black kid eases out of the bodega. This is the other one. They call him Lou-loc. He let off three shots. Nobody even saw him draw his gun. Before they knew what was going on, they were dead."

Cisco made the sign of the cross. He then continued to speak.

"Each Blood had a bullet hole in the eye. Three bullets, three bodies. The guy thinks he's Robin Hood or something. The way I hear it, the boy is a crack shot. He was a pro in LAt. Didn't even flinch when them boys hit the ground. While every one else was trying to figure out what the fuck was going on, these two just strolled off."

Seeing the disapproving look El Diablo was giving him, Cisco attempted to save himself.

"Michael," Cisco said trying to sound confident. "You know I've never been a coward. I have always served this organization faithfully. Some of the Blood chapter leaders and myself decided maybe it would be bottor to just leave them to their little corners than to keep wasting our troops?"

"Cisco," El Diablo said. " You and I came up together, right there in the east los, remember?" Cisco nodded his head as El Diablo continued. "It is for this reason that you still live. I will not tolerate your pathetic ass excuses. The Jamaicans couldn't and the Italians wouldn't; yet you let these crab muthafuckas disrupt our flow? These people need to be dealt with sooner than later."

Cisco tried to muster a smile.

"We are stronger than them, El Diablo. Time is on our side. When an opportunity presents itself, we will crush them."

El Diablo smiled and then said in a pleasant voice, "Cisco, You are one of my oldest and dearest amigo's. I made you overseer of my crew because you are a capable field general as well as a diplomat."

"Gracious, Michael," Cisco said smiling. "That means a lot coming from a man like you."

"But Cisco," Diablo said blowing smoke out of his mouth. "In all the years I've known you, I've never noticed something until now. You are stupid. Common sense isn't one of your strong points.

"Cisco, if you meet a girl and she gives you the crabs, do you wait or do you get rid of them right away?" Before Cisco could answer, El Diablo began speaking again. "I'll tell you. You get rid of them. If you wait, they will multiply and cause you much discomfort."

El Diablo made his way back to the front door with the giant on his heels.

"Cisco!" he shouted over his shoulder. "I will have Harlem and you will get it for me."

Without another word, El Diablo was gone.

*

Lou-loc stepped out of his building and was greeted by the rays of the sun. It was particularly sunny for March. He threw on his sunglasses and proceeded to the car where Gutter was still pounding the horn.

Gutter stepped out of the vehicle and came around to greet his long time friend. As usual, Gutter was G'd up, dressed in gang colors. He had on blue all stars with matching blue laces. Despite the unseasonable heat, Gutter wore an oversized Duke blue devil sweatshirt, probably to conceal whatever firearms he was carrying.

On each wrist Gutter sported two identical blue bandannas. This was to let every one know what gang he was claiming. He tied a blue ribbon in his hair to keep his box braids in a ponytail that rested on his neck. Gutter was the poster boy for gangsters.

The left sleeve of Gutter's sweatshirt was rolled up exposing one of several gang related tattoos. The word "Harlem" was scribbled on his arm in Arabic, the same tattoo that Lou-loc had on his neck, only larger. It was their clique.

When they spoke of Harlem, originally it wasn't in reference to upper Manhattan. It was Harlem Crips, a chapter of the LA gang.

Gutter joined the set back in LA about a year before Lou-loc got quoted. They were both pretty young at the time, but it was the thing to do in California.

When Gutter's father was killed overseas, he and his mother came back to the states to live with relatives. His uncles and cousins were all Crips, so for him, joining a gang was a different story.

When Lou-loc was about ten he and his father were doing some Christmas shopping in the Crenshaw mall. When they were coming out of the mall a group of Bloods surrounded them and demanded the packages his father was carrying.

The packages were to be for the family on Christmas. Lou-loc's father couldn't stand the thought of his family going without on Christmas, so he refused. For his act of bravery, he was rewarded with a chest full of buckshot. The Bloods slapped Lou-loc with the butt of the gun and ran off with the packages.

Lou-loc was horrified. His father lay on the ground bleeding while the poor boy looked on and cried helplessly. From that time on, Lou-loc developed a deep hatred for Bloods. This made his choice to join the Crips that much easier. Over the years, Lou-loc assassinated many Bloods, all in the name of his father.

He and Gutter were two of the youngest members of the Harlem chapter. With neither having a father, they shared a common bond and became close friends. Each was trying to out match the other's thirst for blood and hatred of the rival gang.

The two youngsters were recognized by the other members as loyal and efficient soldiers. They were always down to put in work or take on task for the hood, so they made their way through the ranks quickly by committing gruesome acts of violence. It was made clear to all gangs across LA County that Harlem wasn't to be fucked with.

By the time Lou-loc was nineteen, he and Gutter committed an act that made them legends amongst the homeboys and feared by the law.

At a meeting, the OG's decided that they had enough of a local narcotics detective named O'Leary, who worked the hood. At first they were able to just pay him off, but after a while he got greedy. They were already giving him 40% of their take, but he started demanding 60%. When they refused to pay he took it to the next level.

One of the little players on the set wound up dead one evening. He was found hanging from a tree by his ankles. Inside of his mouth was a note that read, *"Pay or join your friend in nigger heaven."* The police had no idea who had done it or what the note meant, but the homeboys did.

The leaders of the Crip sets had decided that this was a slight to their honor that couldn't go unpunished. O'Leary was, no doubt, the one who had done this, and he needed to be put in his place immediately.

A homeboy by the name of Fat Pat had a sister who worked for the LAPD. She was a Crip supporter, so it was only right that she helped out. She provided the homeboys with detective O'Leary's home address.

The plan was simple. They were to break into O'Leary's house, give him a good beating and bust the place up. It was just to let him know that even a cop could be touched. But in the hood nothing could ever be simple.

The soldiers selected for the mission represented several Crip sets. This was done in order to promote the unification of the C-nation. There was Stan from East Coast Crips, Snake Eyes from Hoover and Gutter, who represented Harlem Crips. Back then, he was still called Lil Gutter. Because Lou-loc and Gutter were crime partners, he volunteered himself for the mission.

The four desperados piled into the Buick they had stolen that morning for the mission and headed for the Carson. The particular house they were looking for was right off Carson Avenue near a housing complex that was still under construction. Carson was a relatively quiet town, but there was a large Crip population. If the need arose, they wouldn't have a problem seeking shelter at one of the homeboy's cribs.

The key to this mission would be Stan. He was one of those high yellow dudes with good hair and green eyes. He had thin lips and a pointed nose. In the right light he could've even passed for a white boy.

The plan was that Stan, dressed in a FedEx uniform, would ring the doorbell. When the detective's wife opened the door, Gutter, Lou-loc and Snake Eyes would rush the house. Once inside, they were to tie up whoever was there and wait for O'Leary to come home.

"A'ight nigga," Gutter said to Stan from his seat in the back. "Once we get up in there, you go on up to the corner and look out for O'Leary's car. There's only one way to come down this street, so you can't miss the nigga. When you see his car, dial my cell. Let the phone ring once, and then hang up. That'll be the signal. You got me?"

Stan, who was in the front seat, took a thumbnail full of cocaine and inhaled it.

"How many times we gotta go through this shit?" Stan asked irritated. "I know what the fuck I gotta do, chump."

"Save all that bullshit, mafucka," Lou-loc said. "If we get caught up in some bullshit, ain't no more YA (Youth Authority). It's the big time, punk."

Stan yawned and lit a joint.

"Lou-loc, stop acting like a bitch. Nigga you ain't even have to come. Always popping some shit. If anything, why we can't just peel this nigga's cap?"

"Because," said Snake Eyes from the drivers seat snatching the joint from Stan. "Killing a law enforcement agent is a capital crime. Which means if we get caught, we get the gas chamber. Stupid muthafucka."

They all laughed.

Snake Eyes was a banger, but he was book smart also. He graduated at the top of his class at Crenshaw high and was currently enrolled in his third year of law school at UCLA. Like Lou-loc, Snake Eyes didn't intend to make a living out of selling drugs.

"A'ight fellas," said Gutter checking his 38. "You ready, Lou-loc?"

For a long moment, Lou-loc said nothing. He just sat there staring at the Tech-Nine on his lap. For some reason this whole situation made him uneasy.

It wasn't that he was scared. Lou-loc had shot more than a few people in his nineteen years on earth, but this was different. They were about to invade a mans home. A police officer at that.

Gutter finally broke the silence. "Yo, cuz," he whispered to Lou-loc, who was sitting next to him in the back seat. "You ain't gotta get dirty this rip. If you want, you can stay in the car and watch our back. Me and Snake can hold this down."

"Nah," said Lou-loc shaking his head from side to side. "Let's do this shit, and get it over with." Lou-loc stepped from the car and tied a red bandanna around the lower portion of his face. Gutter and Snake Eyes stepped from the car and did the same.

As they made their way toward the house Lou-loc stopped short. "One thing fellas," he said in a hushed tone. "We don't touch, his wife and kids. If we gotta peel this nigga, then so be it, but the woman and children go free. Agreed?"

Gutter and Snake Eyes looked at each other puzzled, but nodded their heads in agreement. Stan on the other hand just sucked his teeth and continued carrying his empty box up the driveway. Stan was going to be trouble, and Lou-loc knew it.

Stan walked up the few steps and rung the doorbell while his three henchmen concealed themselves in the bushes. A shadow appeared in the front window. From the silhouette, Stan could tell it was a female, so he put on his super model smile and waved. After a moment or so, Stan heard the front door was being unlocked.

The young lady who answered the door was very attractive. Her long blonde hair was flipped up in the back and held in place by two pencils. She had ocean blue eyes and her lips where full and pink.

Stan openly admired the girl with a lustful look in his eyes. She in turn did the same. The cool breeze coming off the Pacific Ocean caused her nipples to stand at full attention, poking out through her baby doll tee shirt. She shifted her weight from one leg to the other and gave Stan a pleasant smile.

Stan's eyes kept shooting back and forth from her nipples to her too short jean shorts. He was looking at her the way a hungry man would eye a T-bone steak. The funny thing was, she didn't seem to mind. Under different circumstances he would've been trying to holla at her.

After a long silence and a bit of fantasizing, Stan finally found his voice.

"Ah...package for the O'Leary's," he said.

The girl licked her lips and looked Stan dead in the eyes.

"Pretty big huh?" she said seductively. "The package that is."

Stan smiled at her obvious attempt at flirting with him.

"So where would you like me to put it?" Stan asked matching her tone.

Before she could answer, Gutter stepped from the shadows with his gun drawn.

"Don't move, bitch," Gutter snapped.

She looked like she was going to scream until Gutter placed the gun to her head. That changed her mind.

"Let's do a little math, shall we?" Gutter asked backing her into the house. "Scream plus gun equals dead little white girl. You understand?" she nodded her head in agreement. "Good."

Lou-loc and Snake Eyes stepped into the house followed by Stan.

"Yea, I'm gonna get me some of that," Stan said moving towards the already terrified girl. Just when he got within feet of her, Lou-loc stepped in between them.

"We ain't got time for that," said Lou-loc placing a firm hand against Stan's chest. "Besides, you got some where to be don't you?"

Stan wanted to test Lou-loc but thought better of it. Something in the man's eyes told Stan to let it be. He just sucked his teeth and walked out the front door.

Lou-loc watched Stan walk up the street. He and Stan were cool, but Lou-loc knew better than to turn his back on him. After Stan had gone, Lou-loc turned his attention towards the girl. He motioned for her to sit on the couch and then knelt down beside her.

"What's your name?" Lou-loc asked.

When she didn't answer he tried being a little softer with her.

"Look girl, ain't nobody gonna hurt you. Now, tell me your name?"

"T... Tina," she finally blurted out.

"Good," said Lou-loc. "Now we're making some progress. "Next question, who else is here with you?" There was more silence.

"Look bitch," Snake Eyes said as he began, but was cut off when Lou-loc raised his hand for silence. Getting the girl all scared wouldn't help them any.

"Tina," Lou-loc said very evenly. "I told you that no one was going to hurt you, but if you don't cooperate, all bets are off. Now, who else is in the house with you?"

Tina fidgeted on the green sofa for a moment, but when she saw the look on the men's faces, she decided it was best to answer. "My mother and little brother are upstairs in the bedroom. But please don't hurt them. They won't be any trouble?"

"Let us be the judge of that," said Lou-loc. "A'ight boys," he said looking from Snake Eyes to Gutter. "Round them up. Quietly if possible, forcibly if necessary."

Snake Eyes and Gutter made their way upstairs while Lou-loc stayed with Tina. At first there was silence then a scream. As Lou-loc was about to investigate, he heard footsteps coming down the stairs.

Gutter appeared first with a middle-aged woman slung over his shoulder. Her hair was in her face but you could still see the resemblance between her and Tina. The woman's hands and feet were tied behind her as she thrashed wildly on Gutter's shoulder. Snake Eyes followed leading a small boy by the hand.

"What's that all about?" asked Lou-loc.

Gutter tossed the woman on the sofa next to her daughter and let out a sigh.

"Blood, this hoe started tripping. I had to tie her ass up to keep her from wilding out," Gutter said.

"Oh, my God," the woman said frantically. "Did these animals hurt you?"

Tina shook her head in the negative.

"No mom. I'm fine. We'll all be fins as long as we don't give them any trouble."

Mrs. O'Leary looked at her daughter in disbelief.

"Tina, are you insane? *These people* are animals. All they know is violence," Mrs. O'Leary scolded her daughter.

Lou-loc stepped in and tried to defuse the situation.

"Look Miss, you're going to be ok. We didn't come here to harm you or your family."

"You expect me to believe that?" she shot back. "I read about your kind in the news everyday. All you do is kill each other and blame honest white folks for your situation. You bastards are parasites. We've damned ourselves for even bringing you to this country. They should've left you in Africa with the rest of the monkeys and apes.

Gutter took offense to this particular remark. His grandparents had originally come to the states from Algeria. Before Lou-loc had time to react, Gutter was on his feet and moving towards her. He snatched her by the collar of her bathrobe and lifted her to her feet.

"Who are you to judge?" He said in almost a growl. "You say that we are taking from you, but what about what you have already taken from us? Our culture, freedom, dignity...how dare you?"

Lou-loc tried to calm his friend, but Gutter waved him off. With one fluid motion, Gutter drew his weapon and placed it in Mrs. O'Leary's mouth.

"You say you hate blacks so much? Well it was a black woman who saved your life this evening."

Mrs. O'Leary looked at him confused as he tucked the gun back in his belt.

"My poor mother would turn over in her grave if I threw my life away on someone as ignorant as your ass," Gutter said throwing her roughly back to the couch. "I feel no pity for you or your soul for it will surely burn in the Hereafter. It is the children I am concerned for," he said pointing at Tina and her brother.

As Gutter walked away from her, he stopped short.

"Always remember this, ignorance is a very contagious disease. If you pass it on to your children, they will surely share your miserable fate."

Gutter walked over and stood by the window. Lou-loc breathed a sigh of relief. Mrs. O'Leary would probably never have guessed how close she came to meeting her God.

Outside, Stan stood on the corner kicking rocks. He didn't like being outside away from the action. What bothered him more was missing out on his chance with the young white girl.

"Cock blocking muthafucka," Stan said to no one in particular. Who was Lou-loc to be giving him orders? "Fuck Harlem," Stan said kicking a loose stone.

As Stan looked up the street, he noticed a group of young Mexican girls coming his way. They were all wearing bikini tops and too tight shorts. At least the night wouldn't be a total loss, Stan thought as he made his way to intercept them.

"Hola, mommies," Stan said bending into an over exaggerated bow.

"Como esta?" the girls laughed thinking Stan was funny. The girls stopped to see what Mr. funny man had to say.

Stan went right to work snowing the young girls with his best lines. He was so wrapped up in the girls that he didn't notice O'Leary's blue ford bend the corner. That was a mistake that would cost him.

Inside the house the three mock Bloods stood watch over their hostages. Two hours had passed since they entered the house, and there had not been one sign of O'Leary. Lou-loc's stomach started to turn. Something was wrong.

"Where this fool at?" Lou-loc said looking at his watch. "His shift been over and he ain't here."

"Maybe he's out with his girlfriend?" Gutter said taunting Mrs. O'Leary.

"Please don't do this?" Mrs. O'Leary pleaded. "My husband is a police officer."

"We know that," said Gutter. "Why the fuck you think we here?"

"I have money," she said. "If it's money you're after, there's three hundred dollars on my nightstand and some jewelry in my box. You can have it all if you just leave."

"Don't nobody want your money, lady," said Lou-loc.

"Speak for yourself," said Gutter, tossing Lou-loc the cell phone.

"Be on point for the homeboy's call. I'm going upstairs to see what these crackers is holding." Gutter turned and bounded up the stairs.

Outside the house, detective O'Leary exited his car followed by his partner. The men in the house expected O'Leary to be alone, but he wasn't. This would surely affect the equation.

Detective O'Leary was a short squat man with thinning gray hair. His brown suit looked like it had been slept in and his wing tipped shoes looked like they were ready to be retired. From the stains on his shirt, it was fair to say that the man was a slob.

His partner was a bit of a different case. He was a man who appeared to be in his early thirties. He wore an expensive looking blue suit with his tie hanging loose around his neck. His shoes were freshly polished and made a clicking sound on the concrete drive way.

"I don't know, John," he said following O'Leary to the front door. "Seems like for every spook we bust, two more pop up to take their place. Makes you wonder if it's even worth it?"

"All depends on how you look at it Billy boy," said O'Leary lighting a cigarette. "Those poor bastards are doing us a favor. They're killing each other in the streets. And all for what, a fucking color? Property they don't even own?

"I say fuck em all in their black Assess. Basketball dunking sons of bitches. Makes more sense to just step back and let them wipe each other out. I'm just trying to live long enough to collect my pension."

The two men laughed together and headed for the front door. Neither one knowing what waited for them on the other side.

Inside the house, Lou-loc was pacing back and forth over the living room carpet. He didn't feel right about this set up. He was confident in Gutter and Snake Eyes, but he didn't like leaving Stan to cover their Assess.

"Man, why don't you sit your ass still?" said Snake Eyes from the other side of the living room. "You keep working on the rug like that and you gonna leave a trail right to where you stay at," he said jokingly.

Lou-loc gave a halfhearted laugh. Just as he was about to go back to the window, the lock on the front door clicked.

Everything else happened so fast that he barely had time to react. Before he could warn Snake Eyes, O'Leary was stepping into the house. Stan had fucked up, big time

The first thing O'Leary saw when he stepped in the house was his wife sitting on the couch with her hands tied.

"What the hell!" O'Leary shouted. His eyes bulged wide with fear and confusion.

O'Leary was attempting to pull his gun but his partner Billy was a little quicker. The young detective raised his 38 and fired two shots over O'Leary's shoulder. The first one went wild and struck the wall above Snake Eye's head. The second one struck him in the leg and folded him.

Neither one of the detectives saw Lou-loc, who was behind the door near the window. Just as his gut had warned him, everything was going wrong. He still had the element of surprise on his side, so he took advantage of it.

With his free hand he reached from behind the door and grabbed O'Leary by the tie. He yanked him forward and down as hard as he could, tossing O'Leary to the ground. With his other hand he raised the Tech 9 to the peephole and squeezed the trigger. The hollow point bullets shredded the door and most of Billy's skull along with it.

O'Leary made another grab for his gun, but again he was too slow. Before the barrel cleared the holster, Gutter was down the stairs and on him.

CHAPTER 2

"**S**o good of you to join us," Gutter said with a smile. "Don't let me stop you. By all means, reach for it." O'Leary saw the murderous look in the masked mans eyes, and changed his mind.

"Fuck happened in here?" Gutter asked looking from Lou-loc to Snake Eyes, who was on the ground bleeding.

"Ask your stupid ass homeboy," Lou-loc snapped as he rushed over to tend to Snake Eyes. "He let this fat bastard sneak up on us. Phone never even rung."

"Damn," Gutter spat looking at the dead man in the doorway. "You hit bad blood?" he asked Snake Eyes.

"Nah, I think it just scratched me. No thanks to your punk ass homeboy."

No sooner than the words left Snake Eye's mouth, Stan came running in the house.

"Damn, Lou loo, what the hell happened in here?"

Lou-loc shot Stan a dagger (cold stare). When he turned his gaze to O'Leary, the detective was giving him a puzzled look. Strike two for Stan.

O'Leary stared hard at Lou-loc and let the name roll around in his brain. "Lou-loc?" A light of recognition went off in O'Leary's head.

"Lou-loc, huh?" O'Leary said slyly. "You little gang banging muthafucka. I should've known that when you splattered old Billy through the door. Ain't too many pros in LA County can shoot with that type of accuracy. Think you're pretty smart, don't you, *cuz*? Well let me let you in on a little secret. You just killed a cop, and that's a capital offense. It's the gas chamber for you boy.

"If you're Lou-loc, then that black bastard over there must be Gutter? Yea, you fucking apes always roll in packs. At least you fucking coons can keep each other company on death row."

"You always was a dumb ass, Stan," Snake Eyes said as he struggled to his feet. "You just fucked us all."

"Fucked ain't the word," O'Leary said as he got up off the floor. "Kidnapping, breaking and entering, murder...I'm gonna turn the gas on personally for this one."

Stan's eyes began to fill with tears as the panic started to set in. "Oh, yea, you think this is a fucking game?" he said putting the gun to Mrs. O'Leary's head.

"Fall back, player," said Lou-loc. "We ain't gotta go there. Our beef is with this fat bastard, not his family."

"Nah, cuz," said Stan with tears flowing down his cheeks. "I can't go to the pen. No way, no how. it ain't gonna happen.

"Come, on Stan," said Gutter inching closer to him. "Just hold your head, cuz. Everything is blue."

When Gutter got close enough to Stan he lunged for the gun, but it was too late. Pieces of Mrs. O'Leary's skull, as well as brain matter, coated the walls and her son's pajamas.

At that point all hell broke loose. O'Leary went into a rage and caught Gutter with a blind left. The punch caught Gutter off guard and dazed him. As he tried to gather himself, O'Leary followed up with a right to the temple, knocking Gutter to the ground.

Stan tried to turn his pistol on O'Leary, but was a half second too late. O'Leary grabbed Stan's wrist and twisted it until the bones popped. The gun was now O'Leary's.

"Muthafucka!" Lou-loc shouted as he dived through the kitchen's swinging door. He hated to leave the homeboys on Front Street but, he needed to regroup and get the hell out of O'Leary's range.

"Nigger muthafuckas!" O'Leary shouted as he kicked Snake Eyes in his already injured leg. "In my fucking house!" Stan got a kick this time. "You muthafuckas are going down for this one. You're gonna fucking die," he said as he dialed the phone, never taking his eyes off of the fallen soldiers.

O'Leary dialed the phone quickly, constantly looking from the would be killers to the kitchen, where Lou-loc had disappeared. He didn't feel at all comfortable with Lou-loc being out of sight, and armed at that. He knew Lou-loc's reputation from back in the day when he sponsored his first trip to the county. Lou-loc had always been a pretty docile kid, but

God help you if you forced his hand. It was best to get back up as quickly as possible.

"Yea, this is O'Leary," he rasped into the receiver. "My wife's been killed. I got three of the perps in custody, but there's still one somewhere in the house, and he's armed. Hurry the fuck up!" He slammed the phone down.

O'Leary carefully made his way toward the kitchen and kicked the door in, but there was no Lou-loc. The reason for this is because he had slipped out the back and was making his way around towards the front of the house.

Lou-loc peeped in the front window and saw that O'Leary had his back to him. Lou-loc knew there was only one way out. O'Leary had to get hit.

It wasn't like him to kill for free, but he didn't have a lot of choices. It was either die or give up. It wasn't a hard decision, plus he wasn't too fond of the gas chamber.

Lou-loc had managed to slip half way in the front door undetected when Stan did it one mo again

"Help us fool!" he shouted. O'Leary spun around, but Lou-loc was already on the move.

O'Leary let off two wild shots which Lou-loc dodged by dropping into a roll. As Lou-loc was springing to his feet, he let off a short burst with the Tech. The bullets slammed into O'Leary's legs with a sickening thud. As O'Leary was falling, Lou-loc charged him and squeezed the trigger. O'Leary shook left to right from the multiple slugs, and finally he hit the ground.

Lou-loc walked over to O'Leary and looked over the body. O'Leary's face and chest were a mass of red goo and flesh. Lou-loc heard the sirens in the distance and knew it was time to make his exit.

"What about all this?" Stan demanded. "These kids can ID us. We can't just leave them like this. There's more killing to be done, Lou-loc."

"You're right, homes," Lou-loc said. "Y'all give me them slob rags," he directed his crew. They did so, reluctantly.

"What you doing, cuz?" Snake Eyes asked confused.

Lou-loc didn't bother to respond. He took the rags and flipped O'Leary on his back. He got down next to the body and began stuffing the red rags into what was left of O'Leary's mouth.

Tina grabbed her brother's hand and ran for the door. Lou-loc caught her mid-stride and pulled her back.

"Look here, girl," he snapped. "You know what these mean?" He asked showing her the bloody rags.

"Bloods," she said sheepishly. "You guys are bloods. But I promise I won't tell. Just let us go?"

"Now, Tina," he said with a wide grin. "I told you I wouldn't hurt you. Your parents," he said motioning to the corpses, "they weren't supposed to die."

"Listen to me, little one. When the police come you ain't gonna tell them nothing. Do you understand?" She shook her head yes.

"Very good, Tina. Now don't forget, we know who you are. If your story changes when the police get here, we'll know about it."

After he made sure she understood, he made hurried steps towards O'Leary's prone body.

All of the homeboys were looking at Lou-loc odd, but Stan was the only one stupid enough to say something.

"Yo, cuz, that was a good story, but we ain't Bloods and Snake Eyes ain't dead. What's up?" Stan said.

Lou-loc stooped down to pick up O'Leary's gun and turned it on Stan. Before Stan could protest, Lou-loc shot him in the face. Blood splattered all over Gutter and Snake Eyes. Lou -loc wiped the gun clean and put it back in O'Leary's hand. He then wiped the Tech and put it in Stan's hand.

"Stupid muthafucka," he said stepping over Stan's body. "Let's roll peoples."

Lou-loc and Gutter lifted Snake Eyes and helped him out the door. As they exited the house, there were police lights coming from the direction of the Buick.

"Shit," Lou-loc cursed. "This way," he said motioning to a walk space in between some houses. Lou-loc and Gutter half dragged and half carried Snake Eyes through the row of houses and came out on the next street over. They jogged for about another three blocks before they slowed down. At a gas station, they jacked another car and headed back to the hood.

Inside the car, Gutter asked the question that was on every one's mind.

"Yo, Lou-loc, what the fuck was that all about? You know damn well when the police get there that bitch is gonna talk."

Lou-loc smiled devilishly and said, "Shit, I hope so."

Gutter and Snake Eyes looked at each other and then back at Lou-loc.

Lou-loc looked over his shoulder at his confused friends.

"It was part of my plan. When them boys in blue get there, little Tina is going to spill her guts. They gonna see them brim flags I stuffed in ol' boy's mouth and figure slobs pulled the caper. The description she gives them is going to be three black dudes dressed in red, not including Stan. Our deceased friend will take credit for O'Leary and the other two."

Gutter sat back and just stared at Lou-loc.

"You cold muthafucka. That shit is pure genius," Gutter said.

"Ain't it though," Snake Eyes added, For the rest of the ride they laughed at Lou-loc's wicked plan and thought about what to tell the big hommies.

The next morning Lou-loc went out and got the paper. When he opened it up he smiled at the headline: "BLOODS MURDER COP AND HIS WIFE IN THEIR CARSON HOME". Inside there was more: 'Detective John O'Leary,49, and wife Marline, 46, were found murdered in their Carson home late last night. Police arrived on the scene last night after the detective called for back up to apprehend four men who had broken into the house.

By the time they arrived, the detective and his wife were already dead along with his partner, Billy Banks age 33, and another youth, Stanley Jones age 22, of Inglewood. Jones was a long time police informant who had been providing information on both Crip and Blood activity.

"Switch hitting mafucka," Lou-loc thought to himself. All this time and Stan was working for the other side. Goes to show you never really know somebody.

When the news had reached the OG's from East Coast, they wanted to blue light Lou-loc for killing one of theirs. Big Gun, who was Gutter's uncle, stepped up for Lou-loc. He made it clear that if anyone from East Coast touched Lou-loc, Harlem and Hoover would retaliate.

In the weeks that followed, the police were stomping on Blood Assess from Orange County to the Valley. Every top dog on every Blood set were leaned on to give up the killers. With the LAPD, that could hurt.

Things heated up for the Crips also. Not only were the police on them, but the Bloods too. They didn't appreciate all the unnecessary publicity. It was open season on anything blue. That summer, Lou-loc took a bullet to the leg. Suddenly California started to feel very small. So Lou-loc decided he needed a change of scenery, and headed east. That was two years ago.

CHAPTER 3

Lou-loc reclined in the passenger seat, smoking a blunt of Hydro. "If it's one thing I do appreciate about New York City, it's gotta be the Hydro," he said blowing smoke out of the partially open window. "This is some bomb shit."

Gutter was dipping the Camry in and out of traffic on the West Side Highway. Lou-loc looked at the speedometer and the gage read eighty.

"You gonna make us crash, Andretti," Lou-loc said sarcastically. Gutter glanced at his friend and returned his eyes to the road. In spite of Lou-loc's comment, he pushed it to eighty-five.

"Player, you just ain't hip," said Gutter over his shoulder. "This here is New York City, cuz. Everybody out here already drive crazy as hell. It's like they say, 'when in Rome,' right?"

"Well, you still ain't gotta drive all stupid," Lou-loc warned as he passed the blunt. "Man, if you get me stopped with this strap (gun), I'm gonna be tight as hell. Shit, I might let them slobs get at you on the island," he joked.

"Quit bitching, punk," Gutter said as he inhaled the smoke. "Ain't nothing gonna happen to your scary ass. Martina can have you back in one piece."

"Fuck her," Lou-loc said annoyed. "She don't run me."

Lou-loc turned away from Gutter and busied himself by looking out the window. Gutter looked at his friend quizzically.

"Trouble at home, cuz?" Gutter asked with Lou-loc remaining silent. "Don't even play me like that, Lou-loc. We came up on free lunch together. If anybody knows when something is on your brain it's me. Why don't you just spill?"

"Man," Lou-loc said with a sigh. "It's not major. Its like, you ever feel like you might be out growing Sharell?"

"Hell nah," Gutter said speeding past a truck. "Let me put you up on something, cuz. When we moved out here bitches were trying to see us left and right. They were all good to fuck, but that was it. Sharell was the first and only one I clicked with."

Gutter switched lanes without signaling, and nearly collided with an elderly couple in a mini van. "That girl is a gem. Baby go to school at night, and work a state job during the day. You should've asked if she was out growing me?"

Lou-loc smile at his friend. "You right, player. I just be feeling like... maybe Martina ain't that one. I'm trying to get out of this shit, and she trying to pull me deeper in it.

"It's getting to me. If it wasn't for that bun in her oven, I might've bounced already. You dig where I'm coming from?"

When Lou-loc mentioned the baby, Gutter shot him a look. "What?" Lou-loc asked hostilely. "Nigga, if you know something I don't, then spill it?"

Gutter lit a Newport and took a deep pull. "Cuz," he said exhaling the smoke, "I've been your truest, bluest homeboy since that day we jumped your skinny ass on to the set. I would never put you in a cross or question your judgment, but I gotta get this off of my chest." Gutter paused to make sure he had Lou-loc's attention. "You sure that kid she carrying is yours?"

Lou-loc looked at Gutter as if he'd lost his mind. "How you gonna ask me something like that? What the fuck you done heard, Gutter?" No answer. "GUTTER!"

"Alright, Lou-loc. I heard it through the grape vine that Martina been creeping. She been tipping with one of them Inglewood niggaz."

"Creeping, Gutter?"

"Square biz, Loc."

"I don't believe this shit," said Lou-loc pounding the dash. After all the work I been putting in, all for this Bullshit? And she's fucking with a stinking ass brim. Where you get this information, Gutter?"

"Sharell," Gutter said lane hopping, to exit off Christopher.

"How she know?"

"Hoe's gossip, Lou-loc. Few days ago, she was in the nail shop on 126th street. That skinny bitch Nikko was up in there with two of her girls, and shit. You know Nikko don't you? The bitch I was fucking from Martina's old block?" Lou-loc agreed.

"Any how, she was talking about how much fun her and Martina had when they went to that jazz spot out in Long Island. When her girl asked her who she was with, the bitch had the nerve to say, 'Oh, Blood and his cousin Mac, from Inglewood family.' Bitch acting like it's cool to run with them folk.

"Sharell wasn't even gonna follow up with it. She figured maybe the girl was talking about another Martina? That was until the chic she was with asked if you and Martina were still kicking it like that? When Sharell looked up at the mirror, Nikko was looking at her as if to say, *'I hope you heard me?'*

"I'm gonna kill that hoe!" Lou-loc cursed. "How does she think she's getting away with this shit, huh? I ain't no fucking buster. That bitch gotta die, G."

"Easy," Gutter said touching his friend's hand. "You gotta get your shit tight first nigga. You can't be doing shit all wild bill like."

Gutter found a parking lot on Leonard Street and pulled his ride in. Before he cut the engine, he pulled out his twin Glock 18's and placed them under his shirt. Lou-loc placed his gun under the passenger seat.

"Gutter, what the hell are you doing? With all that world trade shit that went down, security got tight down on this end. You gonna fuck around and get locked up.

He waved Lou-loc off. "What ever, bitch. I like to be prepared. You seem to be forgetting two things gangsta. Number one, I'm a foreigner, and number two I'm a Muslim. They ain't too big on either one now a days."

"Gutter, you is about a scary muthafucka if I ever seen one. The military ain't thinking about your ass. They laughed at each other and began walking south to BMCC.

Being around his partner lifted Lou-loc's spirits, but what he heard about Martina still bothered him. He wasn't sure if the information was 100% just yet, so he couldn't wild out just yet. One thing was for sure, he was going to find out sooner than later.

*

The northbound traffic was fairly light for a Thursday afternoon. Cisco wove his red M3 in and out traffic with a vengeance. He was mad as hell, and he wanted the world to know it.

41

"Fuck Diablo!" He said to no one in particular. Cisco was tired of being disrespected. For three long years he ran LC Blood while Diablo ran from a murder charge.

After all this time, and now Diablo wants to come back on the scene barking orders. If it wasn't for Cisco, the great El Diablo would still be hiding in Cuba with his head in the sand. It was Cisco who got the other man to confess to the crime.

The poor soul owed a debt to LC. A large one at that. In exchange for his life, he was to take credit for a murder the police already knew El Diablo committed. They didn't care who it was. As long as they had some one of color to blame for it, they were cool with the arrangement.

The judge handed that simple bastard twenty years. Every one was happy. The police got their murderer, the assistant DA got a promotion, and El Diablo was allowed to come back home. Cisco felt it was a fair deal all the way around.

Through all this, the old bastard didn't even so much as utter a word of thanks.

"Diablo," Cisco said out loud. Devil was a fitting name for that black hearted son of a bitch.

Cisco pulled a tiny cellular phone from his pocket and flipped it open. He quickly scrolled through the phone book until he found the number he was looking for. With a manicured nail, he hit send and waited.

"Hello," came a voice from the other end.

"Como esta?" asked Cisco. "What's going on, Tito?"

"Cisco, to what do I owe this pleasure?" Tito said.

"I think I'll be needing your services, Primo. Are you dressed?"

"Si, Don Cisco. I am still an early riser. Why do you ask?"

"Because," Cisco said getting off the FDR heading south on Park Avenue, "I'm coming to snatch you up. I got some moves to make and I want you with me."

"Drama?" Tito asked sounding more alert now. "Say the word and it's a wrap for whoever."

"Tito, be calm," Cisco said soothingly. "If it were that serious, you'd be the first to know. I'm only a few blocks from you so come on down. We'll talk further when I see you." Without waiting for a response Cisco ended the call.

He pulled the M3 to a stop on 129th street as he waited for a red light to turn green. As he looked out his passenger window, he noticed a group of boys crossing the street. At first he paid them no mind, but at the sight of the blue bandannas hanging from their belts, he felt himself become very angry.

At the sight of his enemies, Cisco reached for the chrome plated 9mm on his lap. One of the boys made eye contact and Cisco put on his mean mug. Cisco decided that if one of the boys recognized him and decided to try him, they would literally *get it at the light.*

The boy slowed his pace and returned Cisco's stare. Cisco spat out the passenger window and raised his gun so it rested on the steering wheel. At the sight of the cannon, the boy turned away and quickly caught up with his boys.

"Puto!" Cisco snarled as he sped off through the now green light.

By the time Cisco made it to 126th and Park, Tito was already standing outside. Tito was one of those people whose appearance didn't match their character. He was a very average looking young man, neither short nor tall. He was slim, but at the same time very muscular. This was no doubt from the years of chopping cane in Puerto Rico. Tito had spend most of his life as a farm boy, and moved to New York as a teenager.

Tito's skin was an even tan complexion, making look like a light skinned black. He wore his hair in a close fade with a part on the left side. His face was covered in a five o' clock shadow where a beard should've been.

Overall, he was fairly young looking in appearance. Except for his eyes. His eyes didn't have the bright youthful luster of a twenty one year old. Tito's eyes were dark and cold. Like someone who had seen many horrors in his time.

Although Tito looked harmless enough, he was anything but. He was Cisco's most brutal enforcer. Tito had developed quite a reputation because of his expertise with blades and his willingness to use them. On the streets he was referred to as 'Major Blood.'

Tito came into the fold shortly after El Diablo's... *disappearance*. He was recruited straight out of Rikers Island's juvenile wing. He was there finishing up an eighteen month bid for slashing an enemy on the streets.

He quickly became a favorite of Cisco's after disfiguring a rival gang member for bumping Cisco in a club. Ever since that incident, he had served as Cisco's body guard and assassin. When Cisco assumed control of LC, he offered Tito a spot as his second in command. Tito declined the position, saying that he preferred to be in the trenches with the rest of the soldiers.

As Cisco sat in his car waiting for Tito to approach, he eyed the predator and admired him. Despite living in a neighbor hood infested with Crips, he continued to dress in red.

He was decked out in a red champion hoodie with red and white Air Force One's. Being that the weather was nice and Tito was still wearing a thick pull over, Cisco knew the man was strapped. And he preferred it that way.

"What's good, Cisco?" Tito asked as he hopped into the passenger seat.

"Fucking street rats," Cisco said looking in the rear view at the young Crip soldiers he had just punked. "Tito, I don't see how you can stand to live amongst these people?"

Tito looked back at the boys then turned back to Cisco. "Fuck 'em," he said in a calm voice. "There are advantages to living amongst the 'Crabs.' In the event that we go to war or something to that affect, they would never think to look for me in their own back yards. Besides, I have an understanding with these young ones around here. They don't fuck with me, and I don't slaughter their families."

The two men enjoy a good laugh, then Tito becomes serious again. "So what has brought you to the slums, Cisco?"

Cisco smiled like the Cat who has just swallowed the Canary. "Tito, my friend, there are about to be some drastic changes in our fair city, and I want to ensure that we reap the benefits. Listen carefully to what I am about to run down to you."

CHAPTER 4

Walking through the halls of B.M.C.C, Lou-loc looked like a lost puppy. He was having a hard time finding the admissions office, and becoming very frustrated. Just as he was about to give up and say fuck college, a feminine voice called to him from behind. "Are you lost?"

Lou -loc turned around ready to tell whoever was speaking to him to fuck off. When he saw the source of the voice, he was speechless. He was standing face to face with the most beautiful woman God had ever saw fit to plant on this earth.

Suddenly everything around him seemed to fade away. All the noise and commotion around him disappeared as he sized up this vision. She was a smooth copper skinned girl. She looked like something straight out of a Cosmopolitan magazine, standing there rocking a peach colored Donna Karen pant suit with the matching shoes. Her hair stopped just before her shoulders and was trimmed into a feathered style. The way it shone she must've just got it done. Her lips were painted a dark brownish color, which complimented her beautiful brown eyes.

Lou-loc let his eyes wonder freely up and down this beautiful creature. The way she stood boasted such confidence. Her athletic figure pressed against the insides of her suit showing off her well developed yet trim, body.

"Well!" She said breaking Lou-loc's trance. "I asked if you were lost? Are you ok?"

Lou-loc mumbled something that sounded like: "I have crossed an entire ocean, and at last I've found you"

"What?" She asked confused.

"Oh...yea," Lou-loc said trying to recover himself, "I mean, yes. I am a little lost. Didn't realize it was so obvious?"

"Not really," she said looking him up and down. "I just noticed you looking around, but not really moving in any direction. I figured you were either lost or waiting for someone?"

"Well actually, a little of both," he said honestly. "I was looking for the admissions office, but I think I've found who I've been waiting for," he said looking her dead in the eye.

She smiled a little and turned her head away. "And what a beautiful smile," he said still looking at her.

"Thank you," she said pleasantly, "but didn't your mamma tell you it's impolite to stare?"

Lou-loc gave her his best smile. "Forgive me," he said bowing slightly, "but you are quite beautiful."

She smiled again. "Thank you for the kind words, but I think it's only fair to warn you that if you're trying to pick me up, it isn't going to happen. I'm not that kind of girl," she said seriously.

"Wait a minute, sweetheart," he said holding up his palms. "It ain't even that kinda party. I got nothing but your best interest at heart. My name is Lou-loc," he said extending his hand.

"Lou-loc?" She asked looking at his hand as if it was a snake. "Your mother named you Lou-loc?"

He was a little surprised by her response, so he hesitated before answering. "Nah. Actually, my full name is St. Louis. St. Louis Alexander, but if you repeat it, I'll just deny it," he said jokingly.

"St. Louis?" she said letting the name roll off her full lips. "That's an unusual name. I like that. What made her name you that?"

He looked at the floor. "That's where she met my daddy. So, do you have a name?" he asked changing the subject.

"Of course I do," she said in a matter of fact tone.

He looked at her confused. "So, are you going to tell me?"

She turned her back and began to walk away. "You can find the admissions office down the hall on the left," she said over her shoulder. Her sudden departure left him standing there stuck on stupid, but he wasn't going to let her slip away like that.

He jogged after her and finally caught up to her at the front door. Lou-loc gently touched her arm to get her attention. "You still haven't told me your name?"

She turned to face him and licked her lips seductively. "St. Louis, I am not presently, nor have I ever been *easy*. So don't get it twisted. You seem like a smart young man. If you really want to get with me, I'm sure you can find a way to reach me." She winked her eye at Lou-loc and strolled out the double doors.

As he watched her walk across the courtyard, so did the rest of the men gathered in front of the school. Even some of the girls took notice of the golden Goddess in the Donna Karen suit.

She moved through the crowds of the adoring people with the grace of a lioness. Lou-loc watched her as she climbed into her green Cherokee Jeep. To his surprise, she turned around and looked directly at him standing out in front, blew a kiss in his direction and merged into traffic. Before she got too far, he made a mental note of her license plate number.

During the registration process, Lou- loc was in a complete daze thinking about the mystery women. He didn't even realize that he had signed up for an introduction to Latino History course. Oh well, he thought. He had business to attend, and no intention on spending any more time at the school trying to get the course changed to something else. He'd just have to do it another time.

When he got outside, Gutter was waiting for him sipping on a pint of Hennessy. "Fuck wrong with you?" Gutter asked his smiling friend. "You all cheeky and shit."

"Fuck you," he said punching Gutter in the arm "I think I just met my future wife?"

"Future?" Gutter asked confused. "What about your current wife nigga?"

"I ain't wetting Martina, cuz. You had to see this broad, Ken. She was all that."

"So you mean to say, a bitch you ain't even bone yet got you open like that?"

Lou-loc shook his head in frustration. "You don't understand, Ken. It's like a feeling you get when you know you've found someone who's right for you. Like God patting you on the shoulder telling you it's alright to love this one. You feel me, nigga?"

Gutter looks at Lou-loc confused. "Nigga, you lunchin' fo real. You been reading that Mase book, or something?"

"I'm trying to have a moment wit a nigga and you acting all stupid and shit."

"My bad, Lou." Gutter says sincerely. "So what's her name?"

"I don't know."

"Where she from?"

"I don't know."

"She got any kids?"

"I don't know."

"Hold on, hold on," Gutter says putting the top back on his bottle. "You talkin' that true love shit, and you don't know jack about this girl? Youz a weird mafucka, Lou."

"What ever, G. I need you to do me a favor?"

"What?"

"Call Yvette and have her run a plate number for me?"

"Lou-loc, you my bluest homeboy, but don't get me caught up in this I spy shit wit you."

"Nigga, the one time I ask you to do me one, and you bitchin' bout it?"

"A'ight, stop cryin' mafucker." Gutter pulled out his phone and dialed a number. "Hello," came a female voice on the other end.

"Yvette girl, what's up?" Gutter said jovially.

"Who dis, Gutter? Don't what's up me, nigga! You had me waiting for yo funky ass all that time, and you ain't never show. What's up wit that?"

"Girl, I got locked up," Gutter lied, "fucking wit that nigga, Rob. Boy had me riding 'round in his whip, and didn't tell me he had a gun. I spent the whole weekend locked up in Yonkers. You know I'll make that shit up to you."

"You better!" She snapped.

"Say, peep game, Vette. I need a favor?"

"Y'all niggaz is all the same. Always want something."

"It ain't for me. It's for Lou-loc. He need you to run this plate number for him."

"Oh yea?" She asked all slick like. "Well, if he want me to do him a favor, he gotta do me one. My girl Sharon been checking for that nigga for a hot minute, but he act like he don't know. I'll run the plate for him on my lunch break, but he gotta go on a double date with me, you and her."

Gutter thought about it for a minute. That girl Sharon got body like a mo' fo, but her face is all jacked up. Lou-loc been ducking her for weeks. He was gonna be salty behind the terms of the deal, but what the fuck? This was his favor.

"A'ight, Vette," he said smiling at Lou-loc. "He'll do it. Call my phone as soon as you get the 411." He hung up with out saying goodbye.

"What'd she say?" Lou-loc asked excited.

"Oh... you straight." Gutter says slyly. "She gonna hook you up in a few. So now you can find out what you need to know."

"Cool, homey. Good looking on that, G."

"You my peoples, Lou."

"Oh, one more thing, G?"

"What's that, homey?"

"What exactly did you tell Yvette I said yes to?"

*

After Yvette got back to Gutter, he began to relay the information to his crime partner. "Well, my friend," Gutter started. "The vehicle is registered to a Ms. Satin Angelino. She's twenty-one, never been married, and ain't got no kids. Her last known address is down in the village. Looks like there might be some hope for you yet, boy."

"Man, I hope so," Lou-loc said seriously. "She could be the one I'm looking to be wit."

"Yea a'ight," said Gutter. "That brings us back to the million dollar question. What about Martina? Fuck you going to do, go home and tell ya wife, 'baby I know we been together for almost two years, and you a few months pregnant, but I've fallen in love wit a broad I hardly know?' Martina's crazy ass ain't hardly having that."

"Apparently you still ain't understanding me," said Lou-loc as he took the bottle of liquor. "To you, shorty, just another face in the crowd, but to me she's the only face.

"Now don't get me wrong. Martina's about to be my baby's mama and all, so you know I got nuff love for her. Funny thing is, I love her, but I can't say that I'm still in love with her. I mean, to be truthful with you, cuz, we ain't got shit in common. I'm tryin' to get out this game while she want me to get in deeper. I don't wanna sell dope all my days.

"I'll be the first mafucker to admit I got side tracked by all this paper here in New York, but dying in these streets," he said with a sweep of his hand, "ain't the way I plan on going out. I gotta see my dream through. I wanna write books, not Obituaries for my fallen comrades."

"Here we go again," said Gutter, snatching the bottle from Lou-loc in mid gulp.

"Fuck you, Gutter," said Lou-loc, wiping his chin. "I ain't hardly trying to preach to you. Lord knows I've done my fair share of dirt. I'll probably do more before it's all said and done. Shit, I'm probably gonna burn in hell for the shit I already done, but that's beside the point. I'm dealing with the here and now, and I wanna do something righteous with my life. You feel where I'm coming from?"

"Yea, I feel you," said Gutter taking a deep swig of the liquor. "But you gotta understand, street life is all some niggaz know. This shit we do put food on a lot of niggaz tables."

"That's true," said Lou-loc. "But for every table we put food on, we take it off three more. You know as well as I do, most fiends will sell their own children for a blast of that shit we serving."

"I understand what you saying, Lou, but a muthafucka gotta eat. A lot of soldiers from our side as well as the others, come from fucked up homes with no daddy, and little to no income. How can we expect them not to take to the streets? If they don't work for us, then it'll be somebody else. Regardless, the call of the streets is too strong for some of us to resist. You of all people should know that, cuz."

Lou-loc looked at him sideways. "I know you ain't even tryin' to run that shit on me, Gutter? You raise a good point, but if that's the case, what the fuck is your excuse? You had both parents around most ya life, and was still doing dirt. Shit your grandfather was a college professor."

"Yea," Gutter said lighting a cigarette, "Gramps was a professor, but he was also a revolutionist. When the Soviet Union tried to bull their way on to Islamic soil, Gramps was right there fighting alongside the Muslims. Being an American citizen, he didn't even have to go. But he did.

"That was Gramps for you. He was a real 'Gangsta.' He lived amongst those people as one of their own. He fought, and eventually died for their independence. When he passed they buried him in the same manner as their other fallen heroes. Gramps is still held in high regards amongst the Arabs who know of his deeds.

"I remember when my aunt Rashia took me to Islamabad to visit his crypt. The way those folks treated us and carried on about him, he must've been an OG or some shit. I couldn't speak their language very well back then, but from what I gathered from what I was able to pick up, 'Kenyatta Hamid Soladine, Sr., was an important man. At least to them he was. Now that's gangsta."

"Yea, it is," said Lou-loc. "But your grandfather wasn't just fighting for the hell of it. He fought with a purpose. What's our purpose?

"Don't get it fucked up. I'll always be down for the set, Crip for life. Right or wrong, good or bad, we click. I just feel like, what the fuck is the point. I ain't got no more tears left in me for the dead. We slaughter each other in the streets, for what? What the fuck is it all about?"

Gutter answered his friends question with one word. "Power."

*

For the next block or so, neither man spoke, each lost in his own thoughts. Lou-loc glanced across the street and noticed a circle of young boys wearing red bandannas. Trapped in the center of the circle was a young white girl. Something about the girl reminded Lou-loc of Tina. She had the same attractive features, except her hair was brown.

A fire began to build in Lou-loc's stomach. For some reason, the sight of the young black boys ganging up on the white girl made Lou-loc angry. So angry, he decided he was going to do something about it. Before Gutter had even realized his partner was gone, Lou-loc was half way across the street.

One of the boys noticed Lou-loc coming in there direction, and stuck his chest out in defiance. "Keep walking, nigga." the boy snarled.

Lou-loc held his hands up, palm's out. "I don't want no trouble, Lil homey. I just came to ask y'all to let the young lady alone?"

Two more of the boys flanked the first one on either side. At the sight of his friends, and Lou-loc's submissiveness, the first boy's confidence was boosted. He had assumed Lou-loc was a punk. You know what they say about 'assumptions?'

From his rear pocket, the boy produced a razor blade and pointed it at Lou-loc. "Breeze, muthafucka," the boy said menacingly. "Or do you want your food ate?"

Without a second thought, Lou-loc went into action. With blinding speed he grabbed the boy's exposed wrist. With a bone popping twist, he forced the boy to drop the razor. With his right index and middle finger, he jabbed the boy in the throat. The boy dropped to his knees, in a fit of coughing. The boy's friends abandoned the girl, and moved to help their fallen soldier. Unfortunately, Gutter changed their mind when he stepped on the curb with twin glocks drawn.

"Make a move." Gutter snapped. "I twist 'slob's' back, young and old. If you don't believe me, take one more step." Seeing that the gunman was dead serious, the boys froze in place. "Damn, and I really wanted y'all to try me."

Lou-loc lifted the boy so that they were nose to nose. "Lil young ass nigga." he spat. "I should take that shank and fuck you wit it. You know who the fuck I am?" Painfully, the boy shook his head from side to side.

"My name is Lou-loc."

"Oh shit!" one of the boys blurted out. He had heard plenty of stories about the executioner called Lou-loc. He didn't know Lou-loc personally, but he knew enough to know he didn't want to bump heads with the man.

Lou-loc eyed the crowd wearily, as the fire in his belly grew. He felt the beast within him cry for release, but struggled for control. "Take them fucking scarves off. All of y'all!" The boys quickly did as they were told. "How old are you, boy?" Lou-loc asked the boy whom he still held in his grip.

"F...fifteen." the boy managed to stutter out.

Lou-loc shook his head in disgust. "You ain't even old enough to wipe ya assess good, let alone robbed some fuckin' body." Lou-loc slapped the boy in the back of the head. "Stupid ass lil niggaz. Y'all need to have ya assess in school. Get the fuck up outta here. If I see any one of y'all sporting a flag on any set, it's a fuckin' wrap. Now beat it."

As the boys were made to leave, Gutter stopped them short. "Hold on fellas," he said putting his guns away. "You run and tell ya peoples, Manhattan is under new management. All slobs will be executed on sight."

Out of no where, Gutter hit the largest of the group square in the mouth. Crimson blood sprayed from the boy's mouth as he crumpled into the arms of his friends. "Now go tell ya bitch ass homeboys that there's a new sheriff in town, and his name is Gutter.

The boys collected their wounded friends and slithered away in disgrace. Gutter threw his head back and had a good laugh at their expense. Lou-loc on the other hand said nothing. He just stood there fuming with his fist balled.

The would be victim placed her hand on Lou-loc's shoulder, breaking him out of his trance. "Thank you," she said in an Aristocratic accent. "Who knows what those animals had planned for me."

Lou-loc spun around suddenly and grabbed her by the wrist. He slowly began to apply pressure until she grimaced in pain. "Look here, bitch," he snarled looking her dead in the eye. "I didn't do shit for your uppity ass, so you might wanna hold off on the gratitude.

"What I did was for those kids. You don't know how tired I am of seeing kids throw their lives away over 'mark' ass muthafuckas like you. There's enough of my Lil brothers behind the wall as it is. All over dumb shit."

"Well...I..." she started, but was cut off.

"Well you what?" Lou-loc snapped. "You didn't mean any thing by it? Man, you crackers kill me. And y'all say we got a lot of excuses. Bitch, raise yo ass up outta here, and take yo ass back to West End avenue. Kick rocks, bitch."

The girl looked back and forth from Lou-loc to Gutter. When she looked like she was about to respond, Gutter stepped in between them.

"Take a hike, shorty," he said very cool. She sucked her teeth but held her comment and walked off.

"Boy, I was beginning to wonder about you," Gutter said slapping Lou-loc on the ass. "Thought them stories about you losing your nerve might've been true. The way you wigged out on them slobs removed any doubt from my mind about your OG status."

Lou-loc rolled his eyes at Gutter and walked off. "Fuck is wrong wit you, cuz!" Gutter shouted after him. "A nigga tryin' to give you ya props, and you get all funny style. Fuck is the deal?"

Lou-loc turned and looked at his friend with sadness in his eyes. "Animals," he said softly. "She called them animals."

"So, what's ya point?" Gutter asked confused. "Fuck them slobs."

"What's my point? Gutter, we used to be just like them. Is that how people see us, as animals?"

"Lou-loc, we wasn't nothing like them Lil niggaz. We respected the G-code as well as our elders. These Lil bastards now a days don't respect shit."

"Fuck the code, Gutter. What about respect for people, or life. What happened to that?"

"I feel where your coming from, cousin, but those rules only apply to civilians. We ain't civilians no more. Ain't been for a long time," he added.

"Don't get all wishy washy on me now, you knew what was up when you got down wit the set. I understand you, Loc, really I do, but I need you to understand me. We're in hostile times, my friend. War could pop off like that. It's them or us, cuz.

"When we get where we need to be, we can all breathe easy, but we ain't there yet. Ain't no days off in this here. Banging is a full time job, and money is sweeter than any motherfuckin' pussy a hoe can lay on you. I don't know about you, Loc, but I'm tryin' to see both. Straight like that.

"Me and you, we started this shit out here together. Nigga we been brothers at arms since writing on the walls counted for putting in work. I need your head to be right if we gonna win this game. Niggaz that don't think right, they go out like Stan. Ain't no way I'm gonna let you go that route, or my mother fucking self for that matter."

"You right, Gutter." Lou-loc admitted. "But you can't say I don't also have a valid point, now can you?"

"Look, just forget it," Gutter said finally tired of arguing. Once Lou-loc got started, he could go on for hours. Gutter knew that he had shit to take care of. "Let's just go check Roc, and get faded. Fuck all this dumb shit. After we get done, you can tip off to see ya little girl friend."

Lou-loc's eyes got a little brighter at the mention of Satin. "I knew that would pick ya spirits up," Gutter said smiling.

"Fuck you, Kenyatta," Lou-loc said playfully.

"Fuck you right back, St. Louis." the two friends shared a hug and a laugh. "You still down for me, Loc?"

"Til the day I leave here, cuz."

"Gangsta?"

"Gangsta."

CHAPTER 5

*T*he Cherokee Jeep moved casually through the traffic on the avenue of Americas. Satin gripped the steering wheel with a manicured hand, and made the 4x4 do as she wished. Much the same way as she did with people. Despite her innocent appearance, Satin was a girl with ambition. She knew exactly what she wanted out of life, and was determined to get it.

When she was very young, she lost her mother to cancer, and her father committed suicide shortly after. The only family she had left were her two brothers and her aunt Selina.

As a child, Satin never wanted for anything. Whatever her aunt Selina couldn't provide for Satin, her older brother Michael stepped up and made sure she got it. It wasn't until she got a little older, that she realized her brother made his income illegally. This made her more hesitant to accept his gifts, but she still let him do for her when necessary.

When Satin was a junior in high school, she revealed to her family her dream of owning her own business, a publishing house actually. Writing was a favorite past time of hers. She took her writing almost as seriously as her income. That was deep for her.

Still they laughed at her and said "A woman's place was in the home and not the business world, which is dominated by men." This didn't deter her one bit. In fact, it only made her work harder at it.

After high school, Satin decided to put college on hold, and took an internship with a local magazine. It was then that Satin decided what she wanted to do with herself. She wanted to start a magazine that catered to the interest of black and Latino women.

The editor, who happened to be a female, was so impressed by Satin's work ethics and ideas, that she decided to hire her as a personal assistant. She even arranged her schedule so that she was able to take Journalism classes at the local community college. She was the only person to ever encourage Satin to pursue her dream.

Satin was definitely on her way up in the world, and she had earned it. But today her mind wasn't on her career. She was thinking about the guy she had met.

"St. Louis," she said out loud, letting the name roll around in her mouth. Such an odd name she thought. Who names their children after cities? But he was very handsome.

She was attracted to him from the first time she saw him, which was actually a few months ago on 125th street. He was going into the movie theater with some Dominican girl. Satin was aware of the fact that Lou-loc had a girl, but truth be told it didn't really matter to her. She wasn't in the habit of breaking up 'happy homes,' but something about him moved her.

Maybe it was his girlish lips, or possibly his eyes. He had very sad eyes. The kind of eyes that only years of pain could bring.

Satin loved those eyes. They were the eyes of someone who had a story to tell. She knew those eyes well because they were once hers.

She remembered the first night she'd seen him. He was rocking a powder blue silk walking suit with some white on white Nikes. His hair was braided in zigzags with blue rubber bands holding them in place. She remembered the butterflies that were driving her stomach crazy, and the feeling of disappointment when the girl walked up and took him by the arm.

"Bitch," she spat. She knew that had to be his girl, but then again it was hard to say. Satin had seen the girl in a few spots, keeping company with several different guys. The thought of the girl already having him, and then being stupid enough to cheat on his fine ass, only made Satin want him more.

When she first saw him, she had assumed he was a thug. The way he carried himself gave her that impression. He walked with a slight 'bop,' and his pants hung off his ass. But when she spoke to him at the school, she was completely taken aback. He was very articulate and soft spoken. Goes to show, you can't judge a book by its cover.

She didn't reveal any of this when they finally met. She could play the game just as well as anyone, if not better. Her reasoning was that she wanted to see how far he would go? Or maybe to see how far she was willing to go?

One thing she did know, was that she was feeling Lou-loc. She just hoped she hadn't ruined it by playing hard to get. Maybe she should've at least told him her name? Fuck it. She knew she'd see him again. BMCC wasn't that big.

Sure, she knew she was wrong for scheming on somebody that already had somebody. But wrong or not, Satin was a girl of ambition, and that overrode her better judgment. When she wanted something, it was in her nature to go after it.

*

Satin parked her car in front of her west 14th street walk up and killed the engine. As she was stepping out of her jeep, a long red Cadillac pulled up to her passenger side. The windows were tinted, so she couldn't see who was in it.

As she closed her driver side door with her right hand, her left dipped into her purse. She fingered her small .22 caliber, and scanned the Caddy for any sign of movement. Growing up in the projects of the lower east, she learned to shoot first and ask questions later. If it was going to pop off, she would be ready.

The driver's side window slid halfway down and revealed a hulking head, wearing dark sunglasses. He smiled at Satin, revealing a moth full of stained yellow teeth. "Long time, Satin," said the giant, trying to sound seductive.

Satin was unsure of the drivers identity, but there was something oddly familiar about his voice. The huge man stepped from his car and made his way to where Satin was standing. As he approached, a light of recognition went off in Satin's head. The massive form, who was now standing six feet away from her, was Rico Runez, also known as 'The Giant.'

"What are you doing here, Rico?" she asked making her pistol visible. "I thought I made it clear to Cisco that his advances were in vain."

"Easy, mama," he said backing up slightly. "It ain't like that. I brought someone here to see you."

"I doubt that there's anyone you know that I'd want to see."

"Oh, but I beg to differ," he said grinning. "I think you'll be quite pleased to see who has come to call on you."

58

As if on cue, a lone figure stepped from the back seat of the car. He was a rather ordinary looking man. He wasn't short, nor was he tall. He had smooth olive skin, and a pencil thin mustache lined his upper lip. A white linen suit hung loosely on his lean frame. The ensemble was a red fedora.

"Hello, Satin," he said calmly. "Are you not pleased to see your big brother?"

Satin stood there with a shocked expression on her face. It had been years since she had last seen her brother, and now here he was. The notorious El Diablo.

Satin quickly composed herself. "Hello, Michael. Or do you prefer 'El Diablo?'"

El Diablo dismissed her comment with a wave of his hand. "Ah, merely a name given to me by some of my associates. Nothing more. So how have you been little sister?"

"Fine, not that you care. It's been, how many years?"

"Aye," he threw up his hands in mock surrender. "Why so cold, Satin. You know I didn't have a choice. Besides, were you not taken care of in my absence?"

"Taken care of?" she started. "You can't be serious? If you call sending your 'Yes man', Cisco here with money, and trying to get in my pants taken care of, yes, I was fine."

"My apologies, Satin. Cisco can be a bit...vulgar, but I will see that he is reprimanded for his actions. But financially, you and the family were good?"

"Yea," she said flatly. "But auntie Selina hasn't been in the best of shape. She's at Saint Vincent's. You been to see her?"

"No," he said sadly. "I feared that I would not be welcomed. Your warm reception has confirmed that.

"I won't take up your time, Satin. I just wanted to see you, and to let you know I'm home. If you should need something, I will send Cisco in case you don't want to see me again."

"Cisco!" she spat. "That's a fucking joke right? Cisco is a piece of shit, who cares about no one but himself. You told him to treat me like a sister, instead he tried to treat me like a whore. Showering me with gifts to gain my affection, 'perro.' No amount of money would ever get me into his bed."

"As I said earlier, Cisco well be dealt with, but let's move on to another topic. How is our brother, Jesus? What's he been up to?"

"In and out of trouble," she said. "I don't blame him, look who his role model is. A fucking king pin."

"Satin, I never meant for things to turn out this way. I only wanted to make things better for our family. Is that so wrong?"

Satin massaged the back of her neck as she looked into his sorrow filled eyes. She knew that he meant well, but his methods were all wrong.

"Michael," she said taking his hand in hers. "I'm a big girl now. I appreciate all that you've done for our family and me, but I don't need a keeper anymore.

"You on the other hand, you need guidance. You have so much, but it is still not enough for you. Your greed is going to be your downfall. Find yourself a nice girl and retire from this game. Please? Why don't you come with us to church, Sunday? We can..."

Satin jumped back startled as El Diablo snatched his hand away. "I'm afraid I cannot, little one. It is as you said, I am Diablo. I fear I would not be welcomed in a house of worship."

El Diablo pulled a piece of paper from his pocket and wrote an address down. "This is where I'll be staying," he said handing Satin the paper. "If you need anything, you can reach me there. It was good to see you, little one."

Without another word, El Diablo turned to walk away with his head hung low. Satin's conscious began to eat away at her. Even though he was a Gangster, they were still family, and Satin new it.

"Michael." Satin called after him. He stopped briefly to see what she wanted, and was surprised at what she did. She ran to him and threw herself into his arms.

"You're an asshole, but we're still family. Welcome home, Michael. Welcome home."

*

A half hour later as Satin watched the car drive off, she couldn't help but wonder, what this turn of events would mean to her life?

CHAPTER 6

Lou-loc and Gutter strolled in silence down Church Avenue in Brooklyn. They were on their way to the meeting with Roc. This was the day they were to meet Anwar, boss of the Al Mukalla Crime Family.

Lou-loc had met Roc once or twice in the past, but he didn't really know much about him. No one did. All Lou-loc really knew, is that Roc was the under boss of the Al Mukalla, and Anwar ran the operation.

The Al Mukalla were a gang of Middle Easterners who operated out of Brooklyn. They had their hands in a little bit of everything. Gambling, loan sharking, guns. You name it, they were in it. They turned a profit from all sorts of vices, but their main source of income was heroin.

Anwar was very careful with the drug trade, only selling to certain people, and never anything under half a kilo. Nobody knew who or where they got their product from, but it was the rawest dope on the streets.

Anwar and his men ruled their little corner of the city with an iron fist. Although they were few in number, they more than made up for it in viciousness. Each member of the organization was ready to die for what they believed in. Niggaz on the streets knew that if you crossed the Al Mukalla, life could become very uncomfortable.

Gutter had gotten connected through Roc. They had met some years ago at an Islamic rally in 'At Taif.' Their two families had a history together that stretched a few years back.

Even though Gutter returned to the states while Roc remained in At Taif, they kept in contact over the years. When Roc moved to New York, he and Gutter resumed their friendship. After a few months of nagging, Roc finally agreed to introduce Gutter to Anwar. The Al Mukalla were very suspicious of outsiders, especially Americans. The only reason Anwar even agreed to meet with Gutter is because he was a Muslim.

Gutter tapped Lou-loc's arm, snapping him out of his daze. "There it is, cuz," he said pointing to a shabby looking corner market.

"That's it?" Lou-loc asked skeptically. "Nigga, you sure?" Gutter didn't even bother to answer. Instead he walked through the front door of the store. With a shrug of his shoulders, Lou-loc followed.

As they stepped through the front door they, spotted Roc behind the counter handing a little girl a pack of skittles and her change. Roc looked up from the his task as if he had sensed their presence, and greeted them with a nod and a smile. The two responded in kind.

Roc was a jovial looking man. He stood at around five feet even. His face was round and pleasant, and he always smiled in public. He was wide at the shoulders, but round at the belly. He actually looked more like a shopkeeper than what he truly was.

Roc was a master killer. Those who didn't know him personally would think he was fat. But under his loose fitting meat cutters smock, was all muscle. Rock was a hulk of a man, with hands like catcher's mitts.

His hands were his favorite killing devices. He would choke his victims, men and women alike, wringing their necks until they snapped. It was through his stone like grip that he acquired the nickname 'Roc.'

At the end of the line were three young men waiting to pay for their 40oz's. All three of the young men were wearing red scarves. They shot at daggers Lou-loc and Gutter, who were dressed mostly in blue. The bandannas on Gutter's wrist confirmed their affiliation.

"Punk ass crabs." mumbled one of the boys.

"What you say, nigga?" said Gutter stepping forward. Sensing that violence was about to erupt, the customers abandoned their purchases and made for the door.

"You heard him, muthafucka," another boy added, "this blood hood, chump. Respect the gangster."

"Fuck you, Lil nigga." Lou-loc spat. "I don't give a fuck what hood we in. My advice to you is, pay for ya mother fucking beer, and beat street. We ain't start this shit, but we sure as hell can finish it. What's up, cuz?"

Lou-loc put a southern twang on the last word just to irk the east coast hoodlums. The challenge had been made. Calling a blood "cuz" was looked at as a disrespect. Lou-loc had deliberately called them out.

The first boy, whom Lou-loc assumed to be the leader of the group, hesitated. Lou-loc possessing an incredible sense of character, knew he had the first boy's heart. However, this didn't hold true for his partner.

From under his sweatshirt, the boy produced a small 22. He was quick, but Lou-loc was quicker. By the time the boy raised his gun, Lou-loc had closed the distance between them, and had the barrel of his Glock to the boy's chest.

Lou-loc smiled and leaned in so he and the boy were nose to nose. "You wasn't trying to draw on me, was you boy?" Lou-loc whispered. The boy saw the savage look in Lou-loc's eyes and suddenly didn't feel so tough. He had no illusions about surviving this encounter.

Before anyone else could react, there was a loud click, and the room went still. Everyone turned to see what the noise was, and were completely thrown off by what they saw.

Standing between isles two and three, stood a little boy. He was skinny, but not too much so. He was some where between frail and recently malnourished. He wore camouflage fatigue pants and a plain tank top. His skin was a dusty brown, complementing the big black curls that danced on his head. Other than one unusual feature, he was just a child. The feature was the sub machine gun he held in his tiny hands.

"Please," said Roc stepping from behind the counter. "Violence nor weapons are permitted here. I would urge you to take heed to the laws of the Al Mukalla, please," he said something in Arabic to the boy with the gun. In response to whatever the command was, the boy pulled a pillowcase from beneath his belt. Roc beaconed him forward, and continued speaking. "Place your guns in the sack, gentlemen."

The boys looked at each other, as if to say: "Is he serious?" The boy waving the .380 Mac convinced them he was. Slowly the boys all began to pull out weapons of all sorts, and placed them in the pillowcase. They were well equipped with various razors, knives, and minor firearms, but the little guardian was walking a little heavier.

"This is some bullshit." one of the boys spat.

"Hey, hey," Roc interrupted. "Don't give me bullshit, my friend. All you little punks around here know Anwar's rule about weapons in his places. Now you all run along. If you don't cause anymore trouble, I might return your guns when the store closes...maybe."

"Come on, Roc," the boy protested further, "you know us, man."

"Yes," Roc said very calmly. "That's the reason I'm having Hassan take your weapons, and not your lives. Now run along, children."

The boys lowered their heads and slunk out of the store. Everyone relaxed after the last of the boys had left the store.

"What was that shit about, Roc?" Gutter asked.

"Nothing for you to worry about, Kenyatta," said Roc. "They're just children. We Al Mukalla keep the peace here. No one would violate a guest of ours, no matter what personal conflicts exist between your factions.

Roc made his way to the front of the store and stared out the window. "You see that?" he asked motioning towards a playground across the street. "That is 'Mukalla Park.' It was built and funded by us. The Al Mukalla.

"Even though we built it, the park is open to all. Children of all races and colors come here to play in safety. We guard it 24/7 with hidden cameras and constant patrols. In that park, no one is allowed to sell or use drugs. The penalty for violating the rule is death. The children are the future of us all, so we must ensure that they grow to fruition."

"That's deep." Lou-loc commented.

"That's Mukalla." Roc responded, "We are about the betterment of our people as well as those in our community. Allah has been good to us and it is only fair that we spread the love to those around us."

"I can respect your gangster, Roc," Lou-loc said.

"And I yours." Roc responded.

"So what's good, Roc?" Gutter interrupted. "I been looking forward to this gathering for some time now. I'm ready to do the damn thing."

"Easy, Gutter," Roc said patting his shoulder. "Anwar is waiting for us in his war room. Before we go to join him, I would ask you also to remove your weapons?"

"What's all this shit about?" Lou-loc asked looking at Gutter. "After what just went down, I'm keeping my strap right the fuck here."

Roc and Lou-loc stared each other down for a moment. Neither men wanted to give ground, but this meeting was in both their best interest. Roc finally broke the silence.

"No disrespect to you," he said looking Lou-loc square in the eye "but it is the policy of our war room. It keeps negotiations from becoming, how do you say...unpleasant?"

"Come on, Loc," said Gutter. "We straight up in here. Let's go along with the program." Gutter handed over his guns, and Lou-loc reluctantly did the same.

"Thank you," Roc said with a smile. "Now if you will please follow me. Anwar is waiting." Roc instructed the little guardian to put the confiscated weapons into the safe and run the register for a while.

He led the two men through the isles and into the back storeroom. It was fairly normal looking as storerooms went. The small area was cluttered with boxes of supplies and file cabinets. There was a large meat freezer that stretched along the entire back wall. Roc turned the knob, and the massive door slid open with a loud hiss. "This way, gentlemen."

Lou-loc looked at Gutter puzzled, and then turned his attention to Roc. "You can't be serious?" he said sarcastically. "You want us to go into a freezer?"

"You Americans are so distrustful," Roc said with a chuckle. "This is the way to the war room. Once you step inside, you'll understand."

Gutter and Lou-loc stepped into the freezer cautiously, with Roc bringing up the rear. Lou-loc had an odd feeling about the whole situation. Once all three were inside, the massive door slammed, and the freezer went dark.

Lou-loc instinctively reached for his gun that was no longer there. "Shit!" he screamed. Infrared beams of light passed over Lou-loc and Gutter's bodies. In his mind, Lou-loc knew he was living his last moments.

The lights continued to sweep over Lou-loc and his partner, but they still seemed to be intact. After a few moments, the beams were gone and the freezer began to rumble. Lou-loc could tell they were descending, but where to, he was unsure. Before long, they were stopped and the freezer was illuminated with some sort of emergency light.

"Hope that didn't unnerve you too much?" Roc said sarcastically. "It was just a sweep for concealed weapons."

"You boys sure are paranoid," Lou-loc retorted with a hint of sarcasm in his voice.

"Afraid we must be," Roc said while unlocking another door that Lou-loc was sure wasn't there when he entered the freezer. "People now a days aren't always honorable. Paranoia will help me to live a very long life."

The three men left the freezer/elevator and found themselves in an underground passage. It was a long corridor that appeared to not have been used in sometime. The walls were crusted with mold and filth. The tiny holes in them showed signs that a gunfight had transpired at some point.

"Must've been quite a gun fight down here?" Lou-loc whispered to Gutter as he examined the holes. Upon closer inspection, he noticed that not all of the specs were holes. Some of them appeared to be covered by glass. Like lenses of some sort. As he turned to rejoin the group, he noticed Roc watching him. Lou-loc was tempted to ask about the holes but he didn't and Roc didn't volunteer the information.

At the end of the corridor, there stood a lone iron door. Along the edge of the door, there was something scribbled in Arabic. Lou-loc couldn't translate the words, but they seemed to mean something to Gutter.

"This is Anwar's war room," Roc said motioning towards the door. "While you gentlemen remove your shoes, I will notify him that you're here." Without waiting for a response, he disappeared behind the door, leaving Lou-loc and Gutter in the hall alone.

Once Lou-loc was sure Roc was out of earshot, he decided to ask Gutter about the writing. "Say, Gutter," he said tapping his friends arm, "what's that writing all about? What that shit mean, cuz?"

Gutter looked at his friend and smiled. "Well, the first part says: 'Justice for the sons and daughters of Allah.' The second part says: 'Death to the Almighty Devil.'"

Lou-loc looked at Gutter confused. "Who or what is the Almighty Devil?"

"America," Gutter said flatly.

A moment later, Roc came into the hallway and summoned them inside. As the two men entered the room, they were quite surprised by what they saw. Unlike the filthy corridor, the room was quite plush. The floors were carpeted from wall to wall, with a high arched ceiling. The interior of the room was soundproofed and completely without windows. A vast network of monitors on the back wall gave off the only light, other than the few scattered candles.

There wasn't much in the way of furniture either. There was a white leather sofa that took up most of the wall to the left of the monitors. In another section of the room, there was a conference table surrounded by seven chairs. In the center of the room sat an oak desk directly in front of the monitors. Even though it was draped in shadows, Lou-loc could tell that someone was sitting behind the desk watching them.

"Please step in," said a voice in clipped English. "Step in and be seated. You are amongst friends here."

Lou-loc and Gutter moved cautiously across the carpeted floor and took up seats on the couch. As Lou-loc sniffed the air, he could smell a familiar aroma through the scented candles. It wasn't a totally unpleasant smell, but it was a familiar one. As quickly as the thought came to him, he pushed it from his mind. There was no way it could be the same smell. Could it?

The figure stepped from behind the desk, snapping Lou-loc from his thoughts. As the figure came into the light, his features became clear to them. He had long black hair that was braided into a ponytail, and tied off with a golden ribbon. His olive toned face was smooth and bare, much like Lou-loc's. The garments he wore were simple. Green army fatigues and a black turtleneck.

Roc stepped in the center of the room and bowed from the waist. "Gutter, Lou-loc, I present to you Prince Anwar Bien Mustaf."

Anwar stepped forward and shook their hands. Anwar was not at all what they had expected. He appeared to be no more that a teenager, but it was his eyes that told a different story. They were the eyes of a warrior.

"Thank you for coming," Anwar said politely. "There is still much for us to discuss. But first, may I offer you some refreshment; soda, juice, liquor?"

At the mention of booze, Gutter was quick to respond.

"Thanks, man. You got any Yak like Henny or something?" Gutter asked.

"Of course I do. That's actually one of my favorite Cognacs. And what will you have?" he asked Lou-loc.

"Same, thanks," Lou-loc responded.

Anwar turned to Roc and said, "Would you mind, brother?"

"Your will is mine," Roc said with a bow. "I'll return shortly." With that he was gone.

Anwar motioned for the two men to join him at the conference table so they could begin the negotiation. "Kenyatta," he said bowing to Gutter, "when Roc told me of your long standing friendship, I asked him why he hadn't brought you to my attention sooner? How could I deny a member of the Soladine family?"

"You are familiar with my family?" Gutter asked surprised.

"Indeed I am. Believe it or not, I owe your grandfather a great debt. When I was a young boy, visiting my family in Afghanistan, the Russians invaded my uncle's village. Your Family helped get us out. "Your grandfather as well as your Father were great men. Even though they were not of our lands, they fought for our people. He was a great asset to our troops, and a martyr to our people."

"Thank you," Gutter said with a nod. All was silent for a moment. It was as if the men were paying their respects to the fallen soldier. Roc came in with the drinks, and took up the seat next to Anwar.

At last, Anwar broke the silence, "Now, to the business at hand. What can the Al Mukalla do for you, Gentlemen?"

"Well, it's like this," Gutter started, "it ain't really what you can do for us, but what we can do for each other. You feel me?

"Me and my partner," he said motioning towards Lou-loc. "We doing big things in Harlem. We got paper coming in, and we holding shit down. We tryin' to step it up, and spread it out, cousin.

"Now things are cool uptown, but the shit is twisted everywhere else. We'd like to expand to downtown and the lower east, but there's too many rival sets. We'd have to spill a good amount of blood to really do us. We ain't really tryin' to go there. Not that we scared or no shit like that, we just don't need the heat."

"And this is to mean what to me?" Anwar asked.

"Hold on Anwar, I'm getting to that. We heard about your little problem out here. Bloods acting all crazy, jacking ya customers and fucking up business. Makes it kinda hard to get ya paper on."

"Very true." Anwar answered honestly. "People are becoming more and more afraid to come out here. We hold sway within the heart of our turf, but we are stretched very thin along our borders. I see you've done your home work, Kenyatta?"

"Thank you, Anwar."

"So, how do you and your bunch propose to help us with our problem?

"Glad you asked," Gutter said with a grin. "We propose an alliance of sorts. Let us set up shop on the Al Mukalla borders. We'll cut you in for 15% of our gross profits in Brooklyn for the first six months, and10% thereafter.

"In return, you hit us wit the dope at a discount. This way, your customers are guaranteed safe passage, your borders are covered, and we get to expand. Everybody gets paid. How you love that?"

Anwar paused for a moment to consider what was being laid out before him. "It sounds good so far, Kenyatta. But I do see a flaw in your plan.

"Allowing your people to operate in our area will be looked upon as a slight to the Bloods in the area. Some might even see it as taking sides. We, Al Mukalla, are what you might call separatists. It is not our way to involve ourselves in outsider feuds.

"It isn't that we are afraid, or don't want to help you. It is quite the opposite actually. It's just that, this... Color War, is not ours. To involve ourselves in this thing of yours, could cause serious problems. If anything negative were to come of this, it would not go over well with my people."

For a long while no one spoke. The Al Mukalla's refusal to aid Harlem in the feud was something Gutter hadn't counted on. Gutter knew that if he couldn't sway Anwar, he would be back to square one.

"I have a suggestion," Lou-loc said, surprising everyone in the room. "I have a way this can work out for us all."

"I'm listening," Anwar said, leaning forward on his elbows.

"Tell me something," Lou-loc started, "if hostile parties were to initiate violence on Al Mukalla turf, and you handled it, would you be in the wrong?"

Anwar looked at Lou-loc puzzled. "Technically no. It is common knowledge amongst all the gang leaders in the area, that we will brook no violations of our set, as you call it."

"Well, there's your solution," Lou-loc said sitting back in his chair.

"I'm afraid I don't follow you, Lou-loc," Anwar said flatly.

"Well, let me break it down to you, Anwar. We'll keep dealing with the problems in Harlem, that isn't a problem for us. Now in Brooklyn, we'll do it like this. We'll handle the new spots, and the threats to the borders. The Al Mukalla will lend additional muscle, when called for. The best part of it is, it'll all be done anonymous if you'd prefer it that way. Other than Gutter and me, none of the homeboys know about this little meeting. If someone were to discover your involvement, it would be as if you were just protecting your turf. No harm, no foul, and we all win."

Anwar sat for a moment rubbing his bare chin. A smile crossed his face as he turned his attention to Lou-loc. "Lou-loc, you are a snake, and a brilliant strategist. You should be with Al Mukalla, my friend. You could've easily been a general in our army back home."

"Thank you, Anwar, but the Crips are my army."

"So, what it is, Anwar?" Gutter interrupted. "Do we do business or what?"

"So eager," Anwar said smirking. "First things first. We need a binding agreement."

"What, like a contract?" Gutter asked.

"Not quite. In olden times, pacts were sealed in blood."

"So, you want us to prick our fingers or something. I ain't too fond of nothing red, but I ain't no punk. Let's do this."

"Not quite what I meant." Anwar corrected. "I had something different in mind. Something to ensure our loyalty to each other in this relationship."

Lou-loc had a bad feeling as to where the conversation was going. "What you talking bout, Anwar?"

Anwar leaned forward and looked Lou-loc dead in the eye. "A life for a life. You kill someone for us, and we for you."

Gutter breathed a little easier. "Shit, is that all? I was more nervous when I thought you wanted me to cut myself. Nigga, I'm always down for a 187. Who you want dead?"

"A local," Anwar started "He runs this little group of five per centers out of Bedstuy. He and his alike are becoming a pain in my ass. Because of certain mutual spiritual beliefs and acquaintances, I can't strike him down directly so I am forced to call on outside help."

"Ain't nothing," Gutter said confidently. "I'll dust his ass myself."

"Afraid not," Anwar interjected, "you are also Muslim, and therefor, it would not be wise for you to embark on such a task. And because of our anonymous relationship, the task cannot be trusted to one of your underlings." Lou-loc definitely didn't like where this was going.

"I do have another candidate in mind," Anwar said a little to cool for Lou-loc's liking. "I nominate Lou-loc."

There it was. Lou-loc had killed quite a few people in his life, but that was before. He had no desire to damn himself anymore than he already was. There was some bullshit about to go down, and he knew it.

"So," Anwar said with a devilish smile, "will you do this thing for us?"

"Go fuck ya self, sand rat," is what Lou-loc wanted to say, but he didn't. "Why you want me to do it?"

"You are my brother's brother. If Kenyatta trust you, then I trust you. Besides, you are one of the most qualified killers I know of." This statement caught Lou-loc off guard.

"Don't look so surprised, St. Louis. I am familiar with your work. To date, you have twenty-three bodies under your belt, two of which were police officers. I know you, Lou-loc."

"Fuck, is you writing my bio or some shit?" Lou-loc asked defensively.

"No need to worry," Anwar assured him, "your secrets are safe with me. In fact, I owe you somewhat of a debt. A few years ago, you murdered a Blood called 'Two Shot.' This particular Blood murdered a cousin of mine in a convenient store hold up. You saved me the trouble of having him executed. Many thanks for that. Now back to the business at hand. If you help us on this, I will make it worth your while.

"There's thirty thousand cash in it for you, and I will owe you a great debt. I have friends in the publishing industry, who owe me favors. Will you do it?"

"Why me?" Lou-loc thought to himself. All he wanted to do was get out of the game, and there was always something to bind him tighter to it.

Lou-loc looked at Anwar, who was waiting for an answer, then he looked at Gutter with hope etched across his face. Lou-loc answered him with one word. "When?"

A broad smile crossed both Gutter's and Anwar's face. "My friends," Anwar said raising his glass, "let us toast to success." Lou-loc was trying to rise above the hood shit, and Anwar had just taken a dump in his lap.

CHAPTER 7

*T*he sun was setting, and evening was approaching as Lou-loc made his way through the streets of the east village. He was having mixed feelings about the day's turn of events. He was happy that his friend was seeing his dream through, but what about his dream?

Lou-loc wanted to distance himself from the set, but something was always pulling him back. It was his sincere loyalty to the set that was slitting his own throat. No sense in worrying over it cause he'd come too far to back out. Against his better judgment, he'd accepted the contract from the Al Mukalla, and in return, they would eliminate a certain rival gangster, to the Crip's claim in Manhattan.

Lou-loc would fulfill his end of the bargain, and then he was going to step to Anwar. That kid was playing some serious mind games, and Lou-loc didn't like it. He valued his privacy, and people invading that, rubbed him the wrong way. Connected or not, he and Anwar were going to have a chitchat. If need be, he could get it too.

Lou-loc pushed those thoughts from his mind and concentrated on the business at hand. He intended to find out what the fuck Martina was up to? After all that he had gone through with his 'baby mamma,' she must've been outta her mind to tip out on him? It was okay though, he had a plan for that ass.

When Lou-loc got to west fourth he ducked into a little corner pub. It was an out of the way little spot filled mostly with Goths and hippies. Lou-loc trying to be as inconspicuous as possible, side stepped through the crowd and took a seat at a corner booth. When Lou-loc was finally able to flag down one of the leather garbed waitresses, he ordered a rum and coke. As he scanned the smoke filled bar, no one appeared to be taking notice of him. He preferred it that way.

After a few moments, the waitress returned with his drink and sat it on the chalky table in front of him. Lou-loc gave her his winning smile, and instructed her to keep them coming. The waitress smiled and made her way back to the bar area. Lou-loc sipped his drink and waited.

About an hour and three drinks later, he spotted who he was waiting for. The man who entered the bar was surprisingly young looking.

In fact, he really didn't look old enough to be in the bar. Strangely enough, no one bothered to stop him or ask to see his ID. It was as if they didn't even notice him.

The stranger must've felt Lou-loc watching him because he turned and stared directly at him from across the room. The stranger held Lou-loc's gaze for a moment, then continued on to the bar. As he passed through, the other occupants gave him a wide berth. Lou-loc continued to sip his drink and wait.

Just as the waitress was leaving Lou-loc's table, a lone figure appeared in front of Lou-loc. He was tall and relatively thin. His skin was dark and smooth against his high cheekbones. With his emerald green eyes, angular chin, and black trench coat, he looked more like a what than a who. Although he appeared to be no more than a high school student, he carried himself like some one of an earlier time. All of his movements were fluid and easy. Lou-loc didn't seem the least bit disturbed by the young man's presence.

Without waiting for an invitation, the stranger sat down with his drink and faced Lou-loc,

"I can tell you don't belong here," the stranger said in a whisper. "What brings you to this part of town, Gang Lord?"

Lou-loc swallowed the last of his watered down drink and sized the stranger up.

"I'm looking for a friend," he responded. "And I am no Gang Lord, Goth boy."

"Fuck you," the stranger snarled.

"Nah, fuck you," Lou-loc shot back. When the two men noticed some of the people turning in their direction, they both burst out laughing. As the threat of violence passed, the patrons went back to their drinks.

"Lou-loc, you are quite dramatic," said the stranger.

"Nah, you the drama king, Cross," Lou-loc responded. "Shit, I couldn't take you on ya worst day."

"Well, that cannon under your shirt would help," Lou-loc said.

"Not much," Cross replied.

"So," Cross began, "this isn't your kind of place. What brings you down here to hob nob with us stiffs? You thinking about coming over to our side?"

"Nah," Lou-loc said shaking his head. "I like getting drunk and going to the beach on sunny days. I ain't quite ready to give that up yet. Thanks though."

"But straight up though, I need a favor. I hate to come down here fucking your groove up, and all but..."

"Go head with that, Lou-loc," Cross cut him off. "If anything, I owe you."

"You don't owe me nothing, Cross. That time them cats shot me you came through for the kid."

"Man, that was just a scratch. That night you found me I was in a bad way. You could've left me out to fry, but you didn't. And even after that, you never told anyone about me. Not even your brother, Gutter."

"You asked me not to say anything, so I didn't. I don't get down like that. Besides, who would've believed me?"

"True. But anyway, what can I do for you? How can a child of Gehenna service the General of Harlem Crip?"

"I need you to do a little detective work, and if it comes down to it, maybe hit something."

Cross picked his still full beer bottle up to his lips but didn't take a drink.

"That serious, huh?" Cross said.

"It might be," Lou-loc said leaning forward as if some one might over hear their conversation. "It's Martina."

"What?" Cross asked shocked. "You want me to kill your girl?"

"Slow down, Cross. I want you to follow her. I think she might be cheating."

"I'm sorry to hear that," Cross said honestly. "So, what's the plan. I mean, if she is cheating, how do you want to handle it?"

"Follow her, see where she goes and who she sees. If she's seeing someone else, kill him. Her, I'll deal with. You'll be paid for your services and you can do what you want with his body. As an added bonus," Lou-loc slid a manila envelope across the table, "those two are suited to your refined taste. You'll get the locations when the job is done."

Cross' mouth began to water as he looked over the contents of the envelope.

"Lou-loc, you've got yourself a deal. I'll get on it tonight."

"Thank you," Lou-loc said standing to leave. "Oh, and Cross, no harm is to come to Martina. Are we clear on that?"

"Don't worry. I won't hurt the little lady, but I can't say the same for her little friend. A slight upon you, is a slight upon me. And that, my friend, is unforgivable."

With that last comment Lou-loc left the bar. He was quite sure that Cross would carry out his wishes to the very letter. He was big on repaying debts owed. Especially those in blood.

*

Cross sat at the table for a few more moments pawing over the envelope. This would be easy. Cross had seen Martina with other men more than once. He just didn't want to hurt his friend by telling him. Many a nights he had wanted to step from the shadows and ravage some young thug pawing at his friend's girl.

Lou-loc had helped Cross a while back. He had always treated Cross with respect and honor. Unlike most of his ilk, Cross would defend Lou-loc's honor and there would be blood claimed for this. Cross just hoped that bitch, Martina, didn't accidentally get caught up in the crossfire.

"Oh, well," Cross thought to himself as he stood to leave. There were always the casualties. For now, that wasn't Cross' concern. The night was young and he was hungry.

CHAPTER 8

Cisco sat in the emergency room waiting area of Roosevelt Hospital waiting for Miguel to bring the car around. He touched the fresh stitches on the side of his face and thought back to the meeting he had with El Diablo a few hours prior.

That bitch, Satin, had told El Diablo of his advances and he was rewarded with twelve stitches in his face.

El Diablo had no patience when it came to his little sister. That just made Cisco despise his former mentor. El Diablo would have his day and LC Blood would belong to Cisco again.

Miguel pulled up in front of the glass doors and beeped the horn. Cautiously, Cisco stepped from the emergency room into the night air. As he slid into the car, he kept looking around as if El Diablo were going to pop out of thin air and cut him again.

"Damn, Cisco," Miguel said looking at the scar. "Diablo fucked you pretty good."

Cisco looked at Miguel coldly, and Miguel knew enough to shut his mouth.

"Don't test me," Cisco snapped. "I've had quite enough of the bullshit for one day, my friend. Did you provide Tito with the information I gave you?"

"Yep. I took care of it as soon as I dropped you off. He said he'd be good alone, but I told him to send Franco and Scales to test their defenses. If they can't get it done, then he'll step to it personally."

"Very good, Miguel. Contrary to popular opinion, you aren't a complete idiot."

Miguel looked at Cisco from the corner of his eye but held his comment.

"The winds of change are blowing, mi amigo," Cisco said while lighting a cigar. "The ways of the old timers are fading. It is time we step into the twenty first century. New times call for new leadership. Wouldn't you say, Miguel?"

Miguel wasn't sure where Cisco was going with the conversation, so he figured it best to just play along. "Si. We need to step it up like the Italians and the Chinese."

Cisco grinned, seeing that he and Miguel were reading from the same page.

"El Diablo has played a large part in the strengthening of our chapter, but he's getting old. He thinks we're still living in the 80's where people still respect and fear a name," Miguel said.

"These are the dog years, Miguel. The only thing people respect any more is money and power. If you want something, you must take it. These old farts are losing their edge. We need fresh blood."

"So, what are you saying, Cisco?" Miguel asked keeping one eye on the road and the other on Cisco.

"What I'm saying is that during my time as boss of LCB, we prospered and made money. When El Diablo is removed from power we will again be the head of the food chain. LCB will be mine again."

"There are others amongst us who feel the same way. They too, would like to go back to living large instead of squabbling and dying over bullshit. By force or by choice, El Diablo will step down."

Miguel knew that Cisco was talking about a mutiny. If anything were to go wrong, those involved would surely become outlaws or be put to death. But on the other hand, if all went well, Miguel would be able to get in on the ground floor.

He didn't know whether he was going to side with Cisco or El Diablo, so Miguel decided to play both ends from the middle. If worse came to worst, he could always inform El Diablo of Cisco's plan. Whichever way it went, there was something in it for Miguel. He figured he might as well play it out.

"I assume you have a plan, Cisco?" Miguel state.

A broad smile crossed Cisco's face. "Indeed I do. Now listen carefully."

*

Satin was coming out of Barnes and Nobles going over the day's events. It was just like Michael to pop up after God knows what from God knows where and expect acceptance. Fuck 'em. He wasn't gonna stop Satin's show.

As she rounded the corner of West 8th Street, she noticed someone sitting on her jeep holding what looked like a stick. It was dark on the block so she couldn't see who it was. Satin quickly retrieved her pistol and moved cautiously towards the jeep. As she got closer to the stranger his features became more familiar to her.

"Holla, senorita," he said getting up off the car. "It's nice to see you again, Satin."

"St. Louis?" Satin said surprised. "How'd you find me?"

"As you said, I'm resourceful. Oh, and you can ice the gat. I'm harmless," Lou-loc said.

Satin blushed and was a little embarrassed that she was still holding the gun. Usually the fact that a stranger had tracked her down would've been creepy, but something about Lou-loc made Satin feel at ease. After an uncomfortable pause, she put the gun back in her purse.

Lou-loc stepped forward and extended his arm. What Satin had assumed to be a stick was actually one long stemmed white rose.

"For you, gorgeous," Lou-loc said handing her the rose.

Satin inhaled the sweet fragrance and blushed like a schoolgirl. "Why thank you, St. Louis. It's beautiful."

"No thanks needed. But do me a favor and cool out on my government. My friends call me Lou-loc."

"So we're friends, huh?" Satin said.

"For now. Maybe further down the road it'll get a little deeper?"

"Let's not get ahead of ourselves, Lou-loc. One step at a time, okay?"

"Fair enough. Listen, why don't we go some where and rap a little. You know, get to know each other?"

Satin's face took on a look of disappointment.

"I wish I could, but I have plans. They're having a black writer's convention at the garden and I want to see if I can get some of these signed," she said holding up her Barnes & Noble bag.

"Damn," Lou-loc said. "Ain't fate a bitch? I come all this way to see you and you hurt my feelings. Guess another time then?"

Lou-loc looked at her with puppy dog eyes and Satin damn near wet herself. Satin wanted this man in the worst kind of way, but she had to be cool about it. As Lou-loc turned to leave, Satin stopped him.

"Hey wait," she said grabbing his arm. "I got an idea. You could come with me. I mean, only if you want to."

Lou-loc had already decided that if need be, he would follow this girl to the ends of the earth, but he couldn't hip her to it. He had to play hard to get so he wouldn't seem thirsty.

Lou-loc scratched his chin and shook his head.

"I don't know, Satin. I'm not even dressed properly. I don't wanna cramp your style."

"Don't be that way," she said rubbing his hand. "You might even enjoy it. You said you wanted to get to know me, right? So here's your chance."

"Okay, Miss Angelino," he said with a smile. "You've convinced me. Give me a sec to make a phone call and we're in the wind," Lou-loc said.

He stepped to the side and pulled out his cell phone and called Martina. She wasn't home so after leaving a message saying that he wouldn't be home til late, Lou-loc turned his attention back to Satin.

"Okay, Satin, everything is kosher. If you like, we can take my car?"

"I told you, I'm not that kinda girl," she said faking an attitude. "We'll go in my car, and if you try something, I will put one in you."

Lou-loc gave her his winning smile and said, "Shorty, I ain't no pervert, that's hard up for a nut. You're safe with me. Shall we, Miss Angelino?" he said extending his arm to her.

"Indeed we shall," she said taking his arm. The two lovers strolled arm and arm to Satin's jeep. They were smiling like they had both hit the lotto as they looked forward to what the future might hold.

*

Martina sat listening to Lou-loc's message while putting lotion on her legs. She was tight at the fact that Lou-loc wouldn't be there tonight, but she didn't sweat it too much. She had plans of her own.

After carefully putting her hair into twists, she pulled her DKNY dress out of the closet. Her nails were painted sunset orange to compliment her gold dress. After she was finished primping she was ready to jet.

After calling a taxi, Martina went downstairs to wait for it. All she could think about was her secret rendezvous. She was so wrapped up in her own thoughts that she didn't notice the red eyes watching her.

Cross crawled along the side of Martina's building watching his prey. He knew she was a bogus bitch, and that just made it harder to keep the beast in check. He wanted to swoop down on her and crush her skull, but those were not his friend's wishes.

Lou-loc was a good man and Cross refused to do him dirty no matter how much it would've pleased his own desires. Hopefully, when Lou-loc realized how much of bitch she was, he'd ask Cross to take her. Until then, he was just going to watch.

The taxi came and Martina got in. Using his extra sensitive hearing, Cross heard Martina give the cab driver an address in Jersey. After the taxi pulled off, Cross released his grip and leapt to the ground. Even though he was at least six feet tall, his landing was as silent as a blade of grass.

Using his powerful legs muscles, Cross was again airborne. Only this time he landed on a custom built Harley with what looked like an infant's skull resting where the head light was supposed to be. With a swipe of his boot, the hog roared to life.

When Martina's taxi had gotten about a block or so, Cross pulled out behind them. Even though it was quite dark, it wouldn't be a problem for someone of Cross' type to follow the taxi. As thoughts of his payment came to mind, Cross licked his cold lips and smiled. Although he couldn't touch Martina, the same didn't apply for her would be lover. Whoever had been foolish enough to cross Lou-loc by shacking up with the whore, had literally stepped into the demon's maw.

Cross and Lou-loc had more than a friendship. They were bound by blood as well as loyalty. It was a bond that Cross took very seriously.

Whoever the poor fool turned out to be that Martina was meeting with, was going to learn that the price of good pussy wasn't always worth it.

CHAPTER 9

Gutter strolled casually from the corner bodega, smoking a black and scratching off his game card. He was proud of how well things went with the Al Mukalla, and even more pleased that Lou-loc had accepted the contract. Soon the dough would be rolling in and their crew would be in good shape.

Lou-loc was a true blue homeboy. Gutter knew that he didn't want to accept the contract, but he did it off the strength of the set. As far as getting down went, you couldn't get no more down than Lou-loc. He was a real nigga.

Gutter felt a little sour about the whole situation. He knew Lou-loc wanted out of the game and all the bullshit that came with it. He wasn't like most niggaz, who wanted to get out because they were scared. Lou-loc wanted out because he was tired of the lifestyle, and Gutter understood that.

The only reason Lou-loc was still putting in work is because of his love for Gutter. All the years they had spent putting in work would soon have to come to an end. Gutter had already decided that once this thing had been done for Anwar, he was going to set Lou-loc free from his oath. The time they spent getting down with and for each other had been sweet, but Gutter knew Lou-loc had bigger plans. He didn't wanna sling no more and Gutter respected that.

Gutter pulled out his wallet and removed a bank deposit slip. After the two grand he had deposited the day before, it had brought the total to twelve thousand. It was money that Gutter had been secretly saving up for his friend. Once their business was conducted, he planned on giving it to Lou-loc to help him out with what ever he wanted to do with his life. It was a good deal of bread, but you couldn't put a price on a friend like Lou-loc.

Gutter was brought out of his thoughts by a flicker of movement in the corner of his eye. With reflexes born from years of street training, he dove to his left and pulled his gat in one motion. Just as Gutter hit the ground rolling, a hail of bullets ripped through the car he had been standing next to seconds prior. As Gutter got to his feet he saw two young men wearing red scarves over their faces charging at him. Gutter's brain screamed out a warning, *"BLOODS!"*

The first Blood raised his Mac 10 to let off another burst, but Gutter beat him to the punch. Gutter let off two quick shots and both hit their mark. The Blood dropped his gun and howled in pain as the first shot slammed into the meat of his thigh and the second shattered his cheek bone.

Gutter took a second to admire his handy work, and that second cost him dearly. As he tried to move out of the second attacker's line of fire, he got hit. The bullet slammed into his stomach and sent him flying backward through the window of a dry cleaners.

As Gutter tried to get to his feet, he was greeted by two more bullets. One struck him in the arm and the other hit him in the chest. This sent his pistol flying. It seemed like the party was over for old Gutter as the Blood called Scales moved in to finish him off.

Gutter was fighting to stay conscious, but it was a losing battle. Scales raised his 45 Revolver and smiled at the fallen gang leader. Just as Scales began to tighten his grip on the trigger, a cry shattered the darkness, *"HARLEM, MUTHERFUCKER!"*

Before Scales even had a chance to turn around, he found himself being ripped to shreds by a hail of bullets. The unknown attacker pressed down on the trigger of his 380 Mac and didn't release his grip until the clip was spent. As Scales lay on his back bleedingand twitching, the stranger stepped over him and bashed his scull in with the end of an oak cane.

Gutter could hear the chaos erupting around him, but couldn't find the strength to move. The stranger was tugging at Gutter and calling his name, but Gutter was having trouble focusing. Between the pain and the loss of blood, he was losing his will to fight. For the briefest of moments, Gutter forced his eyes to focus on the stranger and the face was familiar. It was Snake Eyes. Gutter managed to force a smile onto his lips, and then the darkness claimed him.

*

Lou-loc and Satin sat sipping coffee at a small shop not far from The Garden. They had just come from the convention and decided not to call it a night just yet. At first Lou-loc had been a bit skeptical about going to the event. In fact the only reason he even bothered was to spend some time with Satin.

Once they reached the convention, Lou-loc was quite astounded by the entire affair. There were people and books of all shapes, sizes, and colors. Most of the books on display were books that he had already read. There were a few he hadn't checked out, so he bought them and got them signed by the authors. Some of Lou-loc's favorite writers were at the convention. He wanted to run around grinning and shaking hands, but he couldn't come across as a 'bird' in front of Satin on their first date.

Satin was very impressed by the fact that Lou-loc was so well read. He knew a little something about all of the books there. He had either read them or heard of them. He even bought Satin a book about a girl who wanted to have the best of both worlds. That guy with the dreads that kind of resembles Jerry Rice ten years ago wrote it. He's a brilliant writer and his books are always juicy.

As Satin sat stirring her French vanilla, she decided to pick Lou-loc's brain.

"So, Lou-loc," she said licking her stirrer seductively, "how come you know so much about books?"

"What, you surprised I can read or something?" he asked playfully.

"No, I don't mean it like that. It's just that when you talk about books and writing, there's so much passion in your words."

"Writing is something I'm very passionate about. It's my escape from the hustle and bustle of every day bullshit."

"So you write then?" she asked, leaning in a little closer.
"Sure do." he responded. "I've written two books and a bunch of short stories."

"I'm impressed, Lou-loc. You don't strike me as the type."

"Why, because I rock my pants a little looser than most folks, or cause my hair is all braided up? Tsk, tsk, Satin. How stereo typical of you."

"Cut it out, Lou-loc. You know what I mean."

"I know, I'm just messing wit ya. I get that a lot though. People tend to judge you for face value instead of quality. It's a'ight though, I really don't mind. I kinda like it that way. People tend to give you a wider berth when they think you're some kind of sick cat. And what about you, Satin, what's your story?

"Don't really have one to tell you the truth. Just a young girl trying to work her way through school, and make a better life for her family. Since my aunt's been sick, I've kinda had to bear the burden. You know taking care of my little brother and all."

As Satin spoke, Lou-loc felt closer to her. She was such a deep person, he wanted to hear all she had to tell. Lou-loc moved closer to her and placed his hand on hers. His pager went off, but he ignored it and listened to Satin.

"So, it's just the three of you?" he asked.

"No," she said turning her eyes away, "I have another sibling. An older brother. He doesn't come around much. My aunt calls him a street person. She doesn't agree with his... lifestyle."

"And you, Satin," he asked, "how do you feel about his lifestyle?"

"Well," she started, "I don't condemn it, nor do I condone it. It's just how he is. I wish he would give those damn streets up."

"I see how you feel, doll, but for some of us, the streets are the only way out."

"Oh, you mean like you? Will the streets be your escape as you call it?"

"Hey, hold on now, Satin. I ain't never say I was an angel. I make no excuses for what I do. And as far as your question, no. Believe it or not, I've grown quite tired of the game."

"So, why do you still play it?"

Lou-loc was caught off guard by that question. He didn't really have an answer, so he just spoke from the heart. "I don't know why I play it. I guess because I don't know how to stop playing it."

Satin looked up at Lou-loc with tears in her eyes and shook her head. "Hey, come on," he said moving around the table to her side, "I didn't mean to upset you."

She waved him off, but didn't push him away. "It's not you," she said wiping her eyes, "it's this fucked up world we live in. These streets pull down so many talented brothers like you. I'm just sick of it."

"Satin," he said taking her in his arms, "people can change. Your brother can change, there's still time."

"And you, Lou-loc, can you change?"

"Who knows. Maybe if I had the right person in my life to help me? Will you help me change, Satin?"

Satin looked into Lou-loc's eyes and saw sincerity. This only made her cry more. Here was this man that she hardly knew, and she was falling for him face first. She wanted him, and she knew he wanted her, but what about his girl?

"Lou-loc," she said pulling away, "this can't be. I have to be honest, I want you. I've wanted you from the first moment I saw you going into The Magic Theater. We want each other, but you got a girl, and I can't rock like that."

Lou-loc stepped back completely taken by surprise. How the hell did she know about Martina? He could've lied about it, or denied the fact that he was still with Martina, but he didn't. There was something about Satin that made him want to be totally honest with her. No matter what the consequences.

"Satin," he said, "you're right about me having a lady, I won't lie to you, but it's not what you think. That chic is way bogus. I used to be so in love with her that I was blind to the bullshit she was pulling on me.

"Even as we speak, I got somebody following her. I know she's tipping out on me, but I got no proof. No proof other than what my heart is telling me. I don't even think the baby she's carrying belongs to me?"

Satin looked at the tears welling up in Lou-loc's eyes, and her heart went out to him. She saw so much pain inside him that she had to turn away. Satin knew Lou-loc was the man she wanted to be with, but she was afraid of getting hurt. "So, now what?" she asked.

"Well," he said, "we can wonder what might have been, or we can take a chance on the future, one step at a time."

"One step at a time?"

"One step at a time."

The two of them walked from the shop hand in hand talking, and trying to make sense out of life. Neither one of them noticed the young man in the red sweat suit watching their exit.

*

It was about 3am when Martina finally finished her little date. It was just as Lou-loc had expected, she was tipping. Every time Cross would see them hug or touch each other, he got a thrill. He was going to make this little task as painful as possible.

From the low down Cross had gotten from his associate, Jasper, the man with Martina called himself 'Mac'. He ran a Blood chapter out of Newark. He and Martina had been seeing each other off and on for about three years. Some times as a couple, other times they were just fuck buddies.

Cross really didn't know what Martina saw in the guy. Granted, he was a snazzy dresser. The suit he had on had to cost at least a grand, but his whole MO was tacky. His suit was nice, but his shoes were scuffed and worn. From the smell of the boy, Cross could tell the cologne was cheap.

He wasn't particularly attractive either. He was short with lumpy brown skin and chemical waves. He wore gold caps to hide the few teeth in his mouth that were rotten. What caught Cross' attention the most was the monstrous ruby that he sported on his left pinky.

Cross observed the entire date from a far. Their first stop was a movie theater in the Newport mall. The movie was some ol' corny shit, but that didn't much matter to Martina. She and Mac sat in the back section where they hugged up like young lovers. Cross looked on in disgust as Martina sucked Mac's lil dick for the better half of the movie. The worse part is that she didn't bother to spit.

The two lovers went to different spots around New Jersey having a merry old time. They were the king and queen of shit. Little did either of them know that, biding its time, death trailed not far behind them,.

Cross waited quietly in the shadows of a doorway while Mac kissed Martina, and put her in a taxi. "No sense in tipping the little bitch to the fact that she's busted," he thought to himself. Soon the taxi was well away, and Mac was taking a slow stroll back to his car. A stroll he would never get to finish.

Just as Mac reached for his car keys, Cross leapt out of the darkness with a snarl. He could've taken Mac without making a sound, but it was more dramatic this way. Cross was a sucker for drama.

Mac spun to face what he thought was a stray dog from the sound. He was totally surprised to see a man moving towards him. Mac reached for his gun, but was stopped short by Cross' vice like grip on his wrist. Cross leaned in and twisted his face into a mask of death.

Mac pissed his pants at the sight of this slobbering thing that was standing not even two feet away from him. Cross let out a demonic laugh as he tightened his grip and crushed Mac's wrist. Mac began to whimper, which only excited Cross more. Popping open his switch blade, Cross slashed Mac's face.

The heady aroma of fresh blood sent Cross into a frenzy as he tore savagely at Mac's already shredded face with his teeth. Mac begged and pleaded for his life, but it was too late. The beast had been let loose, and his life was forfeit

CHAPTER 10

When Lou-loc got home, the house was empty. No Martina, no kids. Didn't really surprise him though. She had been slipping out quite often lately. It seemed like every time he was out for extended periods of time, she would slip away, and come home with a lame excuse.

"Fuck her." he thought to himself. If she was doing dirt, Cross would find out. Every time Lou-loc thought of Cross, he felt kind of creepy. Sure they were friends, but he was really out there.

Lou-loc stripped down to his boxers and stood in front of the mirror. He touched the spot where the bullet wound would've been if Cross hadn't helped him. Lou-loc had saved Cross, and Cross had returned the favor down the line. The score was even, but the two chose to remain friends.

Lou-loc flopped down on the bed and sighed. The answering machine light read twenty messages. "Lazy bitch couldn't even clear the machine." Lou-loc didn't care who called, he had some thinking to do. Thinking about Satin.

From the moment he first saw her, she had been on his mind. At first he thought she might've been just a stuck up little chic, but after he had spent time talking to her and getting to know her, he realized he was wrong. She was deeper than he thought possible, and that just made him want her more. Satin was the kinda lady that had ambition. She knew what her goals were, and busted her ass to reach them. She had a deep appreciation for life, and a hell of a lot of class.

Satin carried herself like a lady at all times. She hardly swore, and articulated herself very well when she spoke. Satin was one of those women that when she spoke to someone, her voice commanded their undivided attention. She was definitely someone he could learn from.

It was all like a fairy tale to Lou-loc. They say when you find your soul mate, you know it from your first encounter. Lou-loc was really beginning to think there was some truth to that.

And what about Martina, what if he was wrong? Lou-loc loved Martina, or at least he thought he did. But what if he put his self out there, and she turned out to be a sour apple? Why must life be so hard?

Lou-loc heard the front door click, and knew Martina was home. He quickly closed his eyes and pretended to be asleep.

*

Martina removed her shoes in the hall and slipped silently in the house. She was still a little tipsy from the bottle of Cristal she and Mac had been sipping on. It wasn't the smartest thing in the world for her to do, being pregnant and all, but she figured, "It's only champagne, what could it hurt?"

When she went into the bedroom, she saw Lou-loc stretched across the bed, knocked out.

Sometimes she felt bad for creeping on him, but fuck it. Her logic was: "If he was more sensitive to her needs, she wouldn't have to tip on him." She cared for Lou-loc, that was true enough, but the main reason she stayed with him was because the boy was worth paper. Lou-loc was indeed 'A hustler's hustler.'

When she had first met Lou-loc, she already knew who he was. Her peoples had already hipped her to his steelo. He was a big man in California, but his fame grew when he hit the east coast. On top of all that, he was a pretty nigga. The word was out that Lou-loc was the nigga to get with, and she snatched his ass up.

It wasn't even hard for her to do either. Despite all the dirt he had done, and all the hood shit he was caught up in, Lou-loc was a real sweetheart underneath it all. She just used that to her advantage. Plus, she felt that there wasn't another mami in New York as bad as her. It was common knowledge that Lou-loc had a thing for the Latinos.

Martina walked to the bed and looked down at Lou-loc's sleeping form. She felt kinda bad about her secret rendezvous. Lou-loc was a lot of things, but to her knowledge, he hadn't been unfaithful.

Sometimes she didn't understand why she even fucked with Mac? Lou-loc was better looking, and his paper was just as long, if not longer. The thing with her and Mac was just something that always was. She'd been fucking with him since before Lou-loc came east. Oh well, she couldn't change what was already done.

Maybe she would cut Mac off and be true to Lou-loc? That was a big maybe, considering the baby was probably Mac's. Hell, Lou-loc was already going all out, so why change it? If it ain't broke, then don't fix it.

Martina stripped down to her birthday suit and slid into the bed next to her man. She moved her body against his to steal some of his warmth. She loved him so much, yet she just had such a hard time being true with him always being away. Maybe in time? Maybe.

*

Satin got home that evening with mixed feelings about the last twenty four hours turn of events. First Michael coming back on the scene, and then Lou-loc tracking her down. Her life was definitely becoming interesting.

Satin removed her clothes and put on her white laced night gown. She flopped on her bed and looked at the purple and yellow book Lou-loc had bought for her. Every time she thought of him, her underwear got moist.

He was so damn fine, and he wanted her as much as she wanted him. Satin was far from stupid, she knew niggaz was good for playing games. But the look in his eyes made her realize he wasn't gaming. This man was truly into her. It wasn't unusual for a guy to fall head over heels for her, but that was usually lust. With Lou-loc, it was something much deeper.

Satin had never encountered a man like Lou-loc. He was so passionate about everything. That was odd for a young man, especially a gang banger.

The thought of his gang affiliation presented Satin with another problem. Even though she didn't get down with the whole gang thing, she was guilty by association. What would Lou-loc think if he found out who her brother was?

To her, the whole concept was stupid. Young Blacks and Latinos are killing each other over bullshit. Colors and property that neither side owned.

First it was Michael, and then her youngest brother Jesus. Both had fallen victim to this thing we call street life. Now she had to sit idly by and watch someone else she cared for fall victim.

Then there was the whole 'he got a girl' issue. That dizzy bitch had a grade A winner on her hands, but still felt it necessary to cock her legs for any nigga sportin' a shine. Satin knew how Martina was getting down, but she felt it wasn't her place to put her mouth in that. The good thing was, Lou-loc was finally starting to get wise to her shit.

Satin felt kinda stupid feeling the way she did about Lou-loc. Even though he seemed sincere, she knew that nine outta ten niggaz was full of shit. Again, she pushed those feelings out of her mind. She kept telling herself that Lou-loc was the real thing. Every girl dreams about that knight in shining armor, but she had finally found him. As long as Lou-loc didn't play himself, they'd be all good.

Satin popped some Chamomile tea in the microwave, and lit some scented candles. After her tea was done, she got into bed and tried to relax. Every time she tried to close her eyes she saw Lou-loc. When she inhaled, she smolt his cologne, When she touched her hand, she still felt his print. Satin had a problem, and she knew it. She was in love

CHAPTER 11

Lou-loc was awakened at the crack of dawn by the phone ringing. He was dead tired from the night before, so he decided to let Martina's lazy ass get it. It was probably for her any how.

He heard her mumble a groggy "hello" into the receiver. She sucked her teeth, and began to shake him. Fuck could it be calling him this early?

"Who is it?" he asked annoyed.

"Somebody named Tariq." she replied with attitude.

For a moment, Lou-loc's still half asleep brain couldn't place the name. It was a familiar one, but he wasn't sure where he knew it from. As the fog began to clear, he recognized who the name belonged to. Tariq was the government of his partner Snake Eyes.

"What it is, my nigga?" he asked sitting up right. "Shit, it's like three something in the morning back home. What gives, homey?"

"Ay, what's up, cuz?" Snake Eyes replied. "I ain't home, I'm in New York."

"New York?" Lou-loc asked surprised. "Fuck you doing here, and why you ain't call me to pick you up from the airport? Shit, I would've..."

"Man, this ain't no social call," Snake Eyes interrupted, "we got a situation. These muthafuckas hit Gutter."

Lou-loc could feel all of the blood drain form his face. He couldn't have just heard right. Gutter couldn't be dead..

Fighting back the tears that were trying to make their way to the surface, Lou-loc spoke calmly into the phone. "This shit can't go down like this, Snake. My nigga dead?"

"Nah," Snake Eyes said exhaling, "he still with us. The nigga ain't doing so good though. He was woke for a while, but they got him all doped up. He was asking for you though. How soon can you get here?"

"I'm leaving as we speak. What hospital y'all in?"

"Where else, nigga? Harlem."

Lou-loc let out a slight chuckle, and hung up the phone. Martina was sitting up and looking at Lou-loc inquisitively. He knew she was wondering what was going on, but he ignored her. Lou-loc jumped into his clothes in record time, and was breaking for the door.

"Baby," she called, "what's wrong, is Gutter okay?"

"Nah," he said snatching his car keys from the dresser, "the nigga got shot."

"Oh, my God. Is he okay?"

"I don't know yet. I'm going to the hospital now."

"You want me to go with you?" she asked getting out of bed.

"Nah," he said waving her back down, "I'm going solo. I'll call you when I know something, boo. Go back to sleep and don't worry yourself." Without waiting for her to protest, as she surely would, he was out the door.

*

Martina sat up in the bed not knowing what to make of the situation. She was worried about Gutter. Even though she and Gutter didn't always see eye to eye, that was her man's best friend, so she too had love for him, and wouldn't wish harm on the brother. It could've just as easily been Lou-loc laid up in the hospital, or even worse, the morgue.

With these thoughts in her mind, she began to reflect on the decisions she had forced Lou-loc to make to support their lifestyle. She began to wonder if having the finer things in life was worth her man's life, or her sanity. Suddenly the thought of Lou-loc getting out of the game and living a normal life with her and the kids, didn't sound like such a bad idea.

*

The hospital wasn't far from where Lou-loc lived, so he got there within minutes. He double parked on Lennox and rushed into the emergency room. After some quick questioning, he found out that Gutter was up in ICU, so that's where he needed to be.

Five minutes and an elevator ride later, Lou-loc stepped out of the tiny car into the waiting area. Lou-loc detested hospitals. Ever since he watched his mother wither and die from cancer, they made him uneasy. To Lou-loc, hospitals stunk of death, a smell he was quite familiar with.

95

Lou-loc looked around the tiny green room and looked amongst the different faces. People from all walks of life all gathered together for a common cause. Each and every one there because of a loved one, who was suffering.

Lou-loc shook off his phobia, and strutted through the waiting area. After some searching, he spotted his partner, Snake Eyes, sitting in a corner chair reading a magazine. When he noticed Lou-loc coming his way, he stood up to greet his homey.

"What it is, cuz," he said hugging Lou-loc. "Glad Martina let you shake loose."

"Fuck you, cuz," he said breaking the embrace, "I'm my own man. I do what I want. Plus that's my brother laid up in that piece."

"Fo sho, cuz. But it's good to see you my nigga."

"Snake man, why you ain't call me, and tell you was coming? I could've came and picked you up from the airport."

"Nah," Snake said sitting back down, "I ain't fly, I drove. Shit, you can't take these on no plane," he said pulling his shirt up exposing the butt of his pistol. "And I brought 'Ruby' wit me."

Lou-loc smiled and took the seat next to Snake Eyes. "You still rolling wit that raggedy ass Mac?"

"Nigga," he said adjusting his cane, "call it what you want, but that 'Raggedy Ass Mac,' as you call it, saved the homeboy."

"Nigga, you still putting in work? I thought you was a square peg?"

"Shit, I am. I just passed the bar. I was going to surprise you, ol' hood ass niggaz, and hip you to the fact that I'll be practicing law on the east coast."

"Sho ya right, cuz," he said patting Snake Eyes on the back. "I'm going to need a good lawyer at the rate I'm going."

"Man, don't talk like that." Snake Eye's snapped. "You got a lot of shit wit you, cuz. You just gotta stop jamming ya self with this street shit. It's like my dad used to tell you, 'you a smart nigga, but you ain't got no common sense.'"

"Yea, I remember. How's the old man?"

"He a'ight. Semi retired last year. Him and his girl moved out to the valley. Got a nice little house and a small legal consulting firm. They doing big things."

Before they could roll into more detail about it, Sharell came out of the back. She was a pretty little brown thing. She was thick, yet she wasn't fat. It was all in the right places.

"What's up, Lou-loc?" she said trying to sound strong. Lou-loc could tell from the way her eyes were red and puffed out, that she'd been crying. They didn't make girls like Sharell anymore. She went to church on Sundays, didn't run the streets or use foul language. All she wanted to do was please her man.

"What up, girl," Lou-loc said holding her hand, "you a'ight?"

"I'm cool," she said dabbing her eyes. "Tryin' to be strong."

"I know that's right. How my boy?"

"Doctors ain't really saying much. They saying it's too soon to tell. He's up now, but he's in a lot of pain. He told me to send you in when you got here."

"A'ight, guess I'd better go check him then. You and Snake go on and relax, I'll be back."

Lou-loc got up from his chair and made his way towards Gutter's room. The corridor to Gutter's room was a pale blue, lined with plain wooden doors. All of the doors were the same wood brown with cheap tin lining. The only distinctive features were the cold gray numbers etched on the outside.

Lou-loc strolled through the hall peering into the various rooms inspecting the occupants. All of the patient's faces held the death mask Lou-loc had become so accustom to. Some would make it and others wouldn't. That was just the way shit worked in the hood, actually life in general was kinda like that he reasoned. People were born just to die. Sometimes Lou-loc wondered, "what the fuck is the point?"

Lou-loc stood outside of Gutter's room, opening and closing his hands. He constantly wiped his hands on his sweats, but the moisture never fled. For some reason, he couldn't shake the visions that were bombarding him. They were visions of the time he spent in the hospital with his mother. Some of the patients harbored that same skeletal glare as she did towards the end.

It was painful for Lou-loc to watch his mother waste away like that. After his father was murdered, she was the only person he and his sister had left. She did as best she could with her government checks, but they just weren't enough. That was one of the main reasons that Lou-loc started hustling. He had to man up, and hold his family down.

Lou-loc stood in front of the door and tried to put on his game face. It was hard, but he knew he had to be strong for his brother and the set. When Lou-loc opened the door, he almost broke down at what he saw.

Gutter was laid up in one of those cast iron type beds. There were bandages wrapped around his entire torso as well as one of his arms. He was hooked up to all kind of tubes and devices to monitor his vitals. To see this once proud warrior so helpless, brought a lone tear to Lou-loc's eye. Just as he was about to lose his nerve and back out, Gutter turned around to face him.

"W-what up,... cuz?" he said in a groggy voice. "You... j-just gonna stand there, or come... holla at a nigga?"

Lou-loc put on a false smile and took up a seat at Gutter's bed side. From this close, he got a better assessment of the damage. The would be hit men really did a number on Gutter. His face and arms were covered with bruises and scrapes from falling through the window. The bandages that covered his wounds were soaked through and caked with dried blood. The fucking nurses probably hadn't changed the dressing in a while. But that's how they do you when you don't have any insurance.

Gutter noticed Lou-loc giving him the once over, and spoke up. "Fucking Brims... t-they really tried to do me in, cuz."
"Muthafuckas can't fade you, G," he said patting his friend's hand. "They must ain't know you was invincible."

Gutter tried to laugh, but broke out into a fit of coughing and drooling. Lou-loc took his hand and wiped his friend's chin.

"Easy, soldier," Lou-loc said softly, "we need you healthy. We got big plans, you and me. You gonna fuck everything up by dying, punk."

Gutter regained his wind and began speaking again. "I... think it... was them LC niggaz, cuz. Ain't sure... but think so. I thought... I-I recognized that kid, Scales... remember... from Harlem week... last year? They... done started... s-some shit, Lou."

"I be knowin'," Lou-loc said. "It's going down. We gonna hit these faggots hard for what they done to you, cuz."

"C-contract." Gutter coughed out.

"Nah," Lou-loc shook his head, "I gots to be here wit my nigga. Fuck Anwar."

Gutter gripped Lou-loc's arm so hard that he flinched.

"Business, cuz. You fill that contract and get the ball rolling. We gonna do the damn thing, cuz. Crips stay true to the code. All debts paid in full."

Lou-loc started to protest, but when he saw the look in his friend's eyes he didn't. This was important to Gutter. Lou-loc wanted to believe that his friend would pull through, but in reality, it wasn't likely. The boy was in bad shape. If this was to be Gutter's last request, he would not be denied.

Lou-loc's thoughts were interrupted when Gutter coughed out a word: "Freedom," He said it so low, that Lou-loc almost didn't catch it.

"Freedom," Gutter said again. "When this... bullshit is done... you out." Lou-loc opened his mouth to say something, but Gutter waved him silent.

"Look at me, cuz!" he snapped. "Them niggaz tried to take my... life, I-I ain't salty though. When you in the life... th-this kinda shit happens. I-I don't wanna die in some... funky ass hospital, but if I do... I'll aooopt it. But... I couldn't see you... like this. Imagine how I-I'd feel... escorting lil sis to ya funeral?"

"You know, I ain't no coward," Lou-loc said sharply. "I'm always gonna be down for you and the set."

"T-that's touching, cuz, and I respect that, but let's be real. You got a future in that writing shit. Don't waste ya life. W-when I was stretched out on that cold ass ground bleeding all over myself, it was a fucked up feeling thinking how I was gonna die alone in the street. I don't want that for you.

"Wh-when this is done... you're free of ya oath... and the bullshit that came with it. Take ya lil sis... raise up... better ya self, and teach her a different way of life."

"And what about you, Gutter?" Lou-loc asked, with tears forming in his eyes. "What are you gonna do when you get out of here?"

"You mean if," Gutter said with a smile. "You of all people know my style. I'm gonna get money or get murdered...ain't no gray area.

Hopefully I'll make it outta here. If not, oh well. If Allah decides to call me home, I'm ready to go."

Both of the men sat just staring at each other, neither saying a word. There was an unspoken understanding that passed between the two. Lou-loc had known Gutter for years, and for the first time, he saw something in his eyes that he had never seen before. Fear.

Gutter finally broke the silence.

"I gotta tell you something, cuz. I was gonna surprise you, but I don't know if I'll get a chance to tell you later. I'm going to give you an account number. It's some paper that I've been sitting on. I want you to take the money and..."

Before Gutter could finish his sentence, he was overcome by a fit of coughing. He coughed until blood started spilling from his mouth, and soaking the sheets. Lou-loc not knowing what else to do, called for the nurse.

The doctors and nurses started piling into the room with all types of equipment. They knocked Lou-loc to the side and began working on Gutter. Lou-loc just moved in a daze as the nurses ushered him into the hall so they'd have more room to work.

Snake Eyes and Sharell met Lou-loc in the hallway. "Lou-loc, what's going on?" she asked with tears in her eyes. "Is Kenyatta okay?"

Lou-loc just looked back and forth from her to Snake Eyes. He tried to form words, but his lips wouldn't cooperate. Finally he spoke.

"Just try to stay calm, Sharell. The doctors are working on him. All we can do is wait."

Sharell began to ball right there on the spot. Most of what she was saying was gibberish. She was just rocking back and forth rubbing the iced out cross Gutter had brought her for her birthday.

With Snake Eyes' help, they got her to a chair and tried to calm her. The trio sat in the waiting area hoping the doctors would bring them some positive news. Martina was blowing up Lou-loc's pager, but he ignored it. He sat with his friend trying to be strong for Sharell.

Finally, a thin balding doctor wearing blue scrubs came out of Gutter's room looking exhausted. "Who's here for Kenyatta Soladine?" he asked.

Seeing that Sharell was in no condition to handle whatever news the doctor had, Lou-loc stepped to the plate.

"That would be me," he said walking across the waiting area. Seeing the doctor's uneasiness at his gangsta ass apparel, he extended his hand and introduced himself. "I'm his brother, St. Louis Alexander."

The doctor relaxed a little and spoke in a hushed tone that only Lou-loc could hear.

"Your brother is not doing too good," he said wringing his hands together. "We've managed to stabilize him for the moment, but his vitals are very weak. You and your family are welcomed to stay, but there isn't much you can do for him at this point. My advice would be for you to all go home and get some rest. We'll call you should his condition change."

Lou-loc thanked the doctor and made his way back over to Sharell and Snake Eyes. He felt a little better after speaking to the doctor, but he knew Gutter wasn't out of the woods. Anything could happen. Snake Eyes and Sharell looked at Lou-loc with expectant eyes. He didn't want to alarm Sharell any further, so he figured he'd just tell her a half truth.

"He's stable," Lou-loc said with a huff. "He's still real weak, so we can't see him anymore for a while. They got your number already, Sharell, and I gave them mine. They'll call us if anything changes."

"Oh, praise God," Sharell said wiping her eyes. "I don't know what's wrong wit y'all, Lou-loc. When y'all gonna get out of this life? It's all genocide."

Lou-loc was in no mood to be lectured, but he understood that she was going through something so he tried not to be short with her when he spoke.

"Listen, Sharell, I know you don't dig how we get down, but the end justifies the means. We ain't trying to live like this forever, especially me. As a matter of fact we were just in there discussing the same thing. This life don't love us, and that's real. Everybody comes around in their own time."

"I didn't mean to sound like I was screaming on you," she said composing herself. "I'm just scared. I mean, that's my heart laid up in there. I couldn't go on without Ken. Lou-loc, you like my big brother. If anything were to happen to either one of y'all..."

"Don't even think like that," he cut her off. "Me or that nigga in there ain't checking out no time soon. What kinda nigga would I be if I wasn't there to be best man at y'all wedding?"

He pulled Sharell close and hugged her. "Quit that crying," he whispered in her ear. "Everything gonna be blue. I'm gonna have Snake Eyes take you home while I go handle a few things."

"Lou-loc, I know you. Just let it go," she pleaded. "Hitting them is only gonna make it worse. Let it end with Kenyatta?"

"Oh, nah," he said innocently. "I ain't on it like that. I just gotta go get my paper work right for school," he lied. "Go on and get the car while me and Snake Eyes get Gutter's personals."

Sharell nodded and headed for the elevator. When she was out of ear shot Snake Eyes tapped Lou-loc.

"What you scheming on, cuz?" he asked.

"These niggaz gots to pay," Lou-loc said with ice in his voice. "These muthafuckas got themselves an asshole full of trouble. I want you to go see Wiz at the auto shop up on the point and tell him to get my toy ready. It's going to be a meeting tonight, then I got some shit to take care of."

"You know I'm wit you, cuz."

"Nay, brother. You ain't a combat soldier no more. Fall back and be there for Sharell," Lou-loc said.

"Fuck what ya heard. That's my folks too laid up under the knife. I want in."

"Have it your way then. I'll call you with the details. Right now I gotta breeze," Lou-loc said slapping his homeboy a five then headed for the stairs.

"What you gonna do, cuz?" Snake Eyes yelled after him.

Lou-loc turned around and smiled. "What I do best, my nigga." With that being said he went down the stairs.

CHAPTER 12

*T*he sun was shinning brightly through Satin's bedroom window. As the warm rays moved and danced over her sleeping face, she began to stir. Satin loved the sunshine. That was the reason she had a large picture window built into her loft. The owner was a friend of her aunt Selina, so he didn't complain about the remodeling.

Satin sat up in her round king sized bed and welcomed the new day. She arched her back to stretch and exposed her erect brown nipples that were peeking through her sheer night gown. She slid her long brown legs off the side of the bed and rubbed her manicured feet back and forth over her area rug. There was something about the smooth feel of Persian material on her bare feet that felt good to her.

When Satin recalled the details of her date with Lou-loc she couldn't help but smile. She had been a little skeptical about the whole affair, with him just popping up and all, but he turned out to be a perfect gentleman. He held all the doors for her, complimented her on her outfit, and never once tried to coax her into intimacy. He got a ten for the evening.

Satin padded across her hard wood floor to her walk in closet. She didn't have to work today, so jeans and a Tee shirt were the order of business. Satin laid her clothes across her bed and headed for the shower. Before making it to the bathroom, the phone broke her stride.

Satin answered the phone with a pleasant "hello", and was delighted to hear the gentleman's voice on the other end.

"St. Louis," she sang, "what the deal, papi? I didn't expect to hear from you so soon."

"I didn't disturb you, did I?" he asked.

"Nah, I was up. Thanks for the good time ."

"No, thank you. It was different, but I enjoyed it. What you got planned for this morning?" Lou-loc asked.

"Not much. I'm off today, so I'll probably just chill and catch up on my reading. Why do you ask, you got something planned for me?"

"Can I see you? Maybe take you to breakfast, or something?"

Satin wanted to shout, "HELL YEA YOU CAN SEE ME!" but she knew she couldn't play herself. Instead she responded, "Nah. But if you wanna come over, I know how to cook a little?"

At first Lou-loc was preparing himself for a rejection, but he was pleased to hear that she was willing to see him.

"A'ight," he said coolly. "But since it's ya place, let me cook for you?"

After getting her address, the two hung up. She felt like jumping for joy, but instead she bolted for the shower. Lou-loc said he'd be there in a half hour, so she didn't have much time. Guess she'd save the jeans for another day. She wanted to look good for Lou-loc. Martina's time was just about up, she just didn't know it. Hurricane Satin had arrived, and she planned on staying for a while.

*

Lou-loc pulled his car over on West 8th Street and hopped out in front of a pay phone. He dropped a quarter in and punched the number pad. His cell was in working order, but he made it a point never to talk business on it. To do so was just as good as indicting yourself.

After two rings, a female picked up.

"Hello," she barked in a husky voice. "Who the hell is this and what ya want this damn early?"

"Hey, Kiki," he said pleasantly. "This Lou. Ya brother around?"

"Yea," she growled. "That no good nigga in there sleep."

"I need you to wake him up, ma. Tell him it's important."

"He need to have his ass up any how. Mafucka should be out job hunting instead of laying' up on me and shit."

"You know how it is in the hood, Kiki?"

"I got ya hood, nigga. So what's up, Lou? When you gonna come knock the bottom out this here?"

Lou-loc shook his head. Every time he saw or spoke to Kiki, she was trying to hit on him. At the 'Blue & Gray' barbecue they had last summer, she even went as far as to grab his crotch when Martina wasn't looking.

"Now, Kiki, you know I can't handle that good loving of yours," he lied, "you too much woman for me."

That part was true. Kiki was almost six feet tall, and built like a line backer. She had knocked out quite a few females, as well as a few men. Lou-loc had never just come out and told her he wasn't trying to fuck wit her, cause frankly the girl didn't take rejection well. There was no doubt that he could whip her in a fist fight, but her skills with a razor almost surpassed his own. Plus she was a down ass chic, and he didn't want to hurt her feelings.

"Yea, a'ight," she said slyly. "One day I'm just gonna have to get you loaded and take what I want, wit yo pretty ass." There was no doubt in either of their minds that she meant what she said.

Kiki put the phone down, and screamed for her no good, lazy, dope selling, fake ass gang banging brother to come to the phone. Kiki was a female, but her four letter vocabulary was more vulgar than most of the homeboys.

After a brief exchange of words, her brother finally came to the phone. "WHAT!" he snarled.

"Hold that down, nigga," Lou-loc said in a stern voice, "it's me, fool."

"Oh, my bad, ouz," Pop Top said, realizing who he was talking to, "I thought you was that faggot ass nigga Breeze calling me bout his paper. You know I don't get up till after one, what's the deal?"

"We got a game tonight," Lou-loc said speaking in code. "I need the whole team there, the homey Gutter got hurt, and can't play."

"What?" Top asked in disbelief. "Is it bad?"

"Yea, cuz. He might be out for the season, so you know we gotta play hard. I'm talking free for all." At the mention of violence, Lou-loc could almost hear Top grinning through the phone. That boy loved to put in work, and Lou-loc was well aware of it. That's why he called him first.

"I'm on it, cuz. Time, and place?" Top asked.

"Home court, baby." By this Lou-loc meant St. Nicolas park, but anyone who might be listening wouldn't know that. "I want everyone there at midnight, and I don't mean twelve- 0 - one. You and Snake Eyes will be my co-captains. You in the field, and him in the front office."

"Fo sho," Top said trying to keep his anger in check, "it's on baby."

"Get them niggaz there, cuz."

"You know I will. Let me get up off this jack (phone) so I can make it happen." Without waiting for a response, Top hung up. Lou-loc knew that if anyone could rally the troops, Pop Top could.

Lou-loc dropped a quarter into the phone, and moved on to the next order of business. Lou-loc didn't have Anwar's direct number, so he called the contact that had supplied him with the information. He informed him that the funeral arrangements (hit) would be handled within the next twenty four hours. The contact thanked him and said that he could pick up the floral arrangement (payment) the next evening. With that taken care of, he was ready to go see his sweetheart.

*

After dropping Sharell off, Snake Eyes hopped on the north bound freeway and headed for the Bronx. He really and truly was in a down mood. Not only because his homey was laid up in the hospital, but because of the ripple affect it was having on everyone else. Snake had met Sharell twice before, and spoken to her on the phone dozens of times over the years. He knew she was a good girl and that she loved his friend dearly. He respected her for that. She was in such bad shape that he had to score her some volume so she could calm down. It's fucked up when the ones you care about are really hurting, and there's nothing you can do to ease their pain.

Then there was Lou-loc. After talking to Lou-loc, there was no doubt in his mind as to what he had planned. To a lot of people it wouldn't be a big deal, he'd be just one more nigga, wit a chip on his shoulder. Snake Eyes, however, knew different. Inside the shell of a young man, there lived two people. There was Lou-loc, the intelligent young philosopher, then there was Lou-loc, the assassin. So cold and diabolical that sometimes he even gave Snake Eyes the creeps. Lou-loc was a master schemer, and cold blooded killer, which is why he made OG status so quickly. If you asked for it, you got it, and that's just how it was with him.

It was strange how someone so intellectual and compassionate about life, could take it away so effortlessly. He was like two sides to a coin. Maybe it was the brutal murder of his father that made him like that, or watching his saint of a mother wither away and die? No one really knew what made him tick. Lou-loc was a good dude; there was no mistaking that. But in his heart, he was a killer.

Snake Eyes felt bad for his friend. For as long as he'd known him, Lou-loc had always been a fair man. It just seemed like life didn't want to be fair to him. The G's in the hood expected so much from Lou-loc, and no one ever stopped to consider how he felt. To them, he was just a killing machine, but, Snake Eyes knew different.

Lou-loc was indeed a tortured soul, who would be forever eluded by happiness. He had so much potential, but because of his loyalties, he would be forever limited. On many occasions, Lou-loc had told Snake that sometimes he wished he was dead. He still wouldn't have achieved happiness, but the madness would be over. He would finally be able to rest. That was deep.

Snake Eyes reached the run down auto shop Lou-loc had directed him to in the Hunts point area of the Bronx, and parked his hog around back. The front of the place was littered with beat up cars and trucks. Some in need of repair, others hooked up and ready to go. No doubt, this was the place

Snake Eyes entered the auto body shop, and was overwhelmed by the smell of gas fumes mixed in with sweat and urine. Before he got all the way inside, he was cut off by a hulking Mexican wearing a tattered blue overall. From the look in the behemoth's eyes, he didn't want to make nice.

"Fuck you want, homes?" the Mexican asked, exposing a mouth full of rot, and empty spaces where his teeth used to be.

"Name's Snake Eyes," he said matching his opponent's tone, "I'm looking for Wiz. You him?"

"What you want with Wiz?"

"If you ain't him, don't worry about it."

"I think you better watch your mouth, mafucka," said a voice from behind him. Snake Eyes turned to find himself staring at a gorgeous Mexican woman. She wore a tight fitting leather jump suit, and her silky black pony tail was held in place by a single blue ribbon. Her green eyes looked Snake Eyes up and down like a hungry lioness eyeing a gazelle. This woman was the baddest thing he'd seen since his arrival in the big apple. The only thing that kept Snake Eyes from admiring her further was the fact that she had an AK-47 pointed at his dick

"Maybe you didn't understand my brother's question," said the girl, "so let me try. You got exactly ten seconds to tell me what the fuck you want with Wiz or I'll just make a fucking transsexual out of you. Choice is yours, cuz."

Snake Eyes had no choice but to spill the beans, but he told himself that this bitch would answer for pointing a pistol at him. "Listen, honey, my name is Snake Eyes. Lou-loc sent me up here to pick something up from Wiz."

The girl narrowed her eyes at him and began nodding her head. For the first time, he noticed a small device sticking out from her ear. After a few moments of debating and mumbling in Spanish, she lowered her gun.

"Sorry about that," she said brushing her hair from her forehead. "You can never be too careful. Our shop is smack dab in the middle of enemy territory."

"Ain't nothing," he said relaxing, "I know how it is to live the life. So where is this Wiz?"

"Go on in the back and get yourself a soda. I recommend the orange."

"I don't want a soda," Snake Eyes said confused, "I just wanna get what I came for and bounce."

"Just go to the vending machine and get your soda," she said sounding irritated.

Snake Eyes walked to where the old vending machine sat, and eye balled it suspiciously. The button for the orange soda had a sticker on it that said out of order. He looked back at the brother and sister team, and they were covering their mouths trying to keep from laughing. Seeing that he was getting frustrated, they both motioned for him to push the button. With a shrug of his shoulders, he did. That's when the floor fell from under him.

Snake Eyes' heart plummeted as he fell through the floor and down a circular tube. The only thought flashing through his mind was that he was taking his last breaths. To his surprise, he slid out of the tube and landed hard on his ass.

As quickly as his good leg would allow him, he sprang to his feet and clutched his cane like a club. He quickly scanned the room and noticed he was in some kind of work shop. The floor was littered with old papers and scraps of metal. There were charts and diagrams covering the walls with a large file cabinet of sorts near the hole he exited. In a far corner of the room was a table with all kinds of equipment on it. They were the kind of things one might see in a chemist's lab. Sitting behind the table was the man Snake Eyes was seeking.

Wiz wasn't at all what Snake was expecting. When he stood up and came around to greet Snake Eyes, he couldn't have been any taller than maybe 5'1." He was a short Mexican, with slick black hair, wearing a pair of grease covered khakis with a pearl white Tee shirt. On his face, he wore thick rimmed glasses. Actually, they looked more like coke bottles than glasses. He looked more like a mad scientist than anything else.

"So, you're the lawyer?" Wiz asked extending his hand.

"Yea, the name's, Snake Eyes." he responded shaking Wiz's hand. "Lou-loc, sent me for the package."

"Right, right. Hold up a sec." Wiz walked over to a small freezer unit and removed what appeared to be a box of sorts. After checking the contents of the box, Wiz placed the first box inside of a slightly larger one. The larger box had what looked like a battery attached to the back of it.

"A'ight," Wiz said handing Snake Eyes the box, "tell Lou-loc to follow the instructions to the letter. Once he takes these out of the case, he'll only have a little while before they become unstable. One of those bust in his hand, he's gonna have a serious problem."

Snake Eyes looked at the black box suspiciously. He wanted to ask what was in it, but he figured it wasn't his business. If Lou-loc wanted him to know, he'd tell him on his own. Besides, from the way Wiz was talking, he wasn't sure if he wanted to know.

"Well then," Wiz began speaking, "our business is concluded. That," he said pointing at the file cabinet, "is an elevator. You can take it back to the main floor. Tell Lou-loc that I said good luck."

As Wiz turned to go back to what ever he was doing, Snake Eyes stopped him. "Say, homey, what's wit that vending machine shit?"

"Sorry about that," he said smiling, revealing a mouth full of braces, "I'm afraid my siblings have a weird sense of humor. That's an emergency entrance to my lab. I guess it was their idea of a joke."

"Very fucking funny." Snake Eyes mumbled as he climbed into the tiny elevator.

CHAPTER 13

Satin had just finished putting the finishing touches on her hair when her buzzer rang. She saw Lou-loc when he pulled up in front of her building, so she didn't need to ask who it was. She buzzed him in and then went about making sure all the scented candles were in place and lit.

When she opened the door, Lou-loc greeted her with a smile and a hug. As he stepped in she sized him up. Even though he was conservatively dressed in a gray sweat suit, he still looked as good as ever.

Lou-loc openly admired the decor of her small loft. Her walls were lined with pictures of her friends and family. It was mostly her and an older woman who he would learn later was her aunt Selina. In addition to the pictures, there were artifacts and pieces from various Latino cultures. In one corner there was a book shelf that took up almost an entire section of the wall. In it, she had everything from Tolstoy to McMillan. Lou-loc was quite impressed.

When Lou-loc went into the kitchenette, it was Satin's turn to be impressed. He began to empty the contents of the shopping bag he was carrying onto the counter. Inside the bag there were all kinds of foods. There were fresh fruits, vegetables, pastries, thin steaks, eggs, fresh cheese and an exotic wine that Satin knew ran him quite a few dollars. She had never had a man cook for her before, and here he was not only cooking, but going all out. This was going to be interesting.

Lou-loc noticed Satin staring at the bottle, and felt a little ashamed. The morning had given way to the afternoon, but it was still a bit early to be drinking. The last thing he wanted to do was give Satin the impression that he was an alcoholic.

"I hope you don't mind," he started, "I thought you might like a glass of wine with your meal? I can run out and get some juice if you like?"

"No," she started, "wine will be fine."

Seeing that she wasn't bothered by his beverage selection, Lou-loc relaxed a little.

After washing his hands he began preparing the meal. By the time he was done in the kitchen he had prepared quite the little feast. The steak was lightly breaded and sent waves of pleasure through Satin's taste buds every time she took a bite. The cheese eggs were light and fluffy. They almost seemed to melt in her mouth. In addition to the steak and eggs, Lou-loc had chopped up the assorted fruits and arranged them in the shapes of beautiful flowers. If Satin had any doubts before, she was sure now. She was falling in love with this man.

As they ate they talked about everything from books, to movies, to politics. She knew Lou-loc was intelligent, but she was actually quite surprised at how informed he was. He kept abreast on everything that was going on in the hood as well as in government.

After the meal they moved in to the living room where they sipped hazel nut coffee and ate marble cake.

As the smooth sounds of Billie Holiday seeped from the CD player, Satin couldn't help but to smile at how together Lou-loc was. He even turned off his beeper and cell phone. He didn't think she was paying attention when he did it, but she was. That was very gentlemanly of him, and he scored big points with her for the act.

The morning turned to afternoon, and afternoon started giving way to evening. Satin was having a wonderful time with Lou-loc. As wonderful a time as she was having, the thought of his girl was nagging at her. It was then that she decided to lay her cards on the table.

"Lou-loc," she said touching his hand, "I wanna thank you for such a beautiful day."

"It's cool," he said sliding closer to her. "I enjoy your company, Satin. It wasn't nothing for me to come throw a meal together for you. In fact, we need to do this more often."

"I'd like that," she said. "But there's something I need to come clean about. I know about her. I mean the Dominican girl." Satin expected him to panic, or deny it. To her surprise, he didn't.

Lou-loc stood up, and pulled her to her feet. She wasn't sure what to expect, so she was a bit hesitant. In the back of her mind she hoped that he wouldn't pick now to show his crazy deranged side.

Lou-loc pulled her close to him and spoke in a very soft tone. "Who, Martina? Listen Satin, I ain't gonna bullshit you, or try to lie or no shit. I fucks wit the chic, but it ain't the way you think it is."

"So why don't you tell me how it is, St. Louis?" she said with attitude.

Lou-loc took a deep breath and began speaking.

"Look, ol' girl and me hooked up a few years ago. I heard through the grapevine that she was scandalous, but I don't judge people by what another muthafucka says, so I gave her a play. It was all good at first, but it's like they say, 'old habits are hard to break. A nigga like me, I ain't never been no fool and I don't plan on becoming one anytime soon. I ain't sure, but I got a pretty good idea the girl been putting game on me. I got a homeboy of mine looking into it. Truth be told, I don't love Martina anymore. I've known it for a while, but I was trying to tell myself different. I don't even think that kid she's carrying is mine."

"Oh yea," she snapped, "so why you still with her?"

"I'm just stupid I guess? It's like I was just so used to having some one to take care of, I was afraid of being alone."

"And you expect me too believe that?"

"Truthfully, Satin, and please don't take this the wrong way, it don't make me no never mind if you believe me. I know in my heart what the real deal is. I hope you believe me, but if you don't, I can't stop living."

Satin turned her face away so he couldn't see the tears welling up in her eyes. "I don't know, Lou-loc," she sobbed, "I can't play second fiddle to nobody. No matter how I may feel about you."

Lou-loc wiped the tears from her cheeks. "Listen, baby," he said softly, "I'm gonna run something down to you, and I hope you don't think I'm a sucker for it.

"I know I've only known you for a few days, but I feel like I've been searching for you all my life. I'm falling for you, baby. Wait, let me rephrase that. I've already fallen, and fallen hard."

"Stop it, Lou-loc, just stop it. Don't say things you don't mean."

"Don't mean?" he asked shocked. "I don't bullshit with my emotions, girl. Soon as my man float me the info I need on this phony ass broad, I'm in the wind. She can keep the crib and the rest of that funky ass shit.

"I'm getting out of this game, and that's real. I got some bread put up, and I plan on doing something with my life. If you were to ask me to pick up and leave, I would. Anywhere you want.

"Don't get it fucked up though, Satin. I ain't no trick ass nigga. The reason I'm coming at you like this is because I believe you're the real deal. Now if I'm wrong about you, or you don't feel where I'm coming from, tell me. Let me know that I'm full of shit, and I'll be on my way."

Satin just stood there speechless, staring at Lou-loc with tear filled eyes.

"I see," Lou-loc said sadly. "Thank you for the wonderful day, Satin. I'll always cherish the memories of the brief time we shared together." Lou-loc lowered his head and made for the door.

Satin just stood there for a while weighing her options. She knew guys were notorious for running game, but something in Lou-loc's eyes made her want to believe him. Without giving it a second thought, she dashed out the door to catch up with him.

When she finally caught him, she was surprised to see tears in his eyes. She brushed his cheek tenderly and whispered, "I believe you. I feel the same way you do, baby. It may sound silly, but my heart tells me you're being real. Just don't hurt me like the rest."

Lou-loc tried to muster a smile. He was a little embarrassed that she had caught him in a moment of weakness. Deep down, he really didn't give a shit though. The main thing was that his words rang true.

"Satin," he said playing with her hair, "I'd rather go blind and broke before I caused you to ever shed one more tear over a nigga like me."

"Stay with me?" she pleaded. "I hope you don't think poorly of me, but I want you to make love to me. Seal the deal and become my man?"

Lou-loc reluctantly broke the grip she had on his neck. "I wish I could," he said stroking her cheek, "but I got some things I need to handle tonight. But I'll be through to see you tomorrow."

"You promise?"

"Satin, you are my shining diamond amongst a field of coal. Light the way for me so I can always find you." Lou-loc kissed her softly on her forehead, and made his way down the stairs.

As Satin made her way back inside her loft, she felt as if she was floating. In her heart she knew she had made the right choice. Lou-loc was the kind of man she dreamt about as a little girl, and now she had him live and in the flesh. The fact that he was a gang member didn't even bother her anymore.

Satin went into her bedroom and removed her rosary from the vanity mirror. She knelt beside her bed and started to pray.

"God," she whispered, "I know we haven't spoke much lately, but I need your help on this one. This man that you've sent me is all that I've ever needed or wanted. I might be foolish for falling for him so quickly, but if loving this man is wrong, I'll be damned if I'll be right. So, if you can find it in your heart to make everything okay, let ya girl come out on top?"

*

Lou-loc stepped from Satin's building and took a deep breath. Even the foul ass New York air smelled sweet to him at this point. He knew it was some bird shit letting Satin see him cry, but fuck it. She had assumed his emotional display was over the conversation they had, but that wasn't the case. When he went into the hallway, he cut his cell back on. There were thirteen messages. Eleven from Martina, one from Snake Eyes, and one from Cross. It was the last message that caused him to break down. All he said was that the dog was rabbit, and had to be put down. Lou-loc read between the lines and knew what was up.

As Lou-loc made his way to the car, a young kid wearing a red hoodie pulled up on a mountain bike. "You got a light, Blood?" the young boy capped.

Lou-loc fished his lighter from his pocket with his left hand, and fingered his glock with the right. "Here you go, cuz." Lou-loc wasn't no fool. He knew this kid was working for the other side, but he let him slide with his slick ass comment. Now that he and Satin were on the way to becoming an item, he was floating on air. He didn't really give a fuck about a color.

"Thanks, big homey," the kid said exhaling the smoke from his cigarette. "You better be careful out here with them colors on, dog. This LC Blood hood."

Lou-loc sized the kid up, and there was a striking resemblance to Satin in the boy's features, but he disregarded it. "Look here, lil homey," Lou-loc started, "I'm from the old school. I wear what I want and go where I please. Niggaz don't fuck wit me, and they live to see they next birthday. Ya heard?"

The kid smirked at Lou-loc and asked, "You must be a bad man, huh?"

Lou-loc rolled up his shirt sleeve exposing his tattoo of a six pointed star. "I'm an OG straight outta the jungle. You New York niggaz get up on shit late, and then y'all ain't even putting it down right."

"What you mean?" the kid snapped. "We put it down out here. LC gangsta, take it in blood, nigga," he said throwing up his set (neighborhood).

"That's just what the fuck I'm talking bout," Lou-loc said shaking his head. "Y'all niggaz don't know shit about shit. You rob a few mafuckas, or slash some ol' wine head, and you think that's gangsta? You need to give it up, homeboy.

"Where I'm from, to be down with a set means more than busting ya gun or just being a hard ass. We took care of each other, and our neighborhoods. Y'all niggaz see an old woman struggling, and instead of helping her, y'all wanna get ya jack on. That's ass backward.

"Unity, knowledge, respect, loyalty. That's what we putting down. Y'all 'dead rag' niggaz got the game fucked up. Take my advice, homey, leave this shit to us grown folks."

During the whole conversation all the kid could think of was how much hood fame he could gain by killing this OG Lou-loc turned to walk away, and the kid made his move. From under his hoodie, he pulled a .25 and pointed it at Lou-loc's back. "Crab mafucka," he spat, "I should twist yo shit for coming through here side ways."

Lou-loc turned and looked the kid dead in the eye. From past experience, Lou-loc should have been begging for his life, at least that's what the kid's brain had told him. But Lou-loc didn't even flinch.

The cold look in Lou-loc's eyes made the kid hesitate, and that mistake cost him. With speed born of a life time in the streets, Lou-loc snatched the hand gun and knocked the kid off his bike and onto the pavement. The kid had no doubt that his life was about to end.

Lou-loc leaned over and grabbed a handful of the kid's shirt.

"Stupid ass nigga," he snarled. "I'm death on two legs, mafucka. I should take yo life."

Lou-loc felt the beast raging inside him, and was about to give it release. When he looked up and saw Satin's bedroom light come on, he checked the animal that was his temper. He had to remind himself that he was trying to get away from the hood shit and make something of his life.

"Youz a lucky nigga," Lou-loc said gaining his composure. "I should pop one in yo ass, but I ain't. I'm in a good mood, so you get a pass."

Lou-loc stuffed the .25 in his pocket and kicked the kid in the side of the head, getting blood on his sneakers. "Cross me again, and it's a wrap, blood." Lou-loc turned and headed for his car.

When Lou-loc's car pulled off, the kid sat on the curb and cursed himself for being so weak. He could've made the big time by capping Lou-loc, but instead, he almost got himself killed. He hated Lou-loc, and vowed that he would see him again, and the next time, only one of them would walk away.

CHAPTER 14

Lou-loc parked two blocks from the meeting area. His Techno Marine watch read eleven thirty, so he still had some time before the meeting. Top had rounded up all the troops and Snake Eyes had picked up his package from Wiz. His lieutenants were on point and that's why he chose them. Pop Top was a savage when it came to combat and Snake Eyes was the voice of reason.

All that was left for Lou-loc to do was meet Cross to get the details of his stake out, and give him the address of the young virgins he was promised. Lou-loc still wasn't comfortable with dealing with his friend's eccentric taste, but when dealing with 'licks,' you had to expect the unexpected. Two tears in a bucket, if it got the desired results, it was worth it.

As Lou-loc stood in the shadows of the park side, he felt a presence approaching but couldn't pin point a direction. It was kind of like when you know there's no one else around, but you feel like some one's watching you. Giving substance to his suspicions, Cross came slithering out of the shadows.

"You need to stop sneaking up on people like that," Lou-loc said playfully. "One day you gonna get ya ass shot."

"So," Cross replied. "If I had a quarter for every time some asshole has shot me, I'd be a rich man."

"So, what do you have for me?" Lou-loc asked. "Give it to me straight. I can take it."

For an answer, Cross tossed Lou-loc a paper shopping bag. Lou-loc peeked into the bag and almost hurled. The bag slipped to the ground and the contents fell out. It was a human hand with a ruby ring on the pinky finger.

"I'm sorry, old friend," Cross said sincerely. "That's what's left of the gentleman Martina was creeping with."

Tears welled in Lou-loc's eyes, but he refused to let them escape. His worst fears were confirmed.

"I thought I loved her," he mumbled. "Then she put shit on me."

Cross felt bad for his friend. Even though they were from two different worlds, Lou-loc was his only real friend. One of the few people who didn't shit their pants or run off when they discovered his true nature. Friend was a word seldom used in Cross' world, so his loyalty to Lou-loc was genuine. After all, the same blood ran through both of their veins.

"If it makes you feel any better," Cross said touching Lou-loc's shoulder, "I made his death as painful as possible. He was still alive when I removed his hand."

Lou-loc tried to muster a smile, but Cross knew it was only a mask to hide his pain. The pain Lou-loc felt inside started to fade and was replaced by anger. Every time he wanted to do right, something always went wrong. The beast that he once was cried for release. Tonight Lou-loc would grant the wish.

"Cross," Lou-loc said with glassy eyes, "I need two favors from you."

"Just tell me who, Lou-loc," Cross said, "and he's a dead man."

"Not that kinda favor. I got a lot of shit I need to do tonight. Most of it is fucked up and I need that killer edge. You know what I'm asking for?"

Cross shook his head and said, "Lou, you gotta understand about this thing of ours. I can't keep giving you that shit. The more I give you, the more dependent you'll become. It's like any other drug, and I don't want you to become an addict."

"Don't trip," Lou-loc assured him. "I just need a little something for myself. Just so I'll be able to perform at top efficiency. The second favor I need runs a little deeper than that."

"Well, don't keep an asshole in suspense, what is it?"

"My nigga, Gutter is in Harlem laid up, sprayed up. He ain't doing so good, probably gonna die."

"Lou, I already know what you're gonna ask, but I don't know about doing it," Cross said.

"Cross, that's my heart. If he leave here, I ain't gonna be no more good. I couldn't stand to live if my boy died knowing that I could've did something to help. Don't make me beg, Cross. I need you to do this for me, will you?"

"Lou-loc," Cross said softly. "I hope you realize what kind of position you're putting me in? This thing you're asking me to do could land both of us on a coroner's slab.

"Thanks, Cross. I..."

"Don't thank me," Cross cut him off. "I never said I'd do it. Just know that I might never see another night after this one if I do this thing for you and all because I was your friend. Lou-loc, you saved my life when my own comrades wouldn't help me. You could've left me to suffer and die, but you didn't. For this, I owe you a great debt. In all the years I've been around, I've never met an outsider like you. You murder just like me, but there is still some shred of humanity in you. Too bad I can't say the same for myself. I'm a monster and I can accept what's waiting for me on the other side. It's like that kid said, it's dark and hell is hot. I'm sure that in time I'll find out if there's any truth to it, but don't let yourself fall prey to the same temptations I did. Always remember what I've said to you this night. Nothing is without its price."

Cross closed his eyes and let his thoughts roam.

"Damn you, Lou-loc for putting this load on my shoulder," he whispered. "And damn me twice for being your friend."

*

South of where Lou-loc and Cross were making their exchange, Cisco sat listening to a young man recounting the events of his run in with the notorious Lou-loc of Harlem Crip.

"Are you sure?" Cisco asked the kid while taking a puff of his cigar.

"Yea, I'm sure," the kid went on. "It was Lou-loc. When he showed me his crab ass tattoo, I saw his name under the six pointed star. You shoulda heard how that faggot was talking. He was actin' like LC don't hold no weight down here. I was gonna clip his ass, but he snuffed me before I had a chance to pull out on him," he lied.

Cisco absently rubbed the scar on his cheek and winced from the still lingering pain.

"Tell me this, Jesus," Cisco started. "If that was Lou-loc you bumped into, what was he doing nosing around Satin's building? You think Harlem knows we're behind the hit on Gutter?"

"Nah," Jesus spoke up. "I seen them together before. I think he's trying to fuck, bro."

Cisco's eyes flashed anger. Could Lou-loc be fucking Satin? Just the thought of it sent sharp anger pains through Cisco's temple. He figured if he couldn't have her, no punk ass crab would. Then another thought flashed through his twisted mind. What would the rest of the crew think if they found out that their leader's sister was involved with one of their rivals?

"Jesus, I have a job for you," Cisco said smiling devilishly. "I want you to keep an eye on your sister and find out what the deal is with her and this crab. Don't let her know you're following her, and do not alert El Diablo to the problem just yet. This may work to our advantage. You do this without fucking up, Jesus, and there's a promotion in it for you."

Cisco saw the greed well up in Jesus' eyes. Jesus had no idea that Cisco was using him as a pawn.

"Don't worry, Cisco," Jesus said heading for tho door. "I won't fuck up."

Cisco sat back in his leather recliner and clasped his hands together. This was a situation that would definitely require some watching. Cisco giggled like a school girl as he thought of the look El Diablo would have on his face when he broke the news to him.

*

Lou-loc stood atop the jungle gym looking down at the sea of blue clad soldiers. Even though it was dark, Lou-loc could see each and every member in attendance. He made a mental note of those who didn't bother to show and decided that they would be dealt with accordingly.

At the last minute, they had decided that having all of the homeboys in the park at one time might draw too much attention. They thought it'd be best just to have all of the captains and their lieutenants present, each with a soldier of their choice. Even with this precaution, there were still a good twenty-five of the homeboys present. When Lou-loc's voice finally boomed out, all became silent.

"I wanna thank all y'all niggaz for coming," he said addressing the crowd. "We got pressing business to attend to, so I ain't gonna keep you long. I'm pretty sure all y'all niggaz done heard about what happened to our folk Gutter, so ain't no need for me to go into detail about the shit," Lou-loc said.

"When them faggot ass brims tried to slab Gutter they played themselves," Lou-loc continued. By them even thinking that they could touch an OG, they disrespected us. They basically said fuck Harlem and fuck the whole C-nation. I know mafuckin' well we ain't going for that shit?"

Lou-loc had the crowd in an uproar. There were chants of "fuck Bloods," and threats ridding the world of Bloods.

There was a wicked gleam in Lou-loc's eyes. It had been so long since he had held the reigns of power that he almost forgot what it felt like. The beast was in control, and it howled for blood. The man speaking to the homeboys wasn't St. Louis Alexander the writer, it was OG Lou-loc, head buster, and stone murderer.

Lou-loc waited until the crowd's voices died down before he began speaking again.

"Now," he said waving them silent. "We know it was some brims who did the shooting, but we don't know which set exactly, or who gave the order. But that ain't no big problem.

"This is what we gonna do. I want at least one blood on every set dropped. If you happen to catch more than one body, oh well. I want it to be made crystal clear that we want the nigga or bitch that gave the order. If they don't up em, we keep killing, period. I don't care if we gotta splatter everything red in this city, they better give that mafucka up. Either that, or these streets gonna run red wit them buster's blood."

Lou-loc's speech had the effect he hoped it would. The crowd had become a violent mob. Lou-loc looked down on his crew and smiled like a proud father. These were his children, and if he asked, they would follow him to the ends of the earth.

After the crowd had died down, Lou-loc motioned for Pop Top and Snake Eyes to join him.

"These are the men you will answer to during these troubled times," he said motioning towards the two men. "All you cats already know Top, he'll be over seeing the troops out in the field. But I want to introduce my main man, Snake. I know you see him standing there in his shoes and specks, but don't get it fucked up. He's one of the most cold-blooded studs you'll ever meet. He done saved my ass on many occasions back home in LA, and done dropped quite a few people, so don't let his appearance fool you. He'll also be providing legal services for those of you who'll need it. He's our minister of defense," Lou-loc said.

"These are two of my most trusted partners," he continued. " You show them the same respect that you would show me. Now, y'all niggaz go lay it down. Show these mafuckas that the name 'Crip' still mean something in these streets."

Lou-loc threw up his C's and all the homeboys responded in kind. The crowd filed out with murder on their mind. The park had emptied out leaving only the three leaders.

"That was one hell of a speech," Top said patting Lou-loc on his back. "Shit, I'm ready to go bust on something."

"It's gonna be a lot of heat on us, cuz," Snake commented. "A whole lot of mafuckas is gonna end up on the slab."

Lou-loc looked at his homey and smiled. "I guess the stock in funeral homes is gonna go up, huh? Remind me to call my broker in the morning."

Top thought that the comment was funny, but Snake Eyes didn't see it that way. Unlike everyone else, the murderous gleam in Lou-loc's eyes didn't go unnoticed by him. It was a look that he hadn't seen in a long time. Since the night when Lou-loc had murdered Stan.

"You a'ight, Lou?" Snake asked.

"Never better," Lou-loc said entirely too calm. "You got my package from Wiz?" Snake Eyes handed him a duffel bag and stepped back.

"Yea, I got it," he said. "Man, those is some strange ass Chicanos you fuck wit, cuz."

"Nah, the twins is cool," Lou-loc said. "Wiz, he just a lil different. Y'all niggaz go home and get some rest. I'll call you sometime tomorrow afternoon."

Before waiting for a response, Lou-loc strolled off into the darkness.

As Snake Eyes watched his friend stroll off into the darkness, he shook his head. After what happened to Gutter, Lou-loc's mood seemed to change. He wasn't the ambitious young man that the east coast was molding him into. He was the Cali killer that he used to be. One thing was for sure, there would be a lot of black dress buying in Harlem.

*

After Lou-loc left the park he headed down town and rented a room at the Quarters hotel. When he signed in, he used his real name. The reason for this was so he'd have an alibi as to his whereabouts. After checking in, he slipped out the back and headed home.

When he got there, he had to pause before going inside the house to gain his composure. The voice in his head was screaming for him to kill Martina and be done with it, but he still had feelings for the girl. That and the fact that he didn't wanna make her kids orphans. As soon as he walked in, Martina started up.

"Fuck you been?" she snapped. "I been calling your phone and paging you all day. What, you was laid up wit a bitch or something?" Martina screemed.

"I was busy," he said coolly. "Had to do some running around." Martina wanted to continue the argument but something in his eyes told her to leave it alone.

Lou-loc got a can of paint from under the kitchen sink and walked into the bedroom. When he entered the bedroom, he collected all of Martina's jewelry and dropped it into his pockets. He looked at the five and a half carrot ring that he never had a chance to give her, and shook his head. Next, he went into their closet and removed all of her furs and leathers.

After laying Martina's goods on the bed, he removed his razor blade and proceeded to slash all of her dresses. DK, Versace, Pradda, all turned to confetti. He took all of the clothes he could carry from his side of the closet and placed them in a duffel bag with his jewelry and guns. All of his papers were in a brief case, so he had all bases covered. Strolling like he didn't have a care in the world, he went into the living room and placed his bags by the door.

"Where the fuck you going?" Martina asked rolling her neck. "You just came in this muthafucka, and now you leaving again?"

"Don't worry, baby," he said kissing her forehead. "I gotta drop some shit off to Gutter and make a run. I'll be back tomorrow though. Come here for a sec. *I gotta surprise for you,*" he sang.

At the mention of a surprise her whole attitude changed. Her anger was quickly replaced by greed. On the walk to the bedroom, the only thing that was on her mind was if it was money or jewelry? He didn't come in carrying any bags, so it had to be either or.

Martina's eyes bulged in disbelief at the sight of her shredded clothes and her minks scattered on the bed.

"What the fu..." was as far as she got.

Out of nowhere Lou-loc splashed lavender paint all over Martina's belongings. She stood in the center of all the carnage sack jawed. Lou-loc had laid waste to at least one hundred and fifty thousand dollars worth of goods. Her goods, and that wasn't counting the furs and leathers. Before she even realized what was going on, he had grabbed her by her jaws and lifted her off of her feet.

He looked into her tear filled eyes and spoke in a voice that didn't sound like his own.

"Bitch, I go all out for you and your crumb crushers, and you try to put shit on me?"

"Wh... what are you talking about, baby?" she stuttered.

With his free hand he removed a ruby ring from his pocket. Martina's eyes widened in shock.

"Look, familiar?" he asked.

"Where did you get that?" she stammered out.

"From a dead man, hoe. All this time and you been creeping with a brim? I should twist yo mafuckin' brain." He tossed her onto the bed and put his gun to her heart. "Why?"

"Wait, Lou-loc, let me explain?" she pleaded. "He didn't mean anything to me. You were always gone and I needed someone."

"Gone?" he asked in disbelief. "I'm out there on the grind so you can live good, and you tip out on me? I should crush your heart like you did mine."

"P...please don't kill me?" Martina begged.

"Nah, I ain't gonna kill you," he said putting his gun back in his belt. "You ain't even worth it. Just answer me one thing. Is that baby even mine?" Her silence was answer enough.

"I'm gone, Martina," he said walking away. "Make due with ya bills the best way you can."

"Baby, wait?" she said grabbing his arm. "I know I fucked up and I'm sorry, but don't leave me. Let's try again. I know we can make it work. I couldn't live without you. I love you, daddy."

Lou-loc shook her off his arm.

"Un ass me, bitch. Love? You couldn't even spell love, let alone feel it. If I ever see you again, I might put one in you."

Lou-loc hurried from the apartment before he started to cry. It was hard to say goodbye, but he knew if he stayed he was likely to kill her and anyone else who might be in the house. It was better this way.

As Lou-loc was putting his things in the trunk, he heard Martina shouting from the window.

"You ain't shit, Lou-loc. You just gonna leave me and ya baby? You fucked up my furs and my clothes, but that ain't enough? Youz a crab ass nigga, but that's a'ight. You gonna regret this shit. Believe me, you gonna regret this."

A warning bell rang off in Lou-loc's head, but he shrugged it off. He figured she was just hurt talking out of her ass. He left her broke and bummy. What the fuck could she do to him? Lou-loc hopped in his car and hit the highway to Brooklyn.

Upstairs, Martina's wheels were already turning. She cursed herself for letting Lou-loc get away. She had already dismissed the idea of calling Mac. If Lou-loc knew about him, then nine times out of ten, Mac was already dead.

She was angry and hurt. Her meal ticket had finally run out. She was going to get her revenge though. She needed a way to fix Lou-loc's ass. Then it hit her like a brick. She dug through the pile of clothes and paint until she found the phone. Within seconds, she had reached the party she was seeking.

"Let me speak to Cisco."

CHAPTER 15

Lou-loc parked a few blocks from a bar where his victim was said to be a regular. From the back seat, he retrieved his duffel bag and checked the contents. Inside the bag was an old colt revolver and a small metal box. He opened the box and was greeted by cold air from the cooling system. Inside the box were six bullets, but these weren't regular bullets.

The tips were made of a special plastic designed by Wiz and financed by Lou-loc. Inside the heads of the bullets were a corrosive acid. The plastic that kept the acid from spilling out would burst upon impact. Not only would the acid eat away the casing, but it would also eat away at the victim's insides. No sense in making the job easy for forensics.

Lou-loc placed the gun under his seat and got out of his ride. He walked the few blocks to the bar and stepped inside. There were wall to wall people in the place, so Lou-loc had to look around for a while before he spotted him.

He sat at the bar hunched over a drink, surrounded by a few of his peoples. Even in the dim light his bald head shined like a beacon. His white tank top stood out against his dark skin like two ends of the color spectrum. To Lou-loc, the man they called 'Born' didn't look like he was worth the over priced fee he had agreed on with the Al Mukalla chief, but if Anwar was willing to pay, he would gladly take the money.

When he turned at an angle, Lou-loc could see his iced out medallion swinging form his platinum chain. Lou-loc figured he might as well take that too, after all, he wouldn't need it where he was going. But then again, wouldn't he need all the ice he could carry in hell? Lou-loc chuckled to himself at the little joke and walked happily out of the bar.

After retrieving his glock, as well as the supped up colt, Lou-loc stood in a darkened doorway of a closed auto body shop and waited. It would probably be quite a while before his mark came out of the bar, but patience was always one of Lou-loc's strong points. If need be, he would've waited until day break. That's what made him an effective killer.

*

Mean while, on 114th Street a group of young men were sitting on a stoop drinking and passing blunts. All of the young men sported red head bands. They were Bloods and this was their turf, so as far as they were concerned, they had nothing to fear. If any of the young men could've seen into the future, they might've stayed in bed.

The most animated of the group was a tall light skinned cat named Scooby. Scooby considered himself a hard ass. On Rikers Island, he had earned quite a reputation for himself. He was nice with his hands, and lethal with a shank. Scooby ran his crew with an iron fist, and when he spoke, they listened.

"Fuck them crabs," Scooby said taking a long swig of his 40oz. "Let one of them mafuckas come through here, and it's a wrap. I don't play that shit, dog. I'm the hardest mafuckin' Damou out here."

"What about them folks uptown?" a dark skinned youth named Tick spoke up. "Gutter and them niggaz?"

"Fuck them niggaz." Scooby spat. "You see, I know how Gutter get down. He's crazy, and that's just that. I know what to expect from him, so I ain't worried. It's his partner that gives me the creeps."

"You mean that nigga, Lou-loc?" another youth named Bear added. "Fuck that nigga, he pussy. I seen him on 125th one day while I was wit my bitch. I threw my set up, and he ain't even do shit. Lou-loc soft."

"That's ya problem," Scooby said, "you take everything for face value. My cousin that live out in Torrence, he gave me the 411 on that nut. That kid is the real fuckin' deal."

"Yea," a young boy named B.G. added on, "I heard he killed like a hundred niggaz on the west coast. Shit, they say he went at it with a swat team, and won."

"Those is just stories," Scooby said. "Besides, LC hit Gutter the other day. The way it's looking, his ass is worm food. As it stands, Lou-loc is the only thing between me and controlling Harlem. The nigga might be bout it, but he ain't super man. He bleed like us."

"You better be careful," Tick said. "You plan on going at Lou-loc, you better be ready to get down for real."

"What ever," Scooby said handing Tick his beer. "Hold my shit, nigga, while I go take a leak." Scooby stumbled around the corner to try and find a dark spot to pee. Little did he know, the shadow of death was right on his heels.

Scooby whipped out his joint and began to relieve his bladder. He thought about the line of bullshit that he had fed his peoples. He wished he really was as confident as he had sounded. In all reality, he knew what time it was with Lou-loc. Scooby wasn't a coward, but Lou-loc was somebody who he really didn't want a problem with. Scooby's mind was so jacked up off beer and weed, he didn't even see the figure slithering from under a car behind him.

The figure when standing fully erect was only about five feet five inches tall. Its frame was thin, and haggard. In the proper light, it would've resembled an animated corpse. The only thing protecting it from the elements was a black leather body suit.

The figure roached into a hidden compartment and produced a cord about the width of a string of dental floss. With the grace of a cat, the figure moved toward Scooby. Before the young gang Lord even knew what was going on, the cord was around his neck.

Before the cord was secure, Scooby grabbed for it. As he did so, fire shot through his hand as his middle and index finger tips were severed. The shards of diamond dust woven into the cord severed both flesh and tendon.

The more Scooby struggled, the more excited the figure became. The more excited it became, the tighter the noose got. Scooby tried to scream for help, but all that came out were muffled groans as his life's blood spilled out onto the Harlem street. The cord bit deeper into Scooby's neck until it met bone. Even then, the figure applied more pressure, but the bone wouldn't give. In a matter of seconds, Scooby's head was almost severed, and he was dead on his feet.

After being gone for a while, the others began to worry about Scooby and decided to check on him. All their combined years of street education couldn't prepare them for what they saw when they rounded the corner. Lying on the pavement in a pool of blood was their leader, Scooby.

His head hung at a funny angle, and his face still held the mold of a man attempting to scream. The worst part was, Scooby's dick was still hanging out of his pants.

*

Lou-loc sat across from the bar smoking cigarette after cigarette. The sun would soon be forcing its way up, bumping away the darkness, and exposing Lou-loc. He considered just making the hit inside, but then pushed the thought from his mind. He didn't know the lay out of the bar well enough to try that. The last thing he wanted was to trap himself.

As Lou-loc stepped from the doorway to stretch his legs, his mark came staggering out of the bar. He was flanked by two rugged looking characters on either side. Lou-loc had counted on them being unarmed because they were coming out of a bar, but all hopes of that quickly vanished when one of the body guards produced a pistol from out of a near by dumpster.

Lou-loc stuck to the shadows, and crept to the trios left. As he made his way, he removed the bullets from the case and loaded the colt. Foot by foot he got a little closer. It was still dark, and they were dead drunk so they still hadn't noticed Lou-loc. He was close enough to hit his mark, but he only had six bullets in the colt, and he only had he glock for back up. He needed to be closer to make sure the job was done correctly.

The few yards that separated Lou-loc from his mark were bare. He'd be totally exposed, and should they be lucky enough to get off a shot, he wouldn't have any cover. It was just a chance he'd have to take.

Just as Lou-loc was about to make a mad dash, luck swung in his favor. A group of drunk white kids came stumbling out of the bar laughing and clowning. They just happened to provide enough cover for Lou-loc to move closer.

Lou-loc faked drunk slipping into the crowd. He was staggering and joking right along with the other kids, but he never took his eyes off the mark. He took his glock in his left hand and jammed it into his pocket. With his right hand, he let the colt hang down at his side. The mark still had his back turned, so Lou-loc moved in for the kill.

Just as Lou-loc got close enough to spit on the mark, he turned around and stared him dead in the eye. This is usually the part where the killer says something slick or boast to the mark on how he's going to die, isn't it? Didn't happen that way with this story.

Lou-loc raised the colt and squeezed off two shots. The first shot hit Born square in the forehead with a crunching sound. The second, hit him in the eye and embedded itself in the back of his skull.

The body guards stood there in shock as the acid did its work. Born lay on the ground with blood coming out of his eyes and ears, twitching and convulsing while his blood soaked companions look on in horror. Lou-loc used heir hesitation to his advantage.

Firing through his jacket, the glock boomed to life. The first bullet caught the first body guard in the throat. He tried to cry out, but it sounded more like he was gargling. Lou-loc turned to the second body guard and tore into him with the colt. The single slug tore the left side of his face off.

Lou-loc stood over Born's still twitching body, and put the two remaining colt bullets into his heart. The kid had never did anything to Lou-loc, so there was no reason for him to suffer. It was only business.

The drunken kids had sobered up when they heard the gun shots, and the females began to scream. Lou-loc turned his glock on them and purposely fired two shots over their heads. Some scattered and some hit the floor. Didn't really matter to Lou-loc, he just needed them distracted long enough for him to make his getaway. As he hauled ass down the block he fired four more rounds over his shoulder, that way, any would be witnesses would keep their noses to the ground.

*

Lou-loc drove back to Manhattan just under the speed limit. No sense in getting pulled over, and fucking everything up. Before going back to his hotel, he stopped by the harbor to dump the pistols. He rubbed the guns down with a baby wipe, and tossed them into the water. He didn't care about the colt that was just for the job. It was the glock that hurt him. He'd gotten used to his 'Chrome Misses,' as he called it. Attached or not, the shit still wasn't worth going to jail for.

When he reached his hotel room, he slipped back in the way he left. The hotel only had cameras in the lobby, so he didn't have to worry about his comings and goings being recorded. Once inside his room, he stripped naked and got in the shower.

He felt a little better after washing two day's worth of grit and gun powder off his skin. He lay naked across the hotel room bed and though about the turn his life had taken. Once the brim that ordered Gutter's hit was dealt with, his obligation to the set was fulfilled. He was through with Martina, so he could focus on Satin. He couldn't wait to call her, but it would keep till the morning. Lou-loc stretched out and fingered the small pistol under his pillow. Knowing that he was safe for the moment, he let sleep claim him.

CHAPTER 16

The weeks to come were chaos. The homeboys were putting in overtime. There had been sixteen murders reported, and that's just the ones the police knew about. The bloods fought back, but were swarmed as homies flooded in from the west coast. A lot of people owed Lou-loc favors, and he was calling them in.

Everything was working out just as Lou-loc had planned. He even filled six more contracts for the Al Mukalla. He hadn't intended on coming out of retirement, but Anwar was a good tipper. Lou-loc figured he might as well stack as much paper as he could before he stepped out of the life. The truth of the matter was, the thrill of the kill was sweet to him.

On a different note, Satin, and Lou-loc were getting closer. They were always going here and there, from museums to operas. Satin was putting Lou-loc on to a different side of life. One where he didn't need to hurt people, or have people trying to hurt him. It was different for him going to these places, but it was nice

Lou-loc and Satin were like kids falling in love for the first time. In truth, they were. Neither had ever had someone they could totally give themselves to until they met each other. To fall in love was a beautiful thing, and they were diving in head first.

*

Lou-loc and Satin strolled down the boardwalk in Coney Island, and let the sun beam down on their faces. He pulled Satin to him and kissed her eyelids. They had been seeing each other for over a month now, and it was the happiest six weeks of both their lives. He stared down at her smiling face, and wondered why God hadn't put them together sooner?

"Satin," he said softly, "can I say something, and you won't think I'm being corny?"

"Yea," she said wrapping her arm around his, "what's that?"

"Until I met you, I thought love at first sight was just a phrase. It might sound crazy, but I think I loved you from the first time I saw you.

133

"Don't say things like that."

"Nah, I'm serious. I been hurting inside for a long time. Maybe ever since I lost my dad. When I met you, it's like the pain just faded. You feel me?"

Satin nodded her head and walked up a little. Lou-loc caught up with her, and turned her around to face him. The tears on her cheeks sparkled like diamonds in the afternoon sun. Even crying, she was still beautiful to him.

"It's okay," he whispered as he kissed the tears away, "we got each other now."

"You make me feel so special," She said in between sobs. "I don't want this feeling to ever end. Promise me?"

"Baby, you know I'm here for you. How long, depends on you, but I ain't got no plans to go no where."

There a loud clapping interrupted little moment of tenderness. Lou-loc spun around, and was surprised to see the same young kid he'd almost killed in front of Satin's building. He was dressed in all red, and so were the two boys with him.

"Bravo," Jesus said stepping forward, "what a touching display. I thought I was gonna cry."

"Fuck you want, lil nigga?" Lou-loc snapped. "I gave yo ass a pass one time, but don't push you're luck."

"You got a lot to answer for, crab," Jesus said. "A lot of good soldiers died cause of you."

"Fuck you in yo bitch ass," Lou-loc snapped. "I could give less than a fuck if all you dead rag niggaz curl the fuck up and die. When y'all give up who gave the order on my boy, it all stops. Other than that, suck my dick." Lou-loc grabbed a handful of his crotch for emphasis.

Jesus went for his gun, but Lou-loc was quicker. With a flick of his wrist, a P-89 appeared in his hand. As he began to apply pressure on the trigger, the unexpected happened. Satin jumped in between them.

"Satin, what the fuck are you doing?" Lou-loc asked in disbelief.

"Oh, you didn't know?" Jesus asked putting his gun away. "I know Satin told you, Louie?"

"Told me what?" Lou-loc asked turning his cold glare on Satin. "You know this chump?"

"She should," Jesus said with a grin, "we dropped out of the same pussy. So I guess that makes you my brother- in- law? Yea, me you and El Diablo. Brothers"

When Satin looked at Lou-loc, she saw the hurt in his eyes. She intended to tell Lou-loc, but just never got around to it. The last thing she wanted was for him to find out like this.

"Lou-loc," she said with tear filled eyes, "let me explain."

"You ain't got to explain nothing to me. I understand. Shit, talk about me hurting you?"

"Don't take it like that," she said reaching for his arm. Lou-loc recoiled like she had a snake in her hand. His love for this women was quickly replaced by hate and betrayal. He knew if he didn't leave, someone was going to die.

As Lou-loc turned to walk away, and Jesus left him with a parting thought. "If it'll make you feel any better, those were my homeboys that put the heat to ya man."

The temperature of Lou-loc's blood shot up about 300 degrees. He tried to control his anger because he didn't want Satin to get caught in the crossfire. Even though the bitch had just crossed him, he couldn't bring himself to hate her. Something in the back of his mind told him that there was more to the story. The type of feelings he and Satin shared couldn't be faked.

All that would have to wait for later. The problem he was having now was what to do about the three brims trying to clown him and his comrade? He was out numbered, and he already knew that at least one of them was strapped. Lou-loc felt his anger and hurt welling with every step he took. Lou-loc slowed his steps and exhaled "fuck it."

Lou-loc had been eyeballing a lead pipe sticking out of a trash can. With one hand, he slid his gun into his palm, with the other, he grabbed the pipe and made his move. The three men were still dying laughing when Lou-loc came bull charging their way. Jesus caught it first.

The lead pipe whistled through the air and made a horrible crunching sound against his jaw. Jesus was out on his feet leaving just his partners.

The first homey was reaching under his shirt, but Lou-loc was on him too. He cocked his arm back like a baseball pitcher and sent the bar sailing over in the homeboy's direction. The homey had the 380 halfway

135

out of his pants when the pipe struck the pistol. The hammer jumped and blew a hole in the first homeboy's leg. He wretched in pain and dropped to the ground.

Before he could gather his wits, Lou-loc was on him again. He began to rain kicks and whacks from the butt of his gun on the homey's head. It wasn't even a contest.

When the second homey made a move to flee, he heard the sound of Lou-loc's hammer cock back.

"Ga head, mark," Lou-loc said inching closer. "You wanna be a track star? Nigga, you think you can outrun a bullet? I'll take that bet all day."

"Lou-loc, please!" Satin pleaded. "Don't throw your life away by killing him. Just come with me so I can explain?"

"Bitch," Lou-loc snarled, "you ain't really in no position to make a request. I might just have an extra one in here for you. You crossed me, Satin. You crossed me."

Satin looked out at Lou-loc standing there holding his pistol. Their eyes sharing the same hurt. Any other woman would've been shocked and terrified by the sight of their man about to take a life, but she wasn't. She loved him more for it. To her, that meant he was a man of respect. Respect for himself and those he held dear. This was a man who would kill for the sake of his family.

"You know what, Satin," Lou-loc said easing his finger off the trigger, "I'm gonna let you run your story down to me. I'm probably one of the biggest fools on God's green earth, but I wanna hear it. But I want the truth from you. I ain't in my right frame of mind right now, so if you try to put shit on the game," he paused for a moment, and looked at his gun, "I ain't sure what I'm capable of."

She cautiously move toward Lou-loc. She wasn't worried about him shooting her, but she didn't want to jar him into shooting the homey. "The truth," she whispered, "good or bad, right or wrong. The truth."

"Hold on," Lou-loc said walking toward the second homey. He leaned over so only him and the homey could hear what was being said. "It's a wrap for LC, cuz. A death sentence on the whole set for touching my peoples. You better find a new set to claim, cuz. LC bout to take a nap. If you ain't sleepy, get gone. Pass that along for me, cuz." The second homey nodded dumbly and trotted off.

Lou-loc stooped down over Jesus. "Player," he sang, "wake up, gangsta." Lou-loc slapped Jesus viciously until he began to stir. "Glad to see you still with us. Listen, pimp, I know you can't talk wit ya jaw all fucked up, and shit. I really don't need you to talk though, I just need you to listen. Harlem still holdin' sway uptown. The only reason you'll still be able to eat soup in a few days is because I love your sister.

Lou-loc dusted himself off and walked to join Satin.

"Truth," he whispered to her, "good or bad, right or wrong. Truth. Let's get up outta here. Them people gonna be here soon."

Satin reached out to take Lou-loc's hand but he pulled away. She got the hint, so they made their hurried steps up the boardwalk in silence.

Jesus lay on the ground throbbing in pain. He looked at the two lovers and wondered if he'd made a mistake by provoking this humble man. Satin looked happy with Lou-loc.

He was from a rival set, but he made his big sister happy. Could he be that bad? Jesus didn't have a chance to answer his own question, as unconsciousness dragged him under.

*

In a different borough, several people dressed in red, sipping Remy, sat huddled around a table. These people represented the leaders of blood sets throughout the five boroughs. Each dangerous in his or her own right.

The man who sat at the head of the table was known on the streets as The hawk. He was named so because of his striking resemblance to the winged predator. Hawk wasn't a large man, but was well built. His muscles were visible through his red sweat suit as he scratched his angular jaw. Hawk was a brown skinned man, who stood at maybe five feet ten inches on a good day. His black eyes seemed to look everywhere at once, making him look like he was always scheming. In all truthfulness, he was.

Hawk stood up, slicking down his wavy czar, and addressed the crowd. "I would like to thank you all for coming," he said making sure he made direct eye contact with every member of the council, "before we conduct our business here, I would like to welcome home one of our most out spoken brothers. El Diablo."

"Thank you," El Diablo said receiving applause from the crowd. El Diablo was draped in a black suit with a blood red tie, and shirt. "It's good to be home."

"Yea, what ever. Hawk, why we here?" That was Ruby. She was the only female set leader respected enough to attend the meeting. Ruby was a petite and attractive women. Her skin was the color of autumn leaves with eyes to match. Her hair was dyed blood red, and braided into fish bones. Although Ruby was beautiful, she was vicious and feared for her violent temper. In her ten years of being a Blood, she had been tried for murder seven times, and beat every case. Though she was never convicted, there was no doubt in anyone's mind as to her guilt.

"Always the outspoken one huh, Ruby?" Hawk said not making an attempt to hide his irritation. "Well, being that you asked so nicely, I might as well get to it. I'm sure no one here has missed out on the latest turn of events concerning the Harlem Crips?"

"Missed out? Shit they dropped five of my boys, and that was just last week." This speaker was called Bullet. He was the wiry leader of the hells kitchen bloods. He was quick to shoot off his mouth as well as his gun.

"We've all been having the same problem." Hawk assured him. "All of our respectable sets have taken on casualties. Until now, we haven't generally been bothered by the smaller crew. They have their piece of the apple, and we ours. For some reason they've gotten agitated over something, and have taken to wholesale murder?"

"So fucking what." Ruby snapped. "Let's just hit them back?"

"We've tried that," Hawk said. "It seems like for every one of their troops we kill, they take two of ours. My people uptown can't even get money. Every time we open up shop, somebody in blue comes by shooting.

"The feds are all over everything, making life uncomfortable for our crews. I, as well as our friends out west, would like to put an end to this as quickly as possible. All this attention from the law isn't good for either side. Now we'd like to have a sit down, but it seems like they don't want to talk.

"I know their leader, Gutter. He's not an unreasonable man, but it seems like he's no longer pulling the strings. I'm told that he met with an accident a few weeks ago. I'm not the smartest man in the world, but I'm starting to put two and two together. Would some one care to fill in the blanks?"

"Oh, I'll fill in the blanks," Bullet said sarcastically. "It's that fuckin' nut job, Lou-loc. He's running the show now. Seems one of our brothers ordered the hit on Gutter. When Lou-loc caught wind of what went down, he flipped. Said niggaz is gonna keep dying unless we cough up who it was. Now I ain't no punk or no shit, but that kid ain't got no respect for life, something's gotta be done."

"Fuck, Lou-loc," Cisco spoke up for the first time, "he's a fuckin' man like most of you claim to be, but you're acting like he's God. He can die too."

"Big talk from the Latin Infection." Ruby quipped. "Them two been a pain in your ass since they came out here from Cali. All that shit you popping, and he still ain't dead."

"Who the fuck do you think ordered the hit on Gutter?" Cisco said with a smile.

"And you fucked that up." Ruby shot back.

"I met Lou-loc back when they signed the treaty." Hawk added. "He's an efficient killer, true, but he's not a violent man. Even though we were both two little bad assess from opposite sides of the track, he still treated me with courtesy. He was provoked, and that's what opened this faucet of blood. Now the question is, how do we shut it off?"

"Fuck it," El Diablo started, "I say we pool our resources and put him down."

"You crazier than a shit house rat," said Bullet. "That boy is protected from on high. He get his props from both sides of the coin."

"Bullet's got a point." Hawk added. "I made a few long distance phone calls to get the 411 on our friend Lou-loc. The word is, he and Gutter, are operating independently. The thugs he called in are putting in work out of love for him and Gutter, not their gang. This shit LC done started is personal."

"What the fuck," El Diablo snapped, "he's ordered the assassinations of more than two dozen of our number, and we're supposed to not do anything? I say fuck that nigger."

"Watch your mouth, spic." Bullet mumbled.

"Gentlemen," Hawk interrupted, "slinging racial insults amongst each other isn't going to solve our problem. This mass killing is going to fuck us. We need to come up with a reasonable solution before the feds shut us all down."

"I say we toss him Cisco or somebody," Ruby said. "They started this petty shit, fucking up all our flows. Let their assess roast in the fire."

"Fuck you," Cisco hissed. "Fake ass Charlie Baltimore."

"I say we stand our ground," said El Diablo. "Maybe we can see our way through this, without any taking too many more losses?"

At El Diablo's change of attitude, Cisco began to chuckle. Soon the chuckling became laughter. "I would expect you to take such an attitude about all this, El Diablo. Being that your own sister is sleeping with the enemy."

El Diablo's eyes widened in shock as did the rest of the council's. "What did you say?" El Diablo snarled.

"Please forgive me for bringing it up at such a venue," Cisco said sarcastically, "I wanted to wait until I was sure before I brought it up. Lou-loc has taken quite an interest in little Satin."

"Why do you mock me at a time like this, Cisco. This is not the time or the place for rumors."

"I assure you, Michael, it's all true. If you don't believe me ask Jesus."

El Diablo collapsed in his chair as if all the strength was drained from his body. Never in his life would he have even considered his sister to go over to the other side. She wasn't gang affiliated, but she knew who her peoples were, and she was loyal to her family.

"Well, whadda ya know?" Ruby said grinning. "Hey, Mikey, you got blue in your blood?"

"Now, now," Cisco said standing, "it isn't his fault. He had no idea that his sister was seeing Lou-loc. This, however, has brought me to our solution. A friend of a friend has provided me with the means to get at Mr. untouchable. Lou-loc is a dead man."

140

"Cisco," Hawk started, "even though Lou-loc is out here raising all types of hell, he's still an OG. A made man. If he happens to end up dead, and any one can trace it back to you, there's going to be some really unhappy campers out west."

"I'm not worried. All I need is the support of my brothers on the matter."

"I ain't touching that one," Ruby said flat out. "That kid is connected to some heavy weights. I heard a rumor that the big boys were talking about putting the hurt on whoever hit Gutter. The worst part is, our superiors ain't got a problem with it.

"That shit y'all pulled was stupid. We've kept the peace with them boys for a while, and you fuck it up cause LC wanna be greedy. That was some dumb shit, Crisco."

"What ever. LC will handle it."

"You're right," Hawk said standing. "LC started this shit, so it's up to LC to finish it. No disrespect to you, El Diablo, but I feel that if we went with you on this, we would be dragging the bloods as a whole into this feud. It ain't worth the headaches or the casualties. I'm sure my fellow council members will agree with me on this one?" Everyone nodded their head in agreement.

"Now that that's settled," Hawk continued, "I have a message from our friends of the U.B.N. I was told to deliver it to who ever was responsible for causing all this. The gist of it is, this thing will be settled quickly and quietly. If we can't settle it, then they will send someone who can. In short, gentlemen and lady. When this is all said and done, some of us will find ourselves out of a job and on a slab."

CHAPTER 17

Lou-loc sat on the passenger side of Satin's jeep fuming. In his rage he'd almost forgotten that they'd rode her whip to Brooklyn. If he had actually stormed off during their fallout instead of listening, he'd probably had to hop in a taxi, if he was lucky enough to stop one.

Satin clutched the steering wheel with both hands as she switched lanes without signaling. She kept one eye on the road and one eye on the bulge under Lou-loc's shirt. She wasn't scared, but she was still shaken a bit by the little encounter between Lou-loc and Jesus. Never before had she seen a man go off like that. He was like a wild animal, tearing into the trio. She wondered if she hadn't been there, would Lou-loc have spared Jesus?

"So," Lou-loc said breaking her train of thought, "you said you wanted to explain, I'm still waiting?"

Satin shifted in her seat and tried to find the right words. A way to explain the madness that was her life. If only he could look into her heart, all would be clear. She Loved this man, but didn't know how to express it.

"Lou-loc," she said softly, "I really don't know what to say, so I'll just be honest with you."

"That would be cool as hell, considering you been lying so far," he said sarcastically.

"Lou-loc, please? This is hard enough for me without you making smart ass comments. Now I wanna tell you the real to real, but I ain't gotta kiss yo ass while I'm at it.

"Now, as I was saying, it's true. Diablo and Jesus are both my brothers, but it's not like we're the Partridge family. None of us are that close. Until a few weeks ago, I hadn't seen Michael in years, then he just pops up, and all this shit starts happening.

"Jesus, he's a good kid, but the streets have poisoned his mind. I'm afraid my baby brother has been lost to me for some time. Can't save every one, huh?

"The only person I had in this world was my aunt Selina, God bless her. Then you came along, Lou-loc. You made me feel like it was

142

alright to care about my happiness. I mean look at me. Gangs broke up my family and my dumb ass has fallen for King Crip.

"I don't know what the fuck is wrong with me? Lou-loc, the reason I didn't tell you, because I didn't want to run you off. I was feeling you, and I know you wouldn't have fucked with me if you knew who my peoples were.

"What ever their hangs up are, that ain't got shit to do with what I feel for you, or what you feel for me. With us, it's deeper than a color, or a street. I don't fuck with bangers, but I see something more to you. You have a talent, and a choice. I might be wrong for not telling you, but I'm not sorry. If you decide that when we get back to your car it's a done deal, I'll accept it."

Lou-loc spared a sideways glance in Satin's direction, and saw the tears stream down her face. Even without the steady flow of tears, he knew she was telling the truth. In his heart, he felt as if a weight had been lifted. He had only been with Satin for a short time, but he cared so much for her. Life without her in it was unfathomable. It was kismet.

"Satin," he sighed, "try to understand where I'm coming from. We're at war with these mafuckas and I find out that they yo peoples, how am I supposed to feel? I told you what I just went through wit this bitch Martina, and yet you still holding back secrets? At this point in my life, I can't afford to have people keeping shit from me, especially the ones I love."

"Lou-loc," she sobbed, "I know you love me, at least I hope you do, cause I damn sure got it bad for you. But if you truly love me, get out of the life?"

Lou-loc pulled at his hair in frustration.

"Satin, you know I can't just up and bounce. I got business I needs to handle. The set needs me right now."

"The set?" she asked sorrowfully. "What about me, Lou-loc? I need you too."

"I know, Satin, and I need you, but you gotta understand."

"Lou-loc, the only thing that I understand is that you're the best thing that's happened to me in a long time. I know all about your unfinished business, Lou-loc. I just don't want the business to finish you.

"What about going away, you remember that? You asked me if you could take me away would I go? Yes, I'll go. I've got some money saved that I could put with whatever you have, and I could sell my jeep. We could just go away from here and never come back, okay?"

"Satin," he said touching her cheek, "if only it were that simple. If I were to leave here now, there would be nobody to lead the set. With the way things have heated up over the last few weeks, that would be like leaving a pack of rabid dogs loose on time square. They'd run wild, and things would only get worse."

Satin parked in front of her building behind Lou-loc's car. When Lou-loc reached for the door to get out, she grabbed his arm.

"Lou-loc," she said wiping her eyes on her sleeve. "Where is this relationship going? I mean, I've laid all my cards on the table. I've come clean with you about how I feel, but what have you given back? Where are we going with this, Lou-loc? If I'm setting myself up for a let down, tell me now and we can go our separate ways?"

"Satin," he said, sounding a bit frustrated, "why are you putting me through all this drama?"

"Because," she said matching his attitude, "I want to know where I stand? Where we stand? In my heart, I know you're the person I want to spend the rest of my life with, but how do you feel? You say you love me, but do you love me enough to get out of the life?"

Lou-loc looked into her eyes to see if she was putting game on him, but she was dead serious. From the moment Lou-loc first laid eyes on this Latino beauty, he knew she was special. He knew that Satin was someone he wanted to know more intimately, but he hadn't considered a life long commitment. He had only just begun thinking that far ahead with Martina, and that was after two years. Now here was this amazing woman, whom he had only known a little over a month, asking him to walk the path of eternity. At that moment, everything in Lou-loc's life became crystal clear to him. He knew what he had to do.

"Listen, Satin," he began, "right now I can't promise you anything. Look, once I know Gutter's okay, I'll think about it. If he pulls through, fuck it, I'm getting tired of New York anyway. I hear Florida's nice?"

"You mean it?" she asked smiling. "We can go?"

"Satin, I'm not promising you anything, all I said was I'll think on it. You're my boo, and I love you. It took a while for me to recognize love when I saw it, but you taught me what to look for. I can bend on this one, boo. Just give me a few days to tie up some loose ends and we'll give some serious thought to our future. Now that we've applied for your subscription to 'Modern Bride,' I gotta a move to make."

"Lou-loc," she said stopping him short, "before you leave, there's something I have to give you."

"Okay," he said shrugging his shoulders, "give it here."

"I can't, it's upstairs."

"Okay, but I gotta dip, so let's hurry."

*

Lou-loc followed Satin into her loft apartment not suspecting a thing. Satin continued to play it off like nothing was up, but there was something definitely up. When they got inside she instructed Lou-loc to have a seat while she went and got his surprise from the bedroom.

Lou loc sat on the couch and thought about what his plans were for the future. He had been so caught up in all of the madness over the last few weeks, that he'd forgotten that he was the one who was supposed to be trying to get out of the life. It took a woman like Satin to remind him of where his priorities lay.

"That Satin is one hell of a catch" he thought to himself. Definite wifey material. Sure, he was a little salty for her not being up front with him, but he wasn't actually as mad as he'd acted. He was more hurt than anything. But that was all behind him. Even though he had told Satin he would give it some thought, there was no doubt in his mind about leaving New York.

He reflected on his life and how it would change now that he had Satin in it. One thing was for sure, he had to go legit. Satin wasn't trying to fuck with him if he was still banging, and he respected her for it. Shit, why bother with it? Its not like he had to hustle any more. Lou-loc was never a dumb kid. He always spread his money around wisely. He owned a barbecue joint in Carson that his aunt and uncle ran. It was mainly to make sure that his sister was taken care of and that they were compensated for their troubles. They never asked Lou-loc for anything, but he sent them a few dollars on a monthly basis.

Unbeknown to most people, with the exception of Snake Eyes and his father, Lou-loc had quite a bit of money tied up in legal businesses. In addition to his barbecue spot, Lou-loc was one of the financial backers in a hip hop clothing line. That alone would've put his sister through college, and still kept them well to do.

Overall, his more modest source of legal income was probably security. Lou-loc was the silent partner slash owner in a small security company on the west coast. 'Blue Light Protective Services,' not only provided security for the well off and wealthy, but they also provided services to the dealers who solicited them. Lou-loc understood the game, drug dealers don't have credit cards or checking accounts, so he let them pay cash. Sure, he jacked the price on them, but business was business.

Lou-loc was also one of the few brothers who gave back to the hood. He would donate large sums of money to different charities and community organizations under assumed names. He didn't want the people's praises. He felt what he was doing was his responsibility considering he was one of the people helping pump drugs into the hood, and putting bodies on the slab.

With all that Lou-loc had on the ball, he could've walked away from the game and never looked back. If most people knew the kind of bread Lou-loc was handling, they'd have called him a fool. He wasn't bill gates or even close, but he had more money than a lot of white folks in the game. With all that, Lou-loc still chose to live amongst the dealers and other parasites. After all, they were his people.

After a few moment had gone by, Lou-loc began to get impatient. Satin had been gone about fifteen minutes and he was beginning to worry. Just as he got up from the couch to go check on her, Satin came out of the bedroom, and Lou-loc thought his heart would burst. He was prepared for anything except what he saw.

Satin stepped into the living room wearing a sheer bathrobe that stopped above the knee. Beneath that, she was wearing a transparent gold teddy with the matching garter belt and stockings. When she moved towards him, her dark nipples seemed to be staring him down through the fabric. Lou-loc stood there slack jawed and speechless, staring at the heart shaped muff of hair that became slightly visible as Satin placed one of her tone legs on the arm of the sofa.

"Well," she said in a seductive tone. "You just gonna stare at me all day or what?"

Lou-loc was too dumbfounded to say a word, so she took the initiative. Slow and gracefully Satin moved toward Lou-loc and pushed him back on the couch. She placed one leg on either side of him and slid down onto his lap, where she proceeded to grind back and forth.

"St. Louis," she whispered, while nibbling his ear, "I want you to know how special you are to me. Am I special to you?" she asked while massaging his penis. All Lou-loc could do was nod his head in agreement. "Tell me!" she demanded.

"Ooh, yea," he moaned, "you special, baby."

"How special?"

"Very."

"Oh yea?" she teased while grinding harder. Lou-loc tried to be cool about it, but looking at her perfect body made him want to bust all in his boxers. Even though they had been seeing each other for a while, they hadn't had sex yet. That was the way she wanted it, and he really didn't mind. He could get sex from any bitch in the hood he chose, but with Satin, it wasn't about the sex. He loved who she was, and what she was about.

"Lou-loc, baby," she said while licking his neck and lips, "I love you so much. I want to ask you something, baby, and please don't tell me no. You know how I hate rejection."

"Anything." he panted.

It was then that Satin did the unexpected. She reached behind her neck and let her hair down, but to Lou-loc's surprise, it wasn't a hair clip that was holding it up. Satin held in her hand a platinum men's wedding band. Crisscrossing all around the outside of the band were the prettiest blue diamonds. "Marry me?" she whispered.

Lou-loc's eyes got as big as saucers, and as damp as a London street. He was so shocked, he wanted to break down and cry. But him being gangsta, he didn't.

Satin asking Lou-loc to marry her caught him off guard. A woman asking a man to jump the broom wasn't the traditional way it went, but it

was a new millennium, and women were bolder about the way they did
things. Truth be told, Lou-loc had toyed with the idea of asking Satin
what she thought about the idea, but he didn't want to sound like a corn-
ball or anything. It was just a strange twist of fate that she sprung it on him
first.

"This what you want, baby?" he asked in his Billy D voice.

"More than anything." she replied.

"Then you got that," he said kissing her nose.

Satin put Lou-loc in a bear hug that would rival even big Kiki's.
When she had first purchased the ring a few days prior, she felt like she
was playing herself. She had only known Lou-loc for a short time, but he
felt right to her. Before dropping it on him, she feared that it would scare
him off. She had been wanting to sleep with him, but she didn't want to be
just another piece of ass. She wanted to take what they had to another
level. The marriage proposal to him was the final test, and he passed with
flying colors. If he had said no, she probably would've fucked him anyway,
but after that, she would have kicked him to the curb. "Fuck it. Life goes
on."

A week ago, when the idea of proposing to Lou-loc first popped
into her mind, she immediately asked her aunt Selina what she thought
about the idea. Selina raised her frail frame in the cast iron hospital bed
and looked at her favorite niece through her cloudy gray eyes. Even as an
old woman, there was still something regal about her.

Selina was once the object of many men's affections. Old age had
stolen her beauty, and much of her health, but it couldn't rob her of her
wisdom.

"Marriage," she asked in a heavy Spanish accent, "how long ju
know dees man?"

"For a short time, Tía, but I know he's the one."

"And how ju know dees, mees smarty pants?"

"Because, my heart tells me so."

"Good answer," Selina said patting Satin's hand. "Does dees man
love ju as well?"

"He says he does."

"A man can tell ju any ting he wan, Satin. What he do to proof his
words?"

"Many things, Tía. He's rearranging his whole life style to be with me, because it's what I want."

"Mmm hmm," she said suspiciously. "More talk. What he do that mean something?"

"He spared one of Jesus' stupid little friends, even after the boy shot at him."

"Satin, ju would be with a man who bring death into the world?"

"No, no, it's not like that. You see, Michael, and Jesus' people tried to kill his brother because they are from rival gangs, and..."

"He es a gang meember?" she cut her off. "Ay, Satin, I did no raise ju to be stupid. Ju see what these gangs have done to your brothers, why you geet involved with these people?"

"Tía, you don't understand. He is a gang member. That much is true, but he's not like the rest. He cares about life and about people. He's getting out of the life, so he and I can be together. He loves me, and I love him."

For a long while Selina didn't say a word. She just sat there studying Satin. In her niece's eyes, she saw true love. "Satin," she finally said, "I know jour heart because I've helped you put it back together many a time, after it broken. I see ju really love dis man."

"Oh, I do," Satin said excitedly. "I love him enough to marry him."

"Now hold on," Selina said sternly, "ju moving kinda fast, no?"

"No, Tía. I love this man and want to spend my life with him. He says he loves me also. Me asking him to marry me will be the final test of his loyalty. If he says yes, then even you can't deny that we were meant to be."

"So ju say." Selina responded. "But what about him? Let heem tell me to my face that he love my niece as much as she love heem. When he come tell me, I know if es true."

Satin's lips parted into a wide grin, exposing two rows of perfect white teeth. "I thought you might feel that way. Wait here for a second." Satin jumped up from the bed. After a few minutes, she came back into the room leading Lou-loc by the hand. "Tía, this is my friend, St. Louis."

"Como está usted, senora?" he said in perfect Spanish.

"Buena." she responded. "I see ju speak Spanish?" she asked impressed.

"Yes ma'am. In California it's a mandatory second language."

"My niece tells me many things about you."

"I hope they're good things?"

"Some good, others not so good."

"Well, Miss Selina, I won't lie to you. I've made some poor choices in life, but your niece is trying to help me correct them."

"Good answer. So, meester St. Louis, what are your plans for my baby?"

"To make her as happy as possible."

"Another good answer. She coach you on what to say to me?"

"No, ma'am. I'm just speaking from the heart. I would never attempt to deceive some one as lovely and as wise as you. Even if I could, I wouldn't."

"So far, so good," she said looking at Satin. "I'm just going to come right out and ask you, meester St. Louis, how do you feel about my niece?"

The question caught Lou-loc off guard, but he didn't fluster or hesitate. "I love her, ma'am. I only want to do right by her, for as long as she allows me to."

Selina studied Lou-loc for a long moment. She looked him dead in the eyes to see if there was any hint of a lie in what she was saying. But in Lou-loc's eyes all she saw was sincerity.

"Meester St. Louis," she said holding his hand in hers, "for a long time I've looked after this girl. I've watched her come from a tree climbing little girl, to a beautiful young lady. I am an old woman now, and I fear that my time is short in this world, but I no sad. I know that when I leave here, I will be with my Lord and savior. I need you to promise do some ting for me."

"Sure, if I can," he said sounding a little dumbfounded.

"Take care of her," she said teary eyed. "Allow me to pass on to the kingdom of heaven knowing that my niece is in good hands. Promise me that you will try to do right, and treat her like the queen that she is?"

"I promise," Lou-loc said sounding a little emotional himself. "You have my word." The three of them shared a warm hug and exchanged a few tears. Selina knew that Lou-loc would stay true to his word.

As Satin and Lou-loc made to leave, Selina called her back. She pulled Satin to her and whispered into her ear. "You've made a fine choice, little one. The heart never lies. God bless you both."

Satin left the hospital feeling pleased with herself and her man. To her, a blessing from her aunt was as good as a blessing from God. She was pleased that Selina hadn't mentioned Michael during their visit. She hadn't yet gotten around to telling Lou-loc about her affiliation with the rival gang. That was a week ago.

*

Lou-loc and Satin spent a long time exploring each other in the shadows of scented candle light. It was as if it were the first time for both of them. Not just their first time with each other, but their first time with anyone. Lou-loc was very gentle with her. Each time his tongue stroked her skin, she felt her nerves come alive. He kissed and sucked his way from her eyelids down to her belly. When he got to her vagina, she felt like sparks were going to pop out of her scalp.

At first he did it slow and sensual. He licked around her womanhood and grazed her clit with his tongue. When she tried to push his head down he pulled away and continued to tease her. Once he finally did start handling his business, she was in another world.

The way his tongue worked its way in and out of her spot, she thought she was going to pass out. She began to see spots and blurs with every stroke. It was the first time a man had ever made her orgasm, let alone with his tongue. She was into it and didn't have any shame in her game about showing it.

"Oh, that's it, baby!" she shouted. "That's that shit! Oh, you nasty nigga you!"

After about twenty minutes and a few orgasms, it was time to return the favor. Satin wasn't as experienced as Lou-loc in oral pleasure, but she wasn't no slouch. The warmth from her mouth felt so good to Lou-loc that he wanted to cum prematurely, but being the type of nigga that he was, he wasn't going to let that happen. Her teeth scraped him a few times causing him to flinch, but she still satisfied him. He actually respected her more for not knowing how to give head. That showed that she had either never done it before or didn't have much practice. Unlike Martina, who was a pro.

After a few moments of oral, Lou-loc decided that it was time for him to bust her out. He carried Satin to the bedroom and laid her gently on the bed. Lou-loc slipped on a rubber, and tried to penetrate her. Even with the lubrication from the condom, she was still too tight. He dropped down to his knees and began to lick her spot in an attempt to add more moisture to the mix. Once she was thoroughly lubricated, he eased his way inside of her.

He had only gotten it about halfway in when she began to whimper and cry. "You want me to stop?" he asked concerned.

"You better not," she said seriously. "You don't know how long I've been waiting on this. Just keep going, I'll be alright."

So, keep going he did. It felt like it had been quite sometime since anyone had been inside Satin, and Lou-loc loved her tightness. He stroked her slowly and with care at first, but once they had gotten into a rhythm, she begged him to give it to her harder. Lou-loc was only too happy to accommodate her.

They went at it for a good forty minutes before Lou-loc reached his climax. After a brief intermission they were at it again. This time, they both went at it like wild animals with each one trying to out savage the other. Satin tore chunks of flesh from his back and arms while he plowed into her like a man possessed. Six position changes and an hour later, they lay in each other's arms, and reflected on the lovemaking they had just shared.

It was strange for Lou-loc. For the first time in his life, he felt content. The burdens of the set weren't hounding him, he wasn't looking over his shoulder, and nobody was dying. Even if only for the few moments in the arms of this beautiful women, he was free.

Satin, was so different from, Martina. Martina was ghetto and out spoken, while, Satin was poised and cultured. The two women were like night and day. Each one had her own special qualities, but, Satin added more to the mix.

With, Lou-loc and Martina, it was fucking. No love making, just the two of them going at it with an animal like lust. Not that there was anything wrong with it, but Lou-loc was a hopeless romantic who craved more from a woman.

Satin was a different case. She was like a delicate flower, who he had to handle accordingly. At times she seemed so pure and naive, that he almost felt like he was doing something wrong by sleeping with her. Satin was one of those women who seemed so dependant, but at the same time could stand on her own. She was different and this only further intrigued the young OG.

"What ya thinking about?" Satin asked looking up at Lou-loc.

"Life," he said smiling. The way Satin made him feel was something he'd been searching for most of his life. It was like this brown Goddess was the piece he was missing. It felt so good that he wished it could go on forever. But why couldn't it?

Since he'd been old enough to bang, Lou-loc had been putting in work for the set. He avenged his father's death a dozen times over, and amassed a fair amount of paper. With the money he had put up, and his investments, he was good. Why not lay up with this bad ass bitch and live?

Lou-loc had a good run in the game, but time was getting short. All his niggaz was getting laid, or gotting numbers. Look at Gutter? It pained Lou-loc to think of his ace all tore up and shit, but he had to face the reality of the life he was living. He and Gutter had come up under the same codes, doing the same shit. Lou-loc might have killed a few more people, but Gutter wasn't no saint. He had much blood on his hands.

The situation could've been reversed and that could've been Lou-loc with all those tubes running in and out of him. Satin coming to him was like God had taken a chance and was giving one of His fallen angels a second shot at life. Hell, if that was the case, Lou-loc had no intention on wasting it. He was going to take it and run with it.

"Satin," he said stroking her forehead, "I been...you know, thinking about what you said?"

"And?" she asked.

"Well, I ain't gonna lie, you asking me to marry you was some weird shit, ya know? I don't mean, weird in a bad way. I mean, it caught me off guard."

"Yea," she said getting up, "I played myself, right?"

"Nah," he protested, pulling her back down, "it ain't like that. But are you sure that this is what you want?"

"Listen boo," she said in a serious tone, "life is too short to be pondering over things your heart is already telling you is right. You the one, baby. I don't mean to sound thirsty or like I'm desperate, but that's just how it is. I got a Jones for you, St. Louis Alexander, and I know you got one for me, so why fight it?"

"Damn," he said nodding his head, "that was straight forward and confident. You deep, girl."

"Lou-loc, you know how I'm living, ain't no shame in my game. You're somebody I can build something with. You ain't some simple ass corner nigga still trying to hustle up that Benz. You got yo shit together just like me. You and me could be serious together, as lovers and as partners. But you gotta understand, I can't get wit no street nigga. I know you gonna be you, but lets do it the right way. Ya feel me?"

Lou-loc just sat back and smirked. This was a side of Satin that he hadn't had the pleasure of meeting yet. She was a bull when it came to something she wanted. It was an asset to her numerous other qualities. This was definitely someone he could be with.

"Ma, you make a lot of sense," said Lou-loc. "These streets put age on you quick. I ain't even twenty four yet, and I done been through enough shit to last me two lifetimes. Maybe it is time to give the streets a rest?"

"That's what I'm trying to tell you, Lou-loc. This shit is for the birds. Baby, write ya books and be the star you supposed to be. I've read your work, and I know you can do it."

Satin's words of encouragement gave a boost to his ego. Not only had she taken the time to read the work he'd given her, but she liked it. Martina had never had time to read his work, let alone critique it. There was something special about this women. Even though her peoples were from the other side of the color line, he decided to get over it, and accept her.

"Satin, I want to give you something," he said reaching into his knapsack. He handed her a purple velvet box. When she opened the box, she was enthralled with the crater sized diamond.

"Lou-loc," she squealed, "this is so beautiful. When did you...hold up. I know you ain't trying to pass nothing off to me that you bought for that other bitch you was with?"

"Nah," he lied, "that's just something I bought a while back. I always said I was going to save it for the day I met someone special enough to have it. Low and behold, here you go." It was a little white lie that he told her, but technically, it wasn't that far from the truth. True enough, he had bought the stone for Martina, but she had never actually owned it. Shit, she'd never even seen it.

"That was sweet of you," she said hugging him, "I'll cherish it."

"Just think of it like this," he said while putting their two rings side by side, "we gonna jump the broom, but not no time soon, we gotta get it together first. But these rings will be a symbol of our devotion to each other. When I get my affairs in order I'm gonna cop you a rock so big, that you'll need a wheel barrow to carry it around."

"You're silly," she said kissing him on the cheek.

"Now, I got some moves to make, Satin. I'll come by to check on you tomorrow."

"Lou-loc, don't go?" she pleaded.

"Baby, you know I gotta handle business. I gotta get my affairs in order so we can do us. Within the next few days, we gonna put some distance between us and this shit hole."

"You serious, Lou-loc?"

"Am I serious? Baby, let me tell you how serious I am. When you wake up tomorrow, you go on down and tell your landLord that you'll be moving out soon. I'm gonna float you the bread to pay off your last months rent, so you shouldn't have no static wit the old bird."

"Baby, if you ready to pull up, we can leave tonight," she said eagerly.

"Nah, honey." he waved her off. "We gonna do it right. Take care of your crib and your gig. Within a week, if even that long, we outta here, straight gangsta."

As Lou-loc headed for the door, Satin stopped him short. "Lou-loc," she called out, "I want you to promise me something?"

"Anything, boo. What is it?"

155

"Promise me that we'll always be together? Baby, if I put my feelings into this like I want to, I wanna know that it's something solid, and not just a fling?"

"Baby," he said pulling her close, "you're the rainbow at the end of a storm. I wanna wake up and see your baby doll face next to me in the morning for a lot of years to come. You will forever be my heart, mami. In this life or the next."

"Then promise me, Lou-loc. Tell me that you'll never leave me, and I'm not a fool for loving you?"

"Satin, honey, that's a bona fide guarantee. Now, I gots to raise up and get right.'

She didn't want him to go, but she knew a man had to be a man, so she kissed him good night and let him go. She loved the shit out of Lou-loc. Her biggest fear was that the streets would take him away from her before they really had a chance to appreciate each other. She had always been psychic about things like that.

CHAPTER 18

*T*he penthouse of the Golden Arms apartment building off of Central Park West was about as plush as they came. The decorator, who was imported from France, laid it out to look like a Chinese palace. The walls were decorated with various art works from around the world. They were only prints, but it still gave the apartment an eccentric feel. As opposed to curtains, the windows were all fitted with bamboo shutters.

Expensive furniture filled every room of the apartment. Even the toilet was hand crafted to certain specifications. A red carpet ran from the front door to the living room, giving those who entered the feeling of being a celebrity. The owner liked to stroke his ego that way. This was the domain of Michael Angelino, a.k.a. El Diablo.

El Diablo paced back and forth over his plush living room carpet while Cisco looked on and smiled.

"Michael," Cisco crooned, "you're going to upset your ulcer if you don't calm down."

"Calm down?" Diablo snapped. "You announce to me that my sister is seeing one of the men I'm trying to have assassinated and you do so in front of those fucking apes on the council. Now you tell me, Cisco, how the fuck am I supposed to calm down?"

Cisco leaned back in the recliner and lit a cigarette. He knew he couldn't overplay his hand for fear of ruining everything. He had to nudge El Diablo on for fear of ruining everything. LC Blood would be his, but he had to be patient.

"Michael," he said exhaling a cloud of smoke, "I did things the way I did for your benefit. For one, if I had told you in private, would you have taken me seriously? I told you at the council because I knew that would help you to realize the seriousness of the situation. For two, I wanted all of those fucking "egg plants" to respect our gangsta.

"The streets are watching. Not only are they watching, but they're talking. Some of our cousins, for lack of a better choice of words, feel that since you haven't been on the scene for a while, that you might've gone soft?"

157

"Soft?" El Diablo asked in disbelief. "I have never been weak. El Diablo has paid his dues. There is much blood on my hands, Cisco."

"Oh, it's not to me that you have anything to prove. It's these fucking street rabbles that are trying to tarnish your good name. Then you got this meat ball ass nigga from the other side sporting your sister. What kind of shit is that, Michael? You've got to intervene on this one, boss man. If you let this slide, then it's only a matter of time before you have these fucking tar babies lining up to challenge your authority."

Cisco sat back and let his words sink in. By the way El Diablo was pacing and pulling at his mustache, Cisco knew his speech was starting to take affect. Everything was working out nicely.

"You're right, Cisco. This will not go unpunished. When El Diablo allows his own family to become Judas, he is no longer fit to lead."

"Just what I was thinking," Cisco mumbled under his breath. "I suggest this, Michael. Give me a day or so to confer with my contact. I'll take care of this Lou-loc, but you need to be the one to talk to Satin. We gonna work this shit out, Michael. We just gotta go about it right, you feel me?"

"Yes, Cisco. We have to do it the right way. I'll try reasoning first. If that doesn't work, I'll blow his fucking brains out and put my foot knee deep in Satin's ass. That's what I'll do."

"Bueno," Cisco said standing. "That's the El Diablo I know. Let me get out of here and on my job. I'll be in touch soon, Michael. LC for life!"

As Cisco made his way to the elevator he had to fight back the smile that was forming on his lips. Things were working out better than he had originally planned. Soon, Lou-loc would be dead, El Diablo would either be dead or injail, and he would be the leader of LC Blood once again. Cisco promised himself that once he was returned to power, Satin would pay for trying to give him her ass to kiss. This he was sure of.

*

Lou-loc dipped in and out of traffic feeling himself. He was on top of the world. He had some paper, a bad bitch and a plan. In his mind, he was good and no one could bring him down, or so he thought.

Lou-loc pulled out his cell phone and the first call was to his crooked ass financial planner. He informed her that New York was no longer going to be his residence and that he would be needing some cash to travel with. She assured Lou-loc that he would be receiving the cash within twenty four hours and the necessary paper work would be taken care of. The next call was to Pop Top telling him that there would be an emergency meeting of the set leaders taking place that night. Top kept asking him what the deal was, but Lou-loc wouldn't give. He knew a lot of the homeboys wouldn't be too happy about him getting out, but fuck it. If niggaz really felt that strongly about it, they could see him in the streets. It's not like he was abandoning them. He was just retiring while retirement was still an option.

The hardest part would be saying goodbye to Gutter and Sharell. They were the only family he had on the east coast, so the bond between the three was strong. Sharell had always tried to tell Lou-loc about Martina, but he wouldn't listen. It was too late to change things. Might as well man up and keep stepping.

Lou-loc had already tracked Sharell down at the hospital. Might as well kill two birds with one stone. He could tell Sharell what was up and make his peace with Gutter.

By the time Lou-loc made it to the hospital the sun had set. Looking at the new evening made Lou-loc think about Cross. He wondered if he should track his friend down and tell him that he would be leaving soon. But fuck it, he still had a few days to say his goodbyes.

As Lou-loc made his way through the hospital lobby he tried to find the right words, but he couldn't. How do you tell your best friend, who happens to be in a coma, that you're leaving and that you'll probably never see him again? There was no easy way to say it. Lou-loc promised himself that no matter where he was, if Gutter came out of his coma, he'd be on the first thing smoking back to his friend's side. When he got off of the elevator onto Gutter's floor, Sharell greeted him with open arms.

"Where you been, boy?" she asked giving him her Sunday service smile. "I ain't seen you in so long, I almost forgot what you looked like."

"Ain't nothing, sis. I just been out trying to get my life together."

"Oh yea? I hear that. So you and that fast ass Spanish chic finally parted company?"

"Yea, how you know?" Lou-loc questioned.

"Boy, you know Harlem ain't but so big. She was all out on the block cryin' and shit. She was talking bout how you left her for some square ass young girl."

"Yea, that's my boo."

"Mmm hmm."

"What you mean by that?"

"St. Louis Alexander, you in love?" Sharell asked.

"Girl, you know me better than that."

"Yea, I know you, and that's why I said it. I knew from the first time you told me about her that she was something special. You know, I prayed on it for you, Lou-loc. I asked the Lord to send you someone to set yo ass straight and in comes Miss Satin."

"Yea, Sharell. Satin is all that. She opened my eyes to a lot of shit. I'm trying to find a way out of this hell without doing it the way I've been doing it. We've even talked about getting married."

"Not you, Mr. Player? Marriage so soon. She must've put that thang on you?"

"Nah, it ain't even like that with us. I mean we did the do, but that was after I'd been with her for a while. She's a good girl, Sharell."

"Praise the Lord. I'm so happy for you, Lou-loc. You need a good woman in your life. But how do you plan on truly making this girl happy if you're still caught up in this madness?"

"See," he said timidly, "that's kinda what I came to tell y'all. I'm getting out of New York. I'm getting out of New York and out of the life. I'm done, Sharell. This shit is over for me. I'm just hoping you don't think I'm being a coward for leaving before my man wakes up?"

Sharell's eyes welled up with tears. She rushed to Lou-loc and embraced him.

"Lou-loc," she said sobbing, "I would never think you are a coward for trying to survive. This is what you've always wanted and Kenyatta knew it. There ain't no shame in being tired. We all get that way if we go through enough. The important thing is you're getting out by choice instead of by bullets or bars."

Hearing Sharell's approval of his decision made Lou-loc feel a little better. He had always had a lot of respect for her. She wasn't no hood bitch, yet she wasn't some stuck up chic either. She was just a young lady who had her shit together.

"How's my boy?" Lou-loc asked.

"Well it's hard to really say," Sharell said honestly. "Some days he's good, others not so good. The doctors say his condition is stabilizing, but he's still unconscious. I'm scared, Lou-loc. What if he doesn't wake up?"

"Don't fret that," he said patting her hand. "That boy tough as they come. I've seen Ken pull himself out of more hellified shit than this. It's a small thing to a giant, ma. Bank on that one."

"I hope so, Lou-loc," Sharell said.

"So, how y'all doing as far as bread, honey?"

"Oh, we straight. I got some dough in the bank plus the money Ken got put up. Oh, and Anwar is paying all of his medical bills. He said he's an old friend of the family."

Lou-loc was surprised to hear Anwar's name. How the hell did he even know Gutter was shot up? Them Al Mukalla niggaz was something else. Didn't much of shit go down without them hearing about it. That was some real cool shit that Anwar was paying the bills. Maybe Lou-loc had misjudged the young prince? Well, he'd just have to thank Anwar for what he was doing. But there would be time enough for that later. Now he had to go in and see his friend.

"Sharell," he said. "I'm gonna spend a few with the kid and get some things off my chest. Go on and get yaself a snack." He handed her a fifty- dollar bill.

"Okay, Lou-loc," she said accepting the money. "I'm gonna run down to McDonald's and snatch something up. I already know what you like, so I'll bring it up to you."

As Sharell gathered her purse and made her way to the elevator, Lou-loc couldn't help but appreciate how much of a good woman Gutter had on his side. Why couldn't he had hooked up with her instead of that bitch Martina? Oh well, at least she would see that his man was a'ight and he had Satin in his corner, so they were both in good shape.

Lou-loc made his way down the corridor trying to figure out what to say to his brother. It was best to just open his mouth and let the words flow freely. When he entered the room he almost broke down.

Gutter was laid out in that iron bed looking like death warmed over. There were tubes running in and out of damn near every hole in his body, and a machine helping him breathe. His beautiful dark skin was ashy and drawn in. His hair needed to be braided over and he had lost quite a few pounds. This was not the man he knew.

At first he was mad at Cross. The man had the means to save Gutter and did nothing. But once reason took over, Lou-loc realized there was no reason to be mad at his friend. It was not meant for man to play God. Cross was just playing his part in the natural scheme of things. To be upset with him was selfish.

Lou-loc pulled up a chair beside his bed and took his friend's hand. "What up, cuz? This ya ace boon, Lou-loc. Man, so much shit been going on since you took ya little vacation. The homies been putting in work like a mafucka. We done rode on damn near every blood set in New York. I found out them little marks that put the paper on you was from LC. I put the hurt in their leader's little brother and two of his peoples.

Lou-loc continued on as if he knew Gutter cold hear his every word.

"I took care of that nigga, Born, cuz. In return, Anwar made good on his end and knocked Scooby out the box. We set up the new spots out in Brooklyn and, baby boy, the money is coming in. I got lil Boo and his peoples looking over shit out there cause that's where they peoples is from.

Lou-loc paused and then continued on.

"Peep the fly shit though, cuz. Remember that chic, Satin? That's El Diablo's lil sister. Wait a second before you start preaching. She ain't on it like that. She don't fuck wit them niggaz. She ain't got nothing to do wit the life. She's a good girl. That's my boo now, cuz. It's like you always said, that bitch Martina was dirty. Come to find out, she was fucking wit that lil slob, Mac. He ain't putting his lil dick in nothing no more though, cuz.

Lou-loc paused and put his head down. It was now time for him to say his main reason for being there.

"Guess I should get to the point though? Me and Satin, we in love, cuz. It's the real thing. We even talked about getting married. I know it's sudden, but it's real, G. I'm getting out, cuz. I put in enough work and paid

162

my dues. It's a wrap for me. Them niggaz that tried to one you is dead and buried. We have established ourselves as a super power in Harlem and everybody getting money. We good, cuz. What I really want though, is ya blessing. I'm moving on, cuz. I'm gonna take Satin somewhere and square up. I know you're probably salty wit me, but you know this is how I want it. I've wanted out of this for along time and now I can get it. Maybe get a nice house somewhere, have a few brats, who the fuck knows?

Lou-loc squeezed Gutters hand. He tried to hold back his tears but failed miserably as he continued on.

"Cuz," Lou-loc said sobbing. "I'm sorry for what happened to you. Lord knows I am. If we could've traded places, it'd be me in this fucking meat factory. Before I can do what I need to do, cuz, I need to know we're square. I need to know you're okay with me leaving. Tell me something, cuz?"

Just then Gutter's hand twitched. It was a slight twitch at first, but then there was pressure. Gutter was squeezing Lou-loc's hand telling him that all was well.

Lou-loc's eyes began to well up with tears. He tried to fight them off, but it was no use. The tears flowed freely down Lou loc's cheeks. He wasn't just crying for Gutter though. Lou-loc wept for many reasons. He cried for his father who was gunned down in a mall parking lot. He cried for Gutter's father and grandfather who died for what they believed in. He cried tears for every man he had ever murdered, and the mothers who had to bury their children. He cried for the youth and black America.

*

As Lou-loc bowed over his friend crying, he was unaware of another watching and shedding tears of its own. But these tears were different. These were tears of hatred and tears of vengeance. Tears that come of knowing what one must do, no matter how wrong. These were tears of blood.

163

CHAPTER 19

Satin was on top of the world. The evening breeze was warm on her face as she carried her small bag of groceries back to her loft. Hell, it could've been pouring rain and she wouldn't have cared. Her life was finally beginning to get better. She had been skeptical about coming at Lou-loc the way she did, but her forwardness had paid off once she found out that he felt the same way she did.

It was like her aunt used to always say, "Love is an unpredictable thing. When in doubt, follow your heart." Those words rang true in her situation. She followed her heart and hit a home run. She knew she loved Lou-loc from the first time she laid eyes on him. Their hearts called to each other and now they would become soul mates.

Too bad for Martina. She felt kinda bad about going after him because he had a girl, but it wasn't her fault that the bitch was trifling. She shoulda kept a tighter hold on her man. Oh well, all's fair in love and war. She doubted that Martina would be a problem. Satin was a lady first and foremost, but if the bitch decided to get stupid, Satin had an ass whipping on hold for her.

Satin's thoughts were interrupted when she saw Michael's car parked in front of her building. This drama she didn't need. She was a grown ass woman and Michael could go fuck himself if he had a problem with her being with Lou-loc. Before she could get to the car, Michael hopped out and started towards her.

"Satin," he snapped, "what the fuck is up with you?"

"Nice to see you too, Michael," she said sarcastically.

"Don't play with me, Satin. What's this I hear about you fucking this nigger from the other side?"

"First of all," she said pointing her finger, "his name is Lou-loc. Second, he's not a nigger, he's a writer. And third, we're not just fucking, that's my man."

"Your man? He's a killer. Lou-loc personally executed two of my peoples. Satin, how you gonna fuck with somebody that broke our little brothers jaw?"

"Michael, please. Jesus brought that shit on himself. He started fucking with Lou-loc and got his little ass kicked. The only reason he didn't get himself buried was because of me. Lou-loc loves me, so he let Jesus live."

"Loves you?" Michael said rolling his eyes. "You poor misguided child. He's just fucking you to get at me. This shit is like a fucking slap in the face. You know how stupid this has me looking amongst the other Blood Generals?"

"Michael, you're making yourself look stupid pressing this shit. If you recall, Lou-loc and his peoples didn't start this shit? Y'all the ones that cast the first stone."

"Satin, you don't know shit about shit as far as this goes."

"Michael, don't play me, okay. You don't think I know it was LC who shot Gutter. Jesus already let the cat out of the bag. Shit, why you think he got his jaw broke?"

"Damn, Satin. If I didn't know any better, I'd think you were siding with them black bastards?"

"Oh, please. You know I don't get down with that gang shit in no kinda way. All this sides shit don't mean nothing to mo, oo mioo mo with it. I could care less if the police killed or locked up every one of them dumb ass so called gangsters. For your information, he's getting out of the gang so we can be together. Lou-loc is my man, and that's just the way it is."

"Ya man, Satin? That black son of a bitch don't love you. To him, you another notch on his belt. A fine ass piece of Spanish pussy," Michael said with his words not exactly coming out right, but it was too late to take them back.

That last comment hurt Satin deeply. She and Michael had their differences, but he was still her brother. If anything, she wanted him to be happy. She didn't expect him to accept Lou-loc, but she wanted him to at least understand how she felt.

"Fuck you, El Diablo," she said coldly. "I could give a fuck what you think."

"Now you listen," he said grabbing her by the arm. "I'm your big brother and I know what's best for you. I forbid you to see this 'spook' anymore. I forbid it."

Satin threw her head back and burst out laughing.

"You can't be serious. I'm not the little girl you remember asking for dollars. I'm grown, Michael, G-r-o-w-n, so you can bump your head with the dumb shit."

Satin turned to walk away, but El Diablo wasn't done yet. He spun her around and slapped her across the face. Satin dropped her groceries and stood there in shock. Michael had never put his hands on her before, but there was a first time for everything.

"Satin," he said reaching for her, "I... I'm sorry. I..." Before the words were out of his mouth, Satin had her gun drawn and aimed at his heart.

"You dirty muthafucka," she hissed. "Ain't no man ever laid hands on me, not even our father. Let me tell you something you dope peddling snake. I don't give a fuck what you say. This is my life. Lou-loc and me are going to be together and that's a fact. Now if your small, racist brain can't accept that, o' fucking well. That's the way it is. And if you ever raise your fucking hand to me again I'll empty this clip in your worthless ass. Now can you dig that?" Before he could answer, Satin was strutting towards her building. Before she made her way through the lobby door she took another jab at her brother.

"The next time I have to pull a gun on you it'll be to take your life. Satin disappeared into her building.

Michael stood there at a loss for words. What the fuck was his family coming to? The same little girl he raised had just threatened to kill him. All he wanted to do was look out for his sister's feelings. There was no doubt in his mind as to whether or not his sister loved his rival. But did Lou-loc feel the same? El Diablo knew he had to bring some clarity to the situation, and quickly. This shit was getting out of hand.

*

Cisco stood on the corner of 125th and Park under the Metro North station waiting for Tito to show up. The excitement had him so worked up that he wanted to jump up and down. El Diablo had called and told him about the altercation with Satin and asked his opinion. Cisco played the role of the concerned councilor, but inwardly he jumped for joy.

The mighty El Diablo was playing right into his hands. Within the next day or so he would be the sole controller of LC Blood. Before Cisco could fantasize further, his cell phone vibrated.

"Hello?" he sang.

"Cisco," said the seductive voice on the other end.

"Martina, what a pleasant surprise," he lied. In all actuality, Cisco had no love for Martina. She was loose and had no loyalty. She would sell her mother out to the highest bidder. As foul as she might've been, he still needed her. She would be a key player in his scheme.

"So, what the deal, mami?" Cisco said.

"You know the deal," she quipped. "You got my paper?"

"Listen, sweetheart. Don't put the cart before the horse. You'll get ya bread when the job is done."

"I know you got me, Cisco. I just got shit I need to do, that's all."

"Yea, me too."

"Cisco, why don't you swing by my crib before you turn in for the night."

"Oh yea, for what?"

"Just to chill, you know? Gosh, a bitch can't just wanna hang for old times sake?"

"Yea right. Martina, I know you too well. You always got something up your sleeve."

"Nah, it ain't even like that. But if one thing leads to another, you know?"

Cisco couldn't help but to laugh. Here this bitch was pregnant as all hell and still scheming on cock. Cisco and Martina had hooked up on occasion, but the way things stood, he wanted no part of her. The bitch was a stone snake that didn't have a preference about who she bit. If she was willing to cross a nigga she was supposed to love, imagine what the fuck kinda shit she would get him into? Cisco was arrogant, but he wasn't stupid.

Martina was going on and on about the good times they used to have, but Cisco wasn't really listening. He was too preoccupied with looking for Tito. Just as Cisco was about to bark Martina's head off, he spotted Tito coming down the steps from the Metro North.

"Martina, baby," he said sweetly. "I gotta go handle something and make sure everything is set for tomorrow. Make sure you handle your end. When you make all the arrangements, call me. You understand?" Before she could answer, he hung up the phone.

"Damn," Tito said as he walked up. "These fucking people out here wanna overcharge you for everything."

"Don't sweat it, my man," Cisco said good spiritedly. "It ain't ya bread. So we clear on what's up?"

"Yea," Tito said while lighting a cigarette. "I got it."

"Good, good. Make sure they make the train when it's done. Now for our other problem. Sometime tonight our friend, the giant, is going to meet with an accident. Nothing serious, just enough to sideline him. I'm gonna volunteer you to stand in as El Diablo's bodyguard. When he gets my call, you'll know what to do from there."

"Damn, Cisco. You one cold muthafucka. I'm glad we on the same side," Tito said.

"Tito, you've kept it more than real with me from day one. Didn't I always tell you that I was gonna take care of you? Once I'm running the show, you'll be my number one."

"What about El Diablo? He sure as hell ain't gonna like this."

"Fuck, Diablo. As long as you do what I say, he ain't gonna be in no position to do shit. The NYPD already got a hard on for that nigga. They're gonna jump for joy when this shit pops off. Hell, they're gonna put him under the jail. Just make sure you put them things where they need to be when you go to pick him up."

"I got you, Cisco. Everything gonna be gravy. Straight gravy."

When Lou-loc arrived at the park the rest of his lieutenants were already there. There were six of them in all. There was lil Boo who ran the shop in Brooklyn, B.T. Gangsta from 145th, Moe from Wagner, High side from St. Nicolas, Pop Top and Snake Eyes. The gang was all here, so it was time to do the damn thang.

"What it is, fellas?" Lou-loc asked greeting everyone.

"Ain't nothing," Responded lil Boo. "Life is good, homey, and you the reason for it."

"Hell yea," Moe chimed in. "Shit, these ol' slob ass niggaz is on the ropes, cuz. You Cali mafuckas lay it down for real. Them niggaz that you had out here tore shit the fuck up. That shit had me hyped."

"Right, right," High Side cosigned.

"So what's up, Lou-loc?" Pop Top asked. "I know you ain't called a nigga way down here for nothing?"

"Fo sho, my man," said Lou-loc. "I got something to say to y'all niggaz. Some of y'all might not like it, but it's just the way shit is."

"Well spill, nigga," Top said.

"Well, it's like this," Lou-loc started. "I been banging for the hood for the last twelve years. I done put in work and earned my stripes. As all of you can agree, I'm one of the realist cats in the whole Crip gang. Be it on the east or west coast. That's why this is so hard for me to say. Fellas... I'm out of the game."

The park went so silent you could've heard an ant fart. There was a look of utter shock on all of the homies' faces, all except Snake Eyes. The thought of Lou-loc leaving the gang was inconceivable. He was one of, if not the baddest niggaz on any set. Pop Top was the first one to break the silence,

"What you mean, cuz?" Top asked sorrowfully.

"I mean what I said," Lou-loc responded. "This shit here, it's wearing on my nerves, cousins. All this killing, it can drive a muthafucka batty. It just ain't for me, cuz."

"How you gonna bail on us like that?" High Side asked. "I know how you feel about all this, but you and Gutter started this shit. Y'all showed us how to bang accordingly. That man done did a lot for us, but you the real power behind Harlem Crip' In this little bit of time, you've established us as the strongest set in the five boroughs. You that nigga right now, and you just wanna give it all up?"

"Easy, homey," Snake Eyes butted in. "This nigga here is a ghetto superstar. He got more stripes than most niggaz in the game, and he still here to talk about it. That shit in itself is a blessing. There comes a time in a man's life where he just gets tired, and I guess the homey Loc has reached that point?"

Some of the homies thought it odd that Snake Eyes was speaking up for Lou-loc. They figured that it was because of there long standing friendship and them both being from killer Cali, but it was much deeper than that. Lou-loc had wanted to get out of the game for a long time and Snake Eyes was well aware of that. They had many discussions on the topic and he felt his friend's pain. This was one of the main reasons that Snake's father had helped Lou-loc wash some of his money.

"Listen," Lou-loc started. "It's like this. I'm always gonna be a Crip, that's just a given. But as far as being active in the field, that shit is over. I've killed many a men and caused many a men to get killed. I've put in enough work to earn my freedom. Straight like that."

"Straight like nothing," B.T. said harshly. "We all know when you get in a gang that shit is for life. This ain't no fucking job where you can put in your two weeks notice."

"Ay, watch ya mouth, nigga," Top snapped.

"Nah," Lou-loc said waving Top off. "Let the homey speak."

"Look," B.T. continued, "all I'm saying is this shit ain't kosher. You come all this way to build up your street credibility and now you just wanna walk away? This shit don't sit right wit me, cuz. Maybe the shit niggaz is saying is true?"

"What shit?" Lou-loc asked defensively.

"Well," B.T. sighed, "word is, that you done hooked up wit Diablo's lil sister. Niggaz is saying that this slob ass bitch got ya nose open. What up wit that shit?"

The tension in the air had suddenly become very thick. The knowledge of Lou-loc and Satin's relationship was limited to a select few. Sure some of the homies had seen them together, but no one had ever questioned it. That was Lou-loc's business. By trying to put Lou-loc on Front Street, B.T. was asking for an asshole full of trouble. There had always been bad blood between the two, but it was always kept to ranking on each other. B.T. was testing Lou-loc, and it didn't go unnoticed.

"Why don't y'all niggaz just chill?" Snake Eyes said placing his hand on B.T.'s shoulder.

"Man, fuck that," B.T. said jerking away from Snake Eyes. "Nigga, I don't even know you like that for you to be making suggestions. Only reason mafuckas in the hood even gave you a little respect is because Lou-loc said you was cool. Shit, the way this nigga acting, I'm starting to question his judgment."

170

Lou-loc's eyes became dark and glassy. Pop Top and Snake Eyes had seen this look in his eyes before so they stepped back. It was a look that only came over him when he felt a nigga needed to be taught a lesson.

"Listen, B.T.," Lou-loc said through clenched teeth, "I don't think you really know what's up, so I'm gonna clarify it for you. Satin, that's my boo, true enough. Her brother is a fucking mark and is always gonna be one. I ain't got the least bit of love for that buster ass nigga or none of his peeps. My baby, she ain't got nothing to do wit the life, she's a square broad.

Lou-loc paused briefly and then continued on.

"As far as my situation goes, she don't hold no sway over me. This is something I've wanted for a good while. If you was down from the gate like Snake and Gutter instead of a lil know nothing ass nigga, you'd know this. As far as who I'm wit, and why I'm wit em, that ain't none of your never mind. Let this be the first and last time I gotta remind you of that, cuz."

B.T. matched Lou-loc's stare without blinking. He was a bad ass nigga in his own right. If Lou-loc wanted to get stupid, he'd have gotten down with him. As tough as he was, he didn't want no drama with Lou-loc if he could avoid it. But B.T. being the type of nigga he was, he couldn't allow Lou-loc to play him in front of the crew.

"Let me tell you something," he said putting his finger in Lou-loc's face, "I ain't scared of you, nigga. I know who you are and how you do, so the respect is there. But don't you think for a fucking moment that I wouldn't hesitate to put something in yo ass. This is New York, and we don't play that ol..."

That was as far as he got. Once again, the beast had reared its head and Lou-loc was in battle mode. He grabbed B.T.'s finger and snapped it like a twig. High Side moved to break it up, but Lou-loc moved with near inhuman speed. With his free hand he pushed High Side sending him skidding a good five feet. All of the homies looked on in shock. High Side outweighed Lou-loc by at least twenty pounds, but Lou-loc tossed him like a small child.

B.T. opened his mouth to scream, but Lou-loc silenced him with a straight jab to the lip. Lou-loc pulled his gun and brought it down twice across B.T.'s skull. The gash that opened on B.T.'s head sent blood flying all over the assembled lieutenants.

"Now you get this straight," Lou-loc snarled at his bleeding opponent. "I'm through wit this shit. It's little fuck ass niggaz like you that's fucking the game up now. I'm done, you fucking hear me? I want my life back and ain't nobody gonna stop me from being happy!"

All B.T. could do was cough blood and shake his head. He wanted to put on a show for the homies, but he had no intentions on setting Lou-loc off. He knew the man's reputation for killing and wondered if he would be the latest addition to his list of kills? Luckily for him, Snake Eyes took Lou-loc's arm and pulled him away.

"That's enough, old friend," Snake Eyes whispered. "He ain't worth it. You free, my nigga, and I'll back you on that. Let it go and live your life."

The sound of Snake Eyes' voice seemed to bring Lou-loc back from where ever he had been. The madness had receded and he was himself again. At least for the moment.

Lou-loc looked around at the sea of frightened faces and felt ashamed of what he had done. These were suppose to be his peoples, yet instead of understanding, he saw only fear. He knew it was time for him to get out.

"I... I'm sorry," he said addressing his peoples. "We're suppose to be down for each other and look what the fuck I do. I'm an OG and I ain't supposed to conduct myself in this manner. I'm supposed to be showing y'all younger G's a better way, but instead I personify the old ways. The violent ways. This ain't how it's supposed to be.

Lou-loc looked at each of his homies and continued speaking.

"After tonight, it's a wrap for me, cousins. I'll always be a Crip and I'll always love y'all niggaz, but I'm done with this shit. This is how its gonna go down, and I hope y'all can dig it. Pop Top, you the new leader of our New York chapter. At least until Gutter is up and around. I'm trusting you with this shit because I know you can handle it. Do the right thing, cuz."

"Hey, you know I will," Top said grinning. He had finally got his chance to hold the reigns of power, and he intended to run with it.

"One last thing," Lou-loc said raising his hand. "This mafucka," he said pointing at B.T., who was still rolling around on the ground, "he ain't fit to run shit. He still Crip cause that's his right, but he a soldier now. As my last decree, I want this buster stripped of all rank and title. Youz a grunt now, faggot. Top, I don't give a fuck who you get to replace him, but he's a fucking nobody on set, ya dig?

"I wish you niggaz all the best that life has to offer after I retire. Call on me for guidance whenever you feel necessary. The homey Snake can tell you how to reach me. Now let it be done."

All of the lieutenants who were still able to stand gathered around Lou-loc and embraced him. They were sorry to see their homey step down, but they knew that's what he wanted, and they respected his wishes. Lou-loc had nothing left to prove. In the years during his run he had held the set down and put in much work. In all their eyes, Lou-loc was a stand up nigga. If he wanted his freedom, he was more than welcomed to it. He'd earned it.

*

In another part of town, everything was all good. The Giant staggered out of the east village pub with two young girls on his arm. He had spent a good part of the night, as well as his bank roll, on the girls getting toasted in the bar. He had big plans for the two. Whether they wanted to or not, he planned on fucking.

Being that he was too drunk to perform the task, he decided to let the older of the two girls drive while he freaked off in the back seat with the other. He handed the first girl the keys and watched her shapely little ass as she climbed behind the wheel of the hog. Next, he let the other girl into the back seat, and started around the other side to get in. In his mind, he went over the various demeaning tasks he would have them perform.

As a young man, The Giant never had much luck with women. He was an oversized teenager, who wore hand me down clothes. His shoes would always be busted at the seems because of his oversized feet, and his clothes were always too small. The kids had called him all kinds of cruel names, from tree trunk, to mighty tighty. And these were some of the nicer names.

When El Diablo found him, he was a poor brawler, who fought for money in back room bars and underworld basements. El Diablo took pity on the young man and gave him a job. No longer would The Giant have to wear hand me downs or fight in back rooms just to eat. El Diablo had made him a somebody. A man of power and standing. For that, he would be forever grateful.

As The Giant made his way around the car, he didn't notice the vehicle speeding towards him from the opposite direction. As soon as he stepped into the street, the car clipped his leg sending his large body flying over the trunk. The Giant landed hard on the curb with a sickening thud.

The two women jumped from the car wailing like banshees. All traces of the liquor they had consumed were gone as they looked upon the twisted hulk lying on the sidewalk. The Giant lay sprawled on the ground with his leg twisted at an odd angle. He didn't scream, nor did his cry. The pain was too intense for him to utter a sound. As consciousness fled him, his last thoughts were how would he serve his boss as a cripple?

CHAPTER 20

B.T. gangsta sat in the emergency room looking at his twisted finger while waiting to be seen. Lou-loc had done him dirty and it was all his own fault. If he'd just kept his mouth shut none of this would've happened. Whether he was right or wrong, Lou-loc was going to get his.

With his good hand, he pulled out his cell phone and dialed a number.

"Yo, what up?" he said into the receiver. "This B.T., kid. Peep game. Remember that thing we talked about? Well, the nigga done finally played himself. It's time for our boy, Lou-loc, to take a nap...like in permanent. Make it happen for me, kid."

B.T. nodded his head in agreement to whatever the voice on the other end had said, and hung up. He felt a little better about everything now. He had probably lost the use of his finger, but it was okay. Before the night was over, Lou-loc would lose his life.

*

Lou-loc sat in the passenger seat puffing a blunt while Snake Eyes drove. He felt a little fucked up by what happened, but B.T. asked for it. If he hadn't have tried to be a big shot... Fuck it, it wasn't his problem anymore.

"What's on ya mind, player?" Snake Eyes asked as he pulled up in front of White Castles.

"Ain't nothing," Lou-loc said , exhaling the smoke, "just thinking. Man, I can't believe I'm finally getting out? This shit just seems weird to me, cuz."

"It's about fucking time, nigga. You can't run the streets forever. Eventually, the shit catches up with you. Just be glad you're getting out on two feet instead of on ya back."

"I know that's right."

"So what you gonna do, cuz?"

"Man, I can't call it. Me and Satin gonna get up outta here and live the right way."

"You know my dad is willing to give you a part time job at the firm. You can go to school and still work for him?"

"Nah," Lou-loc said getting out of the car. "If I went back to Cali, wouldn't shit change. Niggaz out there would still try and get me to ride."

"Well," Snake Eyes said joining him, "my job is down in Miami. You could always come down there with me?"

"Miami, huh? Shit, Satin would like that. The weather is always good, and the properties not that expensive."

"Can I ask you something, cuz?"

"Go ahead, man. You know you my nigga."

"You and this girl serious?"

"As a heart attack, cuz. Me and her is the real deal."

"I mean, I don't doubt you, but y'all ain't known each other that long?"

"Snake, my man, love is a strange thing. I know it may sound corny, but when you really love somebody, you just know. Your heart tells you it's right, you feel me?"

"Yea, Lou. I can dig it. As long as you happy, I'm happy for you."

"And that's why you'll always be my nigga."

The two friends shared a manly hug right there in front of White Castles. They didn't care who was looking or what they thought. To them, it was the end of an old life and the beginning of a new one. But their precious moment was short lived as a car screeched to a halt behind theirs.

"Ay," the driver shouted, "which one of you niggaz is Lou-loc?"

Without even thinking, Lou-loc stepped forward. "You know me, cuz?" For an answer, the back windows of the car slid down, and all that could be seen were the flashes from gun muzzles.

Snake Eyes was the first to react. He dove and knocked Lou-loc to the ground. Before Lou-loc could clear his gun from his belt, Snake Eyes was already on one knee firing his .45. Even being partially crippled, he was still quick on the draw.

The first two shots Snake Eyes let off, hit the first gun man, knocking him into the second. The driver tried to peel off, but Lou-loc hadn't showed his hand yet. His kill switch went into overdrive. Taking two mammoth strides, he leapt off the ground and was airborne. He sailed clear over a pile of garbage and landed on the hood of the moving car.

Lou-loc gripped the hood for dear life with one hand and drew his glock with the other. Seeing the fear in the man's eyes, Lou-loc grinned devilishly at the driver. All the color drained from the driver's face as he knew he was taking his last breaths. There was no doubt that the man crouching on the hood of his car was the shadow of death. Without missing a beat, Lou-loc emptied the cannon's clip into the occupants of the car.

The car swerved left to right sending Lou-loc flying into a pile of trash. His back and shoulder hurt like hell, but he would live. Too bad the same couldn't be said about the would be assassins in the car. They were lucky enough to slam into the outer wall of the Adam Clayton Powell building, and mangle their ride.

Lou-loc sprang to his feet with the blood lust fresh in his heart. To his disappointment, there was no one else to kill. Snake Eyes came speeding down the street with the passenger side door open. Without waiting for it to stop, Lou-loc dived in.

Inside the car, Lou-loc tried to get himself calm. This shit was beginning to be too much for him. In just this month alone, there had been numerous attempts on his life. Fuck waiting for Satin to get her affairs in order, they were on the next thing smoking to Miami.

"Snake," Lou-loc said out of breath, "how soon do you think you can get me and Satin to Florida?"

*

Satin paced around her loft fuming. Her earlier encounter with El Diablo had her shaken. She didn't know whether to be angry or afraid. El Diablo had always been stubborn, but never unreasonable.

"Who the fuck does he think he is?" she asked no one in particular. Michael must've been out of his mind to get up in her mix like that. Satin reasoned that she was a grown woman, and could fuck whom ever she chose. Be it Lou-loc or the man on the moon. It was her pussy and her heart.

She touched the sore spot on her cheek where her brother had slapped her, and it only fueled her anger. She wasn't hurt by the slap itself, but it was the fact that he had even been bold enough to raise his hand to her at all. In all her years, neither Michael nor any other man had laid hands on her. One guy she had dated a few years back had grabbed her arm, and that alone landed him in the hospital with a broken nose. Satin might have been petite, but she was far from fragile. Michael had enrolled her in martial arts classes when she was young, so that she would always be able to defend herself.

That fool really had some nerve trying to dictate who she could see. Talking bout "He forbid it," was he out of his mind? But what if he tried to do something to Lou-loc? As soon as the thought entered her mind, she pushed it out. Lou-loc had always been a pussycat around her, but she wasn't fooled. She could tell the man was dangerous, even before he kicked Jesus' little ass. He had always let her assume he was a drug dealer, but it didn't take a rocket scientist to know what the deal was. He was a killer. Lou-loc was the type of man that when he came walking down the street, you got the fuck out of his way. His mere presence exerted menace.

Lou-loc was by far, one of the most intelligent and talented young men she had ever met. The disturbing thing was that he was street poisoned. It was sad when you thought about it. He watched his father get murdered in cold blood, then the cancer took his mother. All he had left was his sister, and he cherished her.

Satin had never met her personally, but they had spoken on the phone on several occasions. Sometimes they would just talk on the phone for hours. Not about anything of any relevance, just girl stuff. Malika was like the little sister she never had.

She wasn't the typical sixteen-year-old little girl. She was very well mannered and polite. She always said please and thank you. Whenever she called the house, it was never, "my brother there?" It was always, "Hello, Satin, how are you today? Is my brother available?" She thought the world of her brother, and the same could be said for him. They were very close, despite their age difference. Satin had promised her that when they got settled, she could come and visit with them.

Satin's thoughts were interrupted by the phone ringing. She wondered who could be calling her at that hour of the night? It wasn't really late, but it wasn't early either. She didn't usually receive calls after ten o'clock. Her heart was suddenly filled with dread. She hoped nothing had happened to her aunt or her man.

"Hello." she answered.

"Hey, boo," Lou-loc said on the other end. "I didn't wake you, did I?"

"Oh, no," she said perking up. The sound of his voice on the phone or in person always made her feel good. "I was just thinking about you. Nothing's wrong, is it?"

"Nah," he said more confident than he was, "I just wanted to touch base with you. Hey, listen. We might be pulling out sooner than we thought."

"Lou-loc, what's wrong?"

"Nothing to worry about, ma. I broke the news to the homeboys. You know, about me retiring?"

"Oh, how did they take it? They didn't have to jump you out or anything did they?"

"You silly. Nah, it wasn't nothing like that. The real soldiers took it like G's. I had to whip that lil nigga B.T. out for talking slick though."

"Lou-loc, you said no more violence."

"Hey, I didn't start. That mafucka had it coming."

"So, Mike Tyson, did you decide where we gonna go."

"Fo sho, lil mamma. What you think about Miami?"

"Oh baby," she squealed, "I've always dreamed about living some where like that. Are you serious?"

"As a heart attack." he joked. "Snake Eyes is setting everything up."

"Oh, baby. I can't believe you're taking me to Florida?"

"Yea, and I was thinking, well if it's okay with you? Maybe we could fly your aunt and my lil sister down that way once we're settled?"

"Yea, that's cool with me. It'd be nice to have them visit with us. That way, the people we love can get acquainted."

"Yea, ma. Plus I'd like for my sister to be the maid of honor when we get married next month."

"Umm hmm. That would be...what did you say?" she asked stunned.

"Satin, honey. I know we said that we'd wait for a while, but maybe we shouldn't? I love you ma, and I want you to know it."

"But, Lou-loc. You don't have to rush and marry me just to prove you love me. Baby, you've given up your whole way of life to be with me. That's proof enough."

"I know, I know. But I want this. I made a promise to myself a long time ago, that if I ever found that special someone, I'd hold on for dear life."

"That is the sweetest thing I've ever heard. If I hadn't already put that thang on you, I'd think you were trying to get into my panties?" They both laughed at that. "So, when do you wanna leave?"

"Like tomorrow," he said seriously. "We'll probably catch a flight tomorrow afternoon or in the evening."

"Tomorrow, why so soon? Something's wrong, isn't it?"

"Nah, I just need to get away from this place. Too many memories, and too many hostile feelings. I just wanna bail before I end up hurting somebody."

"Damn, I haven't even finished packing my stuff."

"Don't worry about that, ma. Just pack a few things, and whatever's personal to you. Don't worry about the rest of your clothes. We starting off fresh, remember? When we hit Miami, we both going shopping. Before we leave, I'll give your key to Snake so he can have your furniture put into storage."

"Well, what about our cars?"

"My other car is already sold, and I'm having my low rider shipped to Florida."

"And my jeep?"

"Fuck it. I'll have Snake sell it and send you the money. I'll buy you another car once we get settled."

"You got it all figured out, huh?"

"You know I do, baby. Look, I'll be by to pick you up in the morning. We gonna swing by the hospital to see ya aunt, then we gone. You okay with that?"

"Well, I guess so. You not coming over tonight?"

"Nah, boo. I got some loose ends to take care of. The dude that's buying my car, is also buying my guns. Shit, I'm retired. Besides, I can't take em on the plane. You go on and get some rest, ma. Tomorrow marks the beginning of a new era for us. Sleep well, boo. I love you, Satin."

"And I love you, Lou-loc." With that she hung up.

Satin sat on her bed with tears in her eyes. Everything was happening so suddenly. Everything that Lou-loc said, he did. He left his gang and was moving her to the beautiful shores of Miami. This was too good to be true. Soon she would be married and living in a beautiful city with the man she loved. After all the heartache she had endured, Satin was finally going to have the story book life she had always dreamed of.

CHAPTER 21

*T*he loud chirping of his cell phone woke Lou-loc from his much needed rest. When he looked at the caller I.D., he recognized the number, so he answered. "Hello, Pam," he said sleepily.

"Well, good morning to you too, Mr. Alexander." said the woman on the other end. "I hope I didn't wake you? But if so, too bad. Now you know how it feels."

"Do you have good news for me, Pam?"

"Don't I always? As per your instructions, I've had most of your accounts transferred to 'Miami First National.' I did some calling around, and arranged for you to meet with a *no questions asked* realtor next week. He says, he has some nice beach front property that you might be interested in. I still haven't found a buyer for your security company, but I'm working on it. I've sent you a travel package with three dummy credit cards via express mail, so it should reach your P.O. box sometime today. Our friends at the shipping company said you can have your car dropped off tomorrow, and they'll have it in Miami no later than next week. Overall, I'd say we're set. Anything else, Mr. Alexander?"

"Yea, stop calling me that. Love you, smart ass."

"Yea, well act like it and hit a sister off wit a lil something something."

"I got you, Pam."

"Yea, what ever, nigga. Bye."

Lou-loc loved Pam like a sister. She was crooked as hell, but also the best at what she did. Pamela Sparks was one of the best money managers on the west coast. She was a sister from the hood that had finally clawed her way out. She was ghetto as hell, but also very professional. Sure, she skimmed a little, and helped drug dealers launder their money, but we all gotta eat. The way Pam was jacking the commission on the brothers in the hood, she was eating like a mafucka.

Pam had a house in the Hills, two Mercedes, a navigator and game. That's what makes the world go round. The nigga wit the most cake, is the nigga wit the most game. A lot of people think its all about

182

heart, or education, but that's all bullshit. It's all about game, and who got the most of it. If yo game was tight, then you was good.

Lou-loc stretched his aching muscles and strolled over to the window. The weatherman had said it was going to be sunny, yet the sky was cloudy. A bad omen, but Lou-loc chalked it up to dumb Meteorologist. Last night's meeting had gone well. Big Mike had given Lou-loc $15,000 for the car and $2,000 for the guns. Considering that it was all cash, he was good.

He had agreed to let Lou-loc use the car for the day, so he was set for transportation. Even though Big Mike wasn't a Crip, he was 'Folks,' and that was just as good. Big Mike was good peoples.

Lou-loc flipped his phone open and dialed Snake Eyes. After about three or four rings, he picked up. "What it is, cuz?" Lou-loc said happily.

"Ain't nothing," Snake Eyes said yawning, "today's the day, huh?"

"Yea, cuz. I'm putting this life behind me and starting over fresh."

"Cuz, you don't know how proud I am of you."

"I be knowing, pimp."

"It's a whole different ball game you stepping into, Loc. I'm gonna introduce you to a totally different hustle, cuz. Them crackers got this game sewed, but slowly but surely, we getting in there. I got big plans for you, Lou-loc. All you gotta do is be willing to put the time in, and we good."

"Hey man, I'm always willing to learn. I'm gonna do the right thing by this girl, Snake. I didn't tell her yet, but I plan on opening up a lil boutique or something for her in south beach. Its gonna be a surprise wedding present for her."

"Damn, nigga. You got it bad."

"Fo sho. I'm in love, cuz."

"Well, Mr. lover man, you just make sure you have your ass at the airport by twelve o'clock. Your flight leaves at one fifteen."

"Cuz, I can't tell you how much I appreciate what you've done for me."

"Man, go head wit that sucker shit. We kin, it's all good. You just make sure you get yo ass back in school, and do right by that girl. We gonna get ya money all washed up, and then you gonna ball like you supposed to, ya heard?"

"Loud and clear, big player. So, I'll meet up with you at about eleven. I'll hit ya phone to let you know where."

"A'ight, cuz. I'm taking my ass back to sleep. Be careful out there, loc."

"I'm out the game, Snake. The rules don't apply to me no more. As of today, I'm a square."

"Yea, well you still watch yo ass, Lou-loc. You got a strap?"

"Nah, I sold em all to Mike."

"Damn, nigga. I'm bout to come through there and lay one on you."

"Be cool, Snake. I ain't going nowhere. When I leave this room, I'm going to pick Satin up, and then I'm coming to meet you. You gonna take us to the airport so you can drop the car keys on Mike. It's cool, baby."

"I ain't feeling this shit, Lou-loc, especially after what happened last night. At least let me send somebody over there to hold you down?"

"Snake, this is me. If I say I'm cool, then I'm cool. Good looking though. I'll give you a call later, homey. Out." Before Snake Eyes could protest, Lou-loc hung up.

All of Lou-loc's bags were still packed from the break up with Martina, so he didn't have to worry about that. All of his guns were gone as well as the excess jewelry he wouldn't need. It was time to go pick Satin up and get on the road.

*

Cisco got up especially early. Usually, he didn't stir from his plush water bed until about eleven or twelve, but today was different. Today was the day he would put an end to Lou-loc and El Diablo. He felt like a kid on Christmas. Late last night, he hadn't gotten the call about The Giant's accident. It was a wasted call because he already knew. He set it up.

Cisco picked up his antique phone and set the ball in motion. The first person he called was Tito. During the brief phone conversation, Tito had informed him that the goods were in place and he was on route to pick up El Diablo. With that taken care of, he called Martina. He could hardly bear to stay on the phone with the woman but for so long. If he didn't need her, he would've just said fuck it, but this wasn't the case. In order for everything to go accordingly, she had to play her part. It was a damn shame what some people would do for money. Martina was going to sell her soul as well as her ex's for a funky ten thousand dollars.

The phone had barely rang twice when Martina snatched it up. "Hello?" she said out of breath.

"What up, Martina? This is, Cisco."

"I was wondering when you would call? You got my paper?"

"You don't waste any time, do you?"

"Life is too short to waste time, especially when it comes to money. Now do you have mine?"

"You'll get your money when the deed is done. We gotta make that happen. As in today."

"Shit, that ain't a problem, pa. I'm about to make the call in a little while."

"Good girl. I owe you one, ma."

"Don't get it fucked up. You owe me ten... $10,000. So listen, when this is all done, how about..." She didn't get a chance to finish her sentence as the line went dead in her ear

Martina sat back on her bed and smiled devilishly. She was finally gonna fix that nigga, Lou-loc. Cisco and them were gonna kick his ass good, or so she thought. She didn't feel one ounce of guilt about what she was doing. She reasoned that once she nursed Lou-loc back to health from his beating, he would realize that she was the one for him and not that uppity bitch, Satin. After she dropped her load, she had something for that bitch too and she had something for Cisco. There was no doubt in her mind that once Lou-loc recovered he was going to kill Cisco. That would take care of the only person that could link her to the scheme.

"You just wait, Lou-loc," she said rubbing her belly, "you'll come back to your senses, and I'll be right here waiting on you."

CHAPTER 22

Lou-loc sat on the couch puffing on a Newport as Satin put the last of her things into her shoulder bag. He looked her up and down and couldn't help but think about how lucky he was. She looked so good, even dressed down.

Satin was sporting a pink Rocawear sweat suit with a pair of pink and white air max. Her silky black hair was wrapped around her head and held in place with pink and white hairpins. Lou-loc's girl was the baddest thing on the streets. Satin wasn't as thick as Martina, but what she lacked in thickness, she more than made up for in character.

"Damn, boo," Satin said as she took one last look at her apartment. "I can't believe we leaving."

"Well, believe it," he said picking up her suitcase. "I told you I was taking you away and I always keep my promises. Now let's get this shit down to the car."

Before Lou-loc was completely out the door his cell went off. When he looked at the caller I.D. he knew just who it was.

"What?" he snapped.

"Damn," Martina whined. "Good morning to you too. What's up, boo?"

"First of all, I ain't ya fucking boo. Second of all, what you want?" Lou-loc said.

"You ain't gotta be all stank and shit, Lou-loc. What's the matter, papi, that bitch you wit ain't treating you right?"

"First of all, what goes on wit me and mine don't concern you. Second of all, what you want?"

"Shit, you in a rush or something?" Martina said.

"Oh, I guess you ain't heard? As of today, I'm out the game. Not only am I out the game, I'm out this city."

"What?" Martina asked in disbelief. "What you mean?"

"Damn, I forgot you kinda slow," he said sarcastically. "It's a wrap, Martina. I'm putting some distance between me and this rotten ass apple. You smell me?"

"Well, let me and the kids come with you. Maybe we can work it out?" Martina pleaded.

"Girl, you crazier than a shit house rat. Me and my boo is gone from here, so you can keep ya drama, ya games and yo kids. I hope you have a nice life."

"How you gonna do this to me, Lou-loc?" she said breaking down. "What about us? What about the baby?"

"Bitch," he said coldly, "don't even play me. You know damn well that ain't my seed, so miss me wit it. Matter of fact, is there a reason for this fucking call?" Satin, seeing her man about to blow his cool, intervened.

"Calm down, baby," she whispered. "The girl is upset, so try to be a little sympathetic to her situation. Be the bigger man that I know you are."

Satin's words calmed him a little, but the anger was still there. "What is it, Martina?" he asked sucking his teeth.

"I didn't call to bug you, Lou-loc," she said trying to sound sincere. "The reason I called is because I'm having a problem with the lease. This dumb ass landLord is talking about putting us out unless you tell him otherwise. You being the lease holder and all, I can't really do shit about it."

"So, what you want me to do?" Lou-loc asked.

"Well, could you just come over here and sign it over to me or something?"

A warning bell went off in Lou-loc's head. Something about the way Martina was coming at him didn't seem right.

"Look, Martina," he started, "I feel for you and all, but I don't think that'll be such a good idea."

"Oh, word?" she yelled into the phone. "You hate me that much to where you'll let me and my kids get thrown out into the streets? Youz a cold ass nigga, Lou-loc."

"Martina," he said getting angry again, "I'm trying to be nice about this shit, but you ain't making it easy. You want me to come all the way

187

from where I'm at to sign a lease? You wilding out. It ain't my fault y'all asses is getting put out. As a matter of fact, you can go straight to..." Satin pinched his arm and kept him from finishing his sentence.

"St. Louis Alexander," Satin said in a stern voice, "I know you ain't gonna do that girl like that? I know she a bitch, but she got little ones. Don't do it for her, do it for her kids. They're innocent in all this. Don't stoop to her level."

"But Satin," he said, "we still gotta go see your aunt, right?"

"We can do that after you sign the lease. It shouldn't take you but a few minutes. We can go to the airport from the hospital."

"Okay, Satin. You lucky I love you," he said playfully.

Lou-loc composed himself and put the phone back to his ear.

"Okay, Martina. I'll be there in about a half hour. Have the paperwork ready. I'm signing the lease, then I'm gone."

"Thanks, Lou-loc. I..."

For the second time that morning, Martina had been hung up on. It was okay though. Mr. OG Lou-loc was about to learn two things. New York bitches are grimy, and hell hath no fury like a woman scorned.

*

Lou-loc dialed Snake Eyes' cell but didn't get any answer. He left a message on his answering machine informing his friend on where he was going. He had intended on having Snake Eyes meet him there, but he'd just have to try him again later. After Lou-loc put the last of Satin's bags in the car, they hopped on the highway and headed uptown. He felt uneasy about dipping through the hood without any type of firearm, but there was nothing he could do about it now. He would be in and out, so he didn't really think anything could go wrong. Besides, that was his hood. Niggaz knew better than to fuck with him.

*

Cisco hung up his phone and a wide grin formed on his face. Things were going well. Now it was time for him to set phase two of his plan in motion. First he called his hired help and gave them their instructions. The next call he made was to El Diablo's cell phone.

"Diablo," he said in a frantic voice, "I hate to bother you, but we've got a problem I thought you should know about."

"What's wrong?" El Diablo asked concerned.

"It's your sister, Michael," Cisco said.

"Satin, what about her?"

"One of my ladies just called me. She said that fucking ape, Lou-loc, is uptown kicking your sister's ass in the street like some whore."

"That muthafucka," El Diablo snarled. "I'll kill that nigger bastard. Where is he, Cisco?"

"It's going on right uptown in front of his old building. It was Martina who called and told me. She said that Satin found out they were still seeing each other and wasn't happy about it," Cisco said giggling to himself as he heard Diablo relaying the info to Tito.

"I'm on my way," El Diablo said out of breath.

"I'll meet you there," Cisco lied. "We'll stomp this ape together."

El Diablo hung up without answering whileCisco sat back in his recliner and turned on the twenty-four hour news channel. It wouldn't be long now. All he had to do was wait.

*

Lou-loc pulled up in front of his old building and got out of the car. As soon as he stepped onto the pavement a cold chill ran down his spine. He shrugged it off as the jitters and continued to stare at the building. This was going to be his last time seeing this building or Martina's funky ass. Good riddance to them both.

"You okay, boo?" Satin asked from the passenger side window.

"I'm cool," he assured her. He didn't want to spook Satin, but something didn't feel right. He saw Martina looking down at him from the window, but she wasn't coming down. And what the fuck was she grinning at?

Martina watched Lou-loc get out of the car and stoop down to talk to Satin.

"So, that's his new bitch, huh?" Martina said to herself.

189

As Martina looked at the features of the small woman in the car, she had to admit, the girl was pretty. As Lou-loc strolled towards the building she put on her brightest smile. Mr. lover, lover was about to get his.

Martina saw El Diablo's red hog bend the corner, and suddenly felt as if something was very wrong. Cisco never said anything about El Diablo being involved. When she saw the gang Lord hop from his car and rush at Lou-loc, she became sure of what she had suspected. Something was very wrong.

"You fucking tar baby, " El Diablo shouted. "Where the fuck is my sister?"

"Huh?" Lou-loc asked dumbfounded by the man in the suit running towards him. "What the hell you talking about?"

El Diablo swung a wild punch at Lou-loc that he easily sidestepped. Without trying to gain his balance, he swung another blow. This time Lou-loc grabbed his arm and rabbit punched him in the stomach, folding him. El Diablo had quite a rep with a blade or a gun, but he wasn't a very good fighter.

"Y.. you, bastard," El Diablo said wheezing. "You hit my sister. I'll... I'll kill you."

"Man, what the hell are you talking about?" Lou-loc asked confused. "Who the hell is your sister?"

"Michael!" Satin yelled getting out of the car.

"Wait a second," Lou-loc said holding his hands up turning to speak to Satin. "This is your brother? This is the *notorious* El Diablo? You can't be serious?"

El Diablo sat on the floor looking from Lou-loc to Satin in a state of confusion. His sister didn't have a mark on her. Her hair wasn't even out of place. Somebody had looped him and he knew just who it was. El Diablo was about to get up and explain himself when he noticed two young boys running up behind Lou-loc. Everything that happened next seemed to go in slow motion.

"Hey, crab muthafucka!" the first boy shouted.

Lou-loc turned around just in time to see the first boy raising a sawed off shotgun and aim it right where he and Satin were standing.

Instinctively, Lou-loc reached under his shirt where his gun would normally be only to find himself clutching air.

The first boy cut loose with the shotgun, tearing off most of Lou-loc's right shoulder. The second boy ran up beside his partner bringing his 'Street Sweeper' into play. Lou-loc only had a fraction of a second to make his next move. He could've tried to run or dodge the shot, but he wasn't concerned with himself. With his good arm, he knocked Satin to the ground and rushed the boys.

The street sweeper rattled to life, and the second boy lit Lou-loc up like the fourth of July. Lou-loc, on his hands and knees, still tried to crawl to the boys. The first boy kicked Lou-loc in the face, flipping him over on his back. Blood spewed from Lou-loc's mouth and nose. He was trying to say something, but at first it was just gibberish. If you listened real close, you could hear him mutter "Satin," over and over.

"This is what you get for fucking wit Diablo, bitch!" he shouted loud enough for everyone to hear. The first boy aimed the barrel of the shotgun at Lou-loc's face and pulled the trigger. Blood and bits off skull splattered all over the pavement and on the front of the building.

The second boy threw up his set and screamed, "LC Blood for life, long live El Diablo!" and with that, the gunmen ran off.

"Lou-loc," Satin whispered as she watched her man's life blood run into the gutter. El Diablo tried to hold her back, but she broke loose and rushed to her man's side. What was left of Lou-loc was enough to make a grown man vomit, but not Satin. She held it down as she kneeled next to her man. His body was a bloody mess and his grill was even worse. Half of his once handsome face was torn to sheds.

"Oh, baby," Satin sobbed. "Why they do this to you, baby? We were suppose to go to Miami. What happened? Look, they messed up your braids."

Satin stroked Lou-loc's bloody skull.

"It's okay," Satin spoke. "I'll just do them over when you wake up. Oh, Lou-loc, why you leave me, papi? You said we were getting married, what happened? You said you always kept your promises."

Snake Eyes pulled up just in time to see his friend stretched out on the ground. When he got Lou-loc's message about going to Martina's, he knew something was fishy. He had just recently signed the lease. They had at least six more months before the lease was up. Tears welled up in Snake Eyes' eyes as he watched Satin kneel over Lou-loc with a vacant look in her eyes. Of all the times he had pulled Lou-loc's ass out of the fire, this was one time he couldn't.

El Diablo walked up timidly and reached out to his sister and spoke, "Satin... I, uh..."

Satin looked at El Diablo's hand like it was a rattlesnake. As she looked up at her brother's sorrow filled face, words rang out in her head: "I'll kill you."

"This is what you get for fucking wit El Diablo...LC Blood," Diablo yelled.

Suddenly all of Satin's sadness was gone. All of the hurt she had felt evaporated, and was replaced by anger.

"You," she whispered, "you did this to him. You and your fucking gang war. Why couldn't you just leave him alone? He was out. He wanted no parts of your feud, but you couldn't let him leave, could you?"

"Satin, I didn't..." he started, but she cut him off.

"We were going to get married on the beach, did you know that?" she asked holding up her now bloody ring. "We were to be married in Miami, Michael. We were going to buy a house and fly aunt Selina down to take care of her, did you know that? You took him from me, you Bastard!"

El Diablo started backing up because he saw madness in his sister's eyes. This was not the little girl he knew. This was somebody totally different. This was a woman who had just lost a lover. He looked to the car to motion for Tito, but he was long gone. It was just brother and sister.

From the car, Snake Eyes watched the whole thing unfolding. When he realized what was about to happen, he moved to stop it, but with his bum leg, he was too slow. Satin's hand dipped into her purse and she came out with her pistol. Without so much as blinking, she squeezed the trigger. She was so distraught that she didn't release the trigger until the clip was empty.

Snake Eyes made his way to Satin and took the gun from her, but it was too late for El Diablo as he lay on the ground with six holes in his

$3,000 suit. His little sister, whom he had raised and nurtured as a child, had sent him home. For him, the game was over.

The police arrived on the scene too little too late as usual. Snake Eyes wasn't there from the beginning, so he couldn't really say what happened, but you know how people in the hood are. They love an opportunity to get a story ass backwards on the news. Snake Eyes was so distraught by the loss of his friend that he didn't much care what they said. He had one brother in a coma and one in heaven. He had seen it so many times that he was numb to it. Another young brother claimed by the streets.

Snake Eyes walked over and looked down at his mutilated friend. Tears flowed freely down his cheeks and he didn't care who saw.

"You're free now," he whispered. "Go on home, cuz. The pain is gone and you're free. I love you, my nigga, and I'm glad you ain't gotta suffer no more. Go on and rest."

Satin walked in a daze as two female officers escorted her to a blue and white. Snake Eyes knew even before the trial that she wasn't going to jail. Her lover was gone, and he took her heart and sanity with him. Satin would spend the rest of her life in a mental institution.

CHAPTER 23

*T*he entire hood turned out for Lou-loc's funeral. Ballers from every coast came to pay their respects to one of God's most thorough soldiers. They laid Lou-loc out in a solid gold casket with a six pointed star carved into it. Because of what happened, they had to make it a closed casket funeral, but there were pictures of him all over. Snake Eyes had placed the picture of Lou-loc and Satin at Six Flags in the casket. He felt Lou-loc would've wanted Satin close to him.

Martina, of course, showed her ass at the funeral. She was crying and falling out in the lap of any nigga that was willing to keep her ass from hitting the floor. On two separate occasions, Snake Eyes and Pop Top had to keep Sharell from swinging on her.

Snake Eyes and Pam took Lou-loc's money and did the right thing with it. With part of the money they started The St. Louis Alexander Scholarship Fund for underprivileged children who couldn't afford to go to college. With the rest of the money they set up a trust fund for Malika so she would have all the advantages life had to offer.

Snake Eyes' last order of business was Lou-loc's work. All his thoughts, memoirs and everything he had put to paper. Snake Eyes made sure it was all published. With the royalty checks, he made sure neither Satin nor her aunt needed for anything. Even though they never asked for the money, Snake Eyes knew. That's exactly how Lou-loc would've wanted it done. Even though they never made it to the altar, Satin was his wife.

*

The seasons changed and made way for the summer. It was back to business as usual. Cisco was especially feeling himself. After the death of El Diablo, he took over as leader of LC Blood. He kind of felt cheated by the way things went down. On the day of El Diablo's death, Cisco had Tito place two guns under the seats of El Diablo's ride. Both of the guns had been used in murders. It was his intention for the police to find the guns, but things had worked out better than he had expected. Satin had whacked the old bastard.

With Lou-loc dead and Gutter being a vegetable, Harlem wasn't holding sway like it was. Pop Top had made a mess of what Lou-loc and Gutter had built. It was chaos uptown. Cisco loved it.

He figured even if Gutter were to snap out of it, he'd more than likely be a crippled retard and posed no threat. The money was coming in and life was good. LC was back on top.

Cisco stood on the sidelines of the West 4th basketball court sipping on his bottle of water. He liked to come down to West 4th to watch the different kinds of people come and go. At this particular moment, he had an eye on this fine little black nurse who was pushing a man in a wheelchair. The man seemed to be in a nod with his bathrobe and dark sunglasses on. He wore a large brimmed hat to shade him from the sun. The nurse was a nice little cinnamon thing with an ass that just called out Cisco's name.

"Hey, mami," he said trying to sound cool.

"Hey yourself," she responded.

"What's up wit you, ma? A nice day like this and you gotta be stuck pushing a wheelchair?"

"Yea, it's a drag, but I gotta pay my bills."

"Ma, I could pay your bills plus give you multiple orgasms. You ain't know? I'm Cisco, LC Blood supreme general."

"Oh, I've heard of you," she said excitedly. "I hear you that nigga?"

"Nah, I'm that spic, but what's the difference?"

"Oh, you all that?" The nurse giggled.

"And then some. Why don't you ditch the cripple and come back to my spot?"

"Sure, I'm wit it," said the man in the wheelchair, catching Cisco off guard.

Before Cisco could respond, the man pulled an eleven-inch hunting knife from under his robe and plunged into Cisco's gut. He stabbed him over and over as tears ran from under his sunglasses.

"You killed my brother, mathufucker!" Gutter snarled. "Die, muthafucka! Die!"

Gutter poked Cisco about thirteen or fourteen times. The funny thing is, that everyone was so wrapped up in the basketball game, no one even noticed Cisco fall to the ground.

"All scores is settled nigga, and that's on Harlem," Gutter said spitting on Cisco's lifeless body as Sharell rolled him away.

"Its over now, baby," Sharell said.

"I know, ma," Gutter said wiping tears from his eyes. "My folk can rest now. You hear me, Lou?" he asked looking to the sky. "You can rest now. All debts paid in full."

Gutter stood up from the bogus wheelchair and took off his bloody bathrobe. He smoothed out his Blue Armani suit and tossed the robe into a dumpster. He and Sharell walked upWwest 4th into the afternoon sun.

*

It was 9 p.m. when Martina walked in with her newborn infant. The sun had set giving way to the darkness. The kids were with her sister, so it was just her and the baby. She put the baby in the basinet and stripped down to her panties and bra. It had been a few months since Louloc was murdered but she still thought of him. If only she hadn't called him that day he might still be alive. Alive and with that bitch. Oh well, neither one of them had him now. But at least she was $10,000 richer for it.

The baby was asleep so Martina decided to take a quick shower. She cracked the window to let in the evening breeze. No sooner than she turned her back the window came crashing in. Before she could react a vice like grip had her by the neck. She kicked and scratched, but the grip was too strong. Finally, she tried to scream but the feeling of her jugular being torn open killed all sound.

The intruder laughed mockingly as Martina's blood sprayed freely from her neck. She felt her strength fading and wondered which fucked up deed she had done that finally caught up with her. She heard the baby crying in the background but could do nothing to help him. Soon the struggle was done and Martina lay lifeless on the floor.

It was a good three days before Martina's sister found her corpse in the bedroom. The stench of the rotting form was so putrid, that the first officer on the scene lost his lunch. The only clues to what had taken place were a bloody cross-smeared on the wall and an empty basinet.

I guess all debts are truly settled?

END.

WHO IS KWAN?

K'wan is without a doubt one of this generations most talented and gritty writers. Born the only child of a poet and a painter, creativity was imprinted in him from day one. In the early years K'wan excelled academically, but like most youth of today, was side tracked by the call of the streets. Through trial and error, K'wan learned the hard way what the fast life has nothing to offer.

After graduating high school, K'wan began to travel the country in an attempt to find his place in the world. For quite some time K'wan traveled from coast to coast doing everything from investment banking, to selling books and magazines door to door in the ghetto's of killer Cali.

It was during a brief stay in the county jail that K'wan discovered he had a flare for writing. With a new found talent and an idea, K'wan hit the streets and began the journey of an unsigned writer.

For years K'wan composed novels and tried to get into the publishing game only to have door after door slammed in his face. That is until he read a book called *Let that Be The Reason* by Vickie Stringer. After contacting the author in search of advice, K'wan ended up getting a book deal. Vickie gave K'wan what no one else would, a chance. This chance bore fruit and the fruit is called *Gangsta*.

Gangsta is the first of many novels pulled from this writer's arsenal. This gripping street tale is sure to leave a lasting impression on the game for many years to come. One thing most people can agree on is not only can you read Gangsta, but you can also feel it.

Thanks to a helping hand, K'wan made his bones with Gangsta and stands as the shining jewel in the *Triple Crown Publication Family*.

K'wan resides in one of New York cities most gang infested housing projects where he continues to create beautiful and touching novels.

K'wan,

You thank me and it is I that owe you thanks.
Do you know how wonderful it feels to put
someone down with something that is positive
and not negative. In my former life, I put
many shorties down with me in the streets to
slang death and destruction. I thought placing a
"bird", "thang" or "kilo" in their hand was
giving them life. A chance. It was a chance to
go nowhere. T.C.P. was a set I ran with back in
my day and we did dirt. I am proud of you, and
so glad to give you a chance for a better life. Do
your thang. Get down for your crown, legally.
Stay down for your Crown, your Triple Crown
and this time when you crown yo'self, pay
yo'self, no Fed, DEA, Local Police, can remove
you from your thrown. Nobody but God, and
you already know what God love?

What That Writer Life Look Like?

Your Sis in the industry

One,

VS

ORDER FORM

Triple Crown Publications
2959 Stelzer Rd.
Columbus, Oh 43219

Name: _____

Address: _____

City/State: _____

Zip: _____

	TITLES	PRICES
	Dime Piece	$15.00
	Gangsta	$15.00
	Let That Be The Reason	$15.00
	A Hustler's Wife	$15.00
	The Game	$15.00
	Black	$15.00
	Dollar Bill	$15.00
	A Project Chick	$15.00
	Road Dawgz	$15.00
	Blinded	$15.00
	Diva	$15.00
	Sheisty	$15.00
	Grimey	$15.00
	Me & My Boyfriend	$15.00
	Larceny	$15.00
	Rage Times Fury	$15.00
	A Hood Legend	$15.00
	Flipside of The Game	$15.00
	Menage's Way	$15.00

SHIPPING/HANDLING (Via U.S. Media Mail)   **$3.95**

TOTAL $_____

FORMS OF ACCEPTED PAYMENTS:
Postage Stamps, Institutional Checks & Money Orders, all mail in orders take 5-7 Business days to be delivered.

. ORDER FORM

Triple Crown Publications
2959 Stelzer Rd.
Columbus, Oh 43219

Name: _____

Address: _____

City/State: _____

Zip: _____

		TITLES	PRICES
		Still Sheisty	$15.00
		Chyna Black	$15.00
		Game Over	$15.00
		Cash Money	$15.00
		Crack Head	$15.00
		For the Strength of You	$15.00
		Down Chick	$15.00
		Dirty South	$15.00
		Cream	$15.00
		Hood Winked	$15.00
		Bitch	$15.00
		Stacy	$15.00
		Life Wtihout Hope	$15.00
		.	

SHIPPING/HANDLING (Via U.S. Media Mail)   **$3.95**

TOTAL $_____

FORMS OF ACCEPTED PAYMENTS:

Postage Stamps, Institutional Checks & Money Orders, all mail in orders take 5-7 Business days to be delivered.